THE MURDER GAME

STEVE LYONS

BBC BOOKS

Other BBC DOCTOR WHO books include:

THE EIGHT DOCTORS *by Terrance Dicks*	0 563 40563 5
VAMPIRE SCIENCE *by Jonathan Blum and Kate Orman*	0 563 40566 X
THE BODYSNATCHERS *by Mark Morris*	0 563 40568 6
GENOCIDE *by Paul Leonard*	0 563 40572 4
THE DEVIL GOBLINS FROM NEPTUNE	
by Keith Topping and Martin Day	0 563 40564 3
THE ULTIMATE TREASURE *by Christopher Bulis*	0 563 40571 6
BUSINESS UNUSUAL *by Gary Russell*	0 563 40575 9

DOCTOR WHO titles on BBC Video include:

THE WAR MACHINES *starring William Hartnell*	BBCV 6183
THE AWAKENING/FRONTIOS *starring Peter Davison*	BBCV 6120
THE HAPPINESS PATROL *starring Sylvester McCoy*	BBCV 5803

Other DOCTOR WHO titles available from BBC Worldwide Publishing:

POSTCARD BOOK	0 563 40561 9
THE NOVEL OF THE FILM *on audio tape*	0 563 38148 5/Z1998

Published by BBC Books,
an imprint of BBC Worldwide Publishing
BBC Worldwide Ltd, Woodlands, 80 Wood Lane,
London W12 0TT

First published 1997
Copyright © Steve Lyons 1997.
The moral right of the author has been asserted.

Original series broadcast on the BBC
Format © BBC 1963
Doctor Who and TARDIS are trademarks of the BBC

ISBN 0 563 40565 1
Imaging by Black Sheep, copyright © BBC

Printed and bound in Great Britain by Mackays of Chatham
Cover printed by Belmont Press Ltd, Northampton

CHAPTER 1

STORM WARNINGS

The weather had turned, more completely and suddenly than nature should allow. Rolling black clouds were interspersed between sun and sea, distant thunder presaging the onset of the storm proper. The horizon was blurred by fine spray and a ferocious wind stung Able Seaman Ben Jackson's face with particles of salt. He closed his eyes against the onslaught, nerves shrieking sympathy with the protesting mainsail. The deck bucked and the liquid uncertainty of seasickness lapped at his guts. HMS Teazer was caught in a ravenous grey whirlpool, lashed by the elements, fighting to escape but already doomed.

When Ben tore open reluctant eyes again, he was elsewhere: staring at a blank white ceiling, brain striving to kick-start foam-wrapped neurons into the task of sifting reality from dreams.

The storm was fictional, which came as a relief. But the ship too was only a fond memory, his despairing pang at this revelation all too familiar. The stomach-ache, sadly, was real, albeit caused not by the sea's unpredictable swells but, more mundanely, by last night's excesses. Thoughts of the spaceport bar's exotic, not to say freakish, mix of customers prompted Ben's half-woken mind to re-evaluate its stance on what was real and what not. Thus had it been since he had stepped into that blue box in Fitzroy Square in the summer of '66, an age of shattered preconceptions ago.

Ben sailed through space and time now, and although

he couldn't claim to have adjusted to the fact, he had at least developed accommodation strategies. It helped to imagine that he had merely traded one type of ship for another, even if this TARDIS was far beyond his understanding. He looked on its owner and pilot, the Doctor, as a sort of surrogate captain; on his fellow human, Polly, as a prettier-than-usual cabin boy. Even the variegated forms of the spaceport's clientele were, at some level, no more alien or incomprehensible than the swinging socialites who inhabited the Inferno nightclub in London.

Ben Jackson's life had become something from a dream; his real dreams, to compensate, offered homesick scenarios of Earth, his one-man quarters and life on the ocean wave. Tonight, such normality had been stolen. In the back of his mind, a nagging voice was trying to explain why.

Ben had dismissed the rocking motion at first, subconsciously categorising it as a holdover from the dream or a symptom of his lingering intoxication. The next violent judder, however, shocked him into alertness and the cold-water realisation that something was wrong. He threw back his bedclothes and headed for the door, colliding with a cabinet instead as the shaking floor took his balance. A bottle of aftershave teetered over the edge of a pristine dressing table and exploded across the polished floor.

He hauled himself to his feet and made another, successful, lunge for the shifting doorway. No time to indulge in self-pity, he told himself. Normally, it was impossible – disconcertingly so – to even tell if the TARDIS was in flight. As Ben raced towards the console room and his captain's side, he wondered what magnitude of storm it would take to upset this vessel.

The Doctor leapt frantically about the hexagonal console, coat tails flapping. His ship's anguish was bludgeoned into his mind, translated into panic and communicated too forcefully by telepathic circuits. A part of him was dying. He batted down switches, stabbed at buttons and coaxed with his thoughts. He tuned out distractions, staying upright despite the upheaval and making himself ignore the anxiety of his companion. Polly Wright clung to the door frame and screamed with each unexpected jolt.

The TARDIS was careening through real space, an unaccustomed condition. The inertial compensators were sluggish with disuse and not designed for manual operation. The Doctor's task, he reflected, was akin to controlling a clapped-out, runaway Cadillac by sticking both hands into its workings and groping for the steering column.

Luckily, he had only to achieve stability for one vital second. Springing towards the bank of take-off controls, he slammed home the dematerialisation levers with a decisive thrust. The engines whined in pain and the Doctor belatedly remembered to cross his fingers.

'What the heck's going on?' The cry came from Ben. He had arrived at Polly's side, face red, pyjamas wet with perspiration. He swayed and looked momentarily nauseous as the floor dropped a few centimetres, then levelled out. Polly gasped and closed her eyes.

The Doctor let out the breath he had been holding and clapped his hands together with satisfaction. 'We had a small collision, Ben, that's all. Everything's OK now.'

Ben looked aggrieved – as much, the Doctor suspected, because he had arrived too late to be useful as because of the mishap itself. '"A small collision"?' he echoed. 'Fair knocked me out of my bed, it did. I thought the old TARDIS had safeguards against that kind of thing.'

'Ah.' The Doctor's guilt was showing and he knew it. 'I'm afraid I disengaged them.' Mindful of his companions' accusing stares, he continued, 'For once, I needed to follow a specific course – and with good reason.'

'Yes, well,' said Polly, apparently recovered now, 'why don't I fetch some tea to calm us down and you can tell us all about it?'

Within minutes, they were seated on wicker chairs in the corner of the room, supplied with mugs of hot tea by the food machine. Ben had changed into a rollneck sweater and slacks and Polly had found time to rearrange her distressed platinum-blonde hair. She looked once more the picture of elegance. The pair sipped at their drinks, while the Doctor ignored his and played with his hands distractedly.

'My intention, you see, was to land aboard a space station.'

'A space what?' asked Polly. The Doctor sometimes forgot that his companions hailed from the mid-twentieth century.

'It's a sort of floating base, Polly, in orbit beyond Earth's atmosphere.'

'Yeah,' Ben chimed in, 'they were talking about them back home, remember? When they sent up a satellite last year. This is the giant-sized version, I suppose.' He looked to his friend for confirmation and the Doctor smiled indulgently.

Polly shivered. 'Oh, I don't see the point. To be stuck miles away from anywhere, alone in outer space…' An expression of distaste completed the sentence for her.

'It's perfectly safe, I can promise you. Except I, erm, made a minor miscalculation with the arrival coordinates.'

'So what's new?' Ben grumbled.

The Doctor affected his best contrite expression. 'We materialised some distance beyond the station, where we were clipped by a passing ship. The TARDIS's shell is virtually indestructible, of course, but the kinetic energy of the collision sent us spinning out of control. I had to steady us long enough to dematerialise again before we hit something else or, worse, breached the interface between the inside and...' He tailed off, aware that the others were looking glassy-eyed. 'Well it's over now, which is the main thing.' He reached for his cup, downed the scalding contents in one gulp and leapt from his seat, invigorated and ready to press on despite the near-disaster.

'What about the other ship?' asked Polly, with characteristic concern. 'Won't anyone be injured?'

The Doctor was already resetting the controls and he answered over his shoulder. 'Their craft was a great deal larger than mine, Polly. Their computer may have recorded a trifling asteroid strike, but beyond that I doubt they even noticed us.'

''Ere,' said Ben suddenly, 'you're not trying again, are you?'

'Oh Ben, the Doctor knows what he's doing.'

'Stuff that, Pol. What if he sinks us good and proper this time?'

'We really have no choice, Ben,' the Doctor insisted, flustered by the interruption. He checked himself and turned to face the young sailor, re-adopting his usual paternal tones as he explained, 'The TARDIS has picked up a distress signal. I have to investigate.'

'Yeah, well.'

'Is there anything we can do to help, Doctor?'

He knew better than to refuse Polly's offer. 'Yes, I think there might be. Ben, you're trained in radar operation, aren't you? Good, now this is similar. I've plotted the course of the signal and I intend to follow it back to its source. It's a rather more accurate method of navigation than the usual one. Polly, I need you over here.' He bustled around the console, manoeuvring his helpers into position. 'Now, as Ben reads out the numbers on his display, I want you to press the corresponding switches. I'll operate the landing sequence from here and prevent any more, ah, accidents from happening.' He came to rest, hands poised over the controls, and treated them both to an enthusiastic grin. 'All clear?'

Ben and Polly exchanged bemused glances, which the Doctor cheerfully ignored. Their tasks were relatively unimportant; he could easily compensate, quietly, for any errors they made. 'All aboard then,' he announced, 'for the Terran space station Galaxian in the year two thousand, one hundred and thirty-six.'

Polly spent longer than she had meant to in the TARDIS's wardrobes. By the time she returned to the console room, the Doctor had completed his environmental checks and he and Ben were listening to the faint, anonymous message again.

'Doctor, need your assistance urgently,' implored a thin, male voice against a background of wheezing interference. 'Hotel Galaxian, Earth orbit, alien involvement. Please help.' At this point, the words dissolved into a blast of static. There was no way to know if the message had ended or had simply been interrupted.

The Doctor's brow was furrowed and he tugged at his lower lip as he pondered over what he had heard. 'I don't recognise the voice – but somebody clearly knows of me. Apart from the personal address, to have used that particular distress frequency... why, that doesn't come into general use for another three centuries. And yet, I don't remember...' He glanced up and saw Polly, and his expression immediately cleared. 'Ah, here you are. All ready to go?'

'I'm not sure. What do you think of this?' She indicated her newly chosen gear doubtfully: a plain, salmon-pink T-shirt and faded blue jeans of a fit that left little to the imagination. They were a far cry from her usual miniskirts and the clinging fabric felt awfully restrictive. 'If we're to visit the future again, I don't want to look like some sort of nineteen sixties throwback.' She was still stinging from the comments drawn by her style of dress on Vulcan, some time ago.

'Sure,' said Ben, 'we're off to rescue some poor geezer from alien monsters – last thing you need is to find out you're not with it any more!'

'You'll be fine,' said the Doctor. His tone was diplomatic and kind, but one glance at his own battered frock coat, checked trousers and untidy mop-top hairstyle made Polly fear his opinion was worth little. He was like a cross between Charlie Chaplin and one of the Beatles, she thought. As he scurried out of the TARDIS, she looked to Ben for more encouragement.

'You don't think it's a bit too basic, do you?'

'No worries, Duchess. You couldn't look common wrapped in a sheet of wallpaper!' As usual, there was a mocking quality to his voice, so she couldn't be sure if he had meant to compliment or insult her. She stuck out her tongue at him, just in case.

They emerged, finally, into a deserted hall, laid out like a dining room or restaurant. The neatly arranged rows of wooden tables seemed to be awaiting many visitors, but a closer inspection suggested that few, if any, had been here in months. The elaborately patterned red-and-gold wallpaper had faded and a thin film of dust clung to every surface. In contrast, a number of lush green plants broke the straight-lined monotony. The TARDIS had landed in a corner formed by a trellis meeting the wall, the weather-beaten blue box in keeping with its surroundings for once. Polly hadn't expected to be greeted by such a prosaic scene, and the words of the message came back to her.

'Did I hear something about a hotel, Doctor? I thought we were going to a space station.'

He laced his fingers together, his expression apologetic. 'I think you should look behind you, Polly.' She turned and immediately threw a hand over her mouth to stifle a gasp.

One wall of the room was transparent and concave, affording a breathtaking view of the cosmos: more stars than Polly had ever seen, freckled like a rash across an impenetrable blackness which lasted for ever. Her world shifted beneath her and she closed her eyes to steady herself, trying to banish a ridiculous image of drifting through the unending dark in a fragile soap bubble, a whisper from death. She felt Ben's comforting hand on her shoulder. 'Hey, come on Pol. I'm a bit queasy myself but the Doc said it's OK, right?'

'I know, I know. I'm just being silly. It took me by surprise.' Polly opened her eyes and tried to smile bravely.

'It's an understandable reaction,' the Doctor assured her. 'And, until you get used to it, I suggest we find an environment which doesn't offer quite the same perspective.'

'A room without a window,' Ben translated. 'Good idea.'

As they headed for the door, the leaves of an overhanging pot plant brushed against Polly's arm. She was vaguely disappointed to learn that it was plastic.

The station's corridors were in the same state as its restaurant, with carpet frayed and wallpaper peeling. The trio made their way along a wide, gently curving passage which, Polly imagined, would eventually prove to be circular. She already felt better: like the TARDIS, this place offered a perfect gravity and atmosphere. Without visual evidence, it was hard to imagine they weren't safely on the ground.

The Doctor had taken the lead, dropping into his accustomed role as keen lecturer. 'You see, the Galaxian was Earth's first offworld tourist attraction. In its early days, interstellar travel was frightfully expensive and there was really nowhere to go to. For a more modest fee, you could hop on to a shuttle flight and take your holidays here – in space, as it were. It was a popular idea in its time.' His enthusiasm waned visibly as he cast an eye about himself. 'That time, I fear, is long past.'

'Is this what we're standing in, then?' asked Ben. An indented wall panel held a photograph of an alarmingly lopsided, vaguely spherical construct, which tapered to a point at both top and bottom. Its fine detail was hidden by shadow, but its edges glistened attractively in reflected sunlight. It was an impressive picture, but Polly had had enough modelling experience to know how cameras and lighting could fabricate the most alluring lies.

'It looks like a child's top!' she commented, and immediately suffered a mental picture of what would happen if it spun.

The Doctor had already moved on, speed-reading a row of ivory-framed certificates with insatiable curiosity. 'Commendations for the hotel's design and engineering principles. Awards from the corporate sector, too. Of course, a venue like this would have been convenient for international business meetings. And prestigious.'

'In its time,' Ben reminded him.

'Hmmm, yes. Well, every dog its day, Ben – and the Galaxian's day ended with widespread colonisation. Package tours to other worlds became commonplace and the novelty value just wore off. I'd be surprised if it's still in business at all.'

'Well somebody must be here,' said Polly, 'to have sent a signal.'

'Quite. And I wonder whereabouts we might find them.' The Doctor had stopped at another panel, on which a plan was displayed. Polly craned over his shoulder and saw that it was a cross-section of the hotel. Its centremost – and widest – level, she noticed, was reserved for docking and cargo storage. Above it, tiers numbered A1 to A10, in ascending order, were used primarily for accommodation. Below, levels B1 down to B10 boasted amenities including a pool, gymnasium and crèche. It could have been almost any hotel on Earth, but for its odd shape.

'Erm, Doctor…' Ben began.

'The main residents' bar, perhaps. Or we could ask at reception, see if anyone has checked in –'

'Doctor!' Ben's second, more urgent, call succeeded in getting his attention. 'I don't think we'll have to look far.'

Polly heard the approaching footsteps a second after the Doctor did. Without her realising he'd moved, he had somehow placed himself protectively in front of his companions. Ben seemed to resent this and he jostled for pole position. Polly held her breath and shrank back against the wall. But the young man who jogged around the bend of the corridor posed no visible threat.

'Hello. Wait up there. I've caught you at last. We're not using this area, you know, but thanks so much for coming.' He came to a stop as he reached them, too winded to speak. Polly and Ben exchanged playful looks, recalling their earlier conversation. The newcomer was in his mid-twenties, about their age, and extravagantly dressed in a wide-collared purple silk shirt, a spangly silver jacket and spectacles which boasted huge, circular lenses and a lurid pink frame. For a second, Polly thought this might be what the best-dressed people were wearing this season – but then, she would hardly have emulated them even with the benefit of foreknowledge. Fashion was one thing, style quite another.

'Geoff Hornby,' the fashion victim introduced himself, shaking each of their hands in turn. 'I didn't think anyone else would make it, after World Corps did away with the flight and all. I thought we'd have to cancel, but with you three we've got just enough players. Where did you come from, anyhow? Thomas told me you'd arrived, but he said no ships had docked. Some sort of T-mat equipment -'

'Or something,' said the Doctor, smoothly cutting into

the flow. 'I'm the Doctor and these are my companions, Ben and Polly. You say you were expecting us?'

Hornby looked uncertain before the Doctor's probing gaze. 'You are here for the mystery game, aren't you? "Murder in Space"?'

'Ah yes, the game. Of course!' The Doctor underscored his words with an enthusiastic clap. Ben opened his mouth to protest, but was not given the chance. 'We are in time, I hope?'

'We kick off at fourteen hundred,' said Hornby. Then, glancing at his watch, he amended: 'At least, we were supposed to. I'll have to get hold of the others, let them know it's all on again. We haven't even allocated characters yet. Come on, I'll take you to reception and sort out some rooms.'

'Without a view, I hope,' Polly muttered.

Hornby set a brisk pace into a connecting corridor, still chatting away. 'I don't mind telling you, this weekend has been murder to organise.' He barked a short laugh at his own accidental pun. 'First, World Corps leave the hotel in a mess, then they go and cancel the public shuttle. I end up with a grand total of seven players – which is all those who could make their own way here – and one of them has dropped out. Too busy, she's decided. I'm not counting you three, of course. Have you played many RPGs?'

Polly was caught off guard by the sudden question. 'I don't even know what one is,' she confessed.

Hornby's look suggested that he found such ignorance incredible, but the Doctor came to the rescue as usual. 'An acronym for role-playing games. Like acting really, but without a script. For the duration of the game, we each have to pretend to be someone else.'

'You'd be the expert on that,' said Ben, unkindly.

'Oh, that sounds like it could be fun,' decided Polly.

Geoff Hornby was studying her keenly. 'You know, I can just see you in the role of Dame Natasha Moneybags. She's an heiress who likes to flaunt her wealth. She's not very nice, though. She thinks most of the other characters are beneath her. Could you do that?'

'Sounds perfect to me,' said Ben, with a broad grin.

Polly shot him her filthiest look. 'How about you, then?' she asked him. 'Who can you play?'

'Aw, I'm not cut out for this acting lark, Pol. When they handed out parts for the school play, I was lucky to make the back end of the donkey.'

'Oh I don't know Ben,' said the Doctor, 'I think you underrate yourself. You might just enjoy it.'

The group arrived at the head of a grand staircase, which swept down towards what could only have been the main reception area. Polly was pleased to note, as they trotted downward, that this part of the hotel had at least been cleaned. The decor was a little more recent, too, but there was still nobody in sight.

'Is yours the only party in the hotel?' the Doctor inquired.

'It is,' said Hornby. 'World Corps stopped taking bookings long ago. I told them I could fill their bedrooms if they let me run games here free of charge. I won't be dealing with them again though, not after the mess they've left me in.'

They reached the great, curved, polished-oak reception desk, where Hornby passed his hand across a white plastic panel inlaid into the wood. Polly leaned forward and read the inscribed legend WAVE FOR ATTENTION beneath it. She was constantly intrigued by the marvels that future generations took for granted.

Hornby didn't wait long before hopping over the desk and setting to work at a computer terminal. 'I doubt if anyone will come. Do you know how many staff World Corps have sent to run the Galaxian this weekend? One. The rest were supposedly on board the flight they so mysteriously cancelled. Thank goodness for Thomas, that's all I can say. I'll issue you with keycards, but you'll have to see Ms Hayes before you leave to sort out payment details. She's World Corps's representative, by the way. Their only representative.' The computer spat out three small, gold-coloured plastic cards, which Hornby passed to the Doctor. 'If you'll hang on a minute, I've got briefing packs and costumes behind here too. We'll sort out yours now.'

'Costumes too. How marvellous!'

'There's some great stuff here,' crowed Hornby, perked up by the Doctor's gushing enthusiasm. 'I've found the most wonderful little number for Dame Moneybags. I've even got an authentic uniform for the policeman character and real medals for the Admiral.'

'A naval man!' exclaimed Polly. 'There you are Ben, the perfect part for you. You'll even get a promotion out of it.'

'Leave it out, Pol.'

'Splendid!' said the Doctor, as if his every problem had been solved. 'I've always said there's nothing like a bit of make-believe to take your mind off your troubles.'

Ben glared at him mutinously.

'I just don't see what he's playing at!'

'You know the Doctor, Ben.'

'Do I?' Ben brushed the admiral's uniform off an easy chair and dropped heavily into its place. An implausible number of medals jangled protestingly. Immediately, Polly was on her feet, retrieving the garment and brushing it down. Ben wished she wouldn't bother. A dull, persistent ache was building behind his eyes and he looked at his bed longingly. 'I knew the old Doctor, you knew where you stood with him. But this one…' .

'I thought you were over all that. I thought you trusted him now.'

'He's decent enough, yeah. I'm just not sure he's all there sometimes.'

'What a horrid thing to say!'

'Well look at him, Pol. We're supposed to be investigating a mayday, but oh no - one whiff of a chance to dress up and go playing and he gets all gooey-eyed. It's like there's a big kid trying to get out of him.'

'And what would you do?' countered Polly, with a hint of irritation. 'We don't know who sent the signal, nor what kind of danger he might be in. All we do know is that Geoff Hornby has never heard of the TARDIS, which rules him out. The Doctor just wants us to keep a low profile until we can work out what's happening - which means joining in with this… PRG thing.'

Ben sighed, accepting her logic. 'I suppose you're right, Duchess. I just wish he'd tell us where he's at more often. I never know what he expects of us.'

'And what would you prefer, Ben Jackson? Some bluff old sea captain with an eyepatch and a parrot on his shoulder, barking out orders?' Polly thrust a hand behind her back and closed one eye, pulling her face into an exaggerated grimace. 'Splice the mainsail, Jackson, and shiver me timbers against these Cybermen, me hearty!'

'Very funny,' said Ben, laughing as he hurled a cushion

in her direction.

'Have a bit of confidence,' said Polly seriously, 'in yourself if not in the Doctor.'

Ben pouted, recalling the previous night: Polly dragging him around the spaceport bar, mixing freely with Venusians and Draconians and those suspicious-looking things from Alpha Centauri; slipping into conversation with creatures of all shapes and colours; getting away with questions that Ben would never have dared ask, while he just stood there nodding politely and taking refuge in his beer.

'I'll show you confidence,' he retorted, hoisting his costume with determination. 'A shilling says I find out whodunnit before you can.'

Polly breezed towards the door. 'Two shillings says I find the killer before you've even worked out who the victim is.'

'You cheeky little…' Ben went for the pillow again and Polly dived out of the room, giggling.

When she had gone, Ben allowed his cheerful façade to drop. Not that it had been entirely for her benefit: her visit had bucked up his spirits somewhat. Still, he was suffering from minor dehydration, lack of sleep and the knowledge that, once again, the TARDIS had landed them smack in the middle of an uncomfortable situation.

He drew back the curtains, which he had closed for Polly's comfort. The windows on this side of the station, at this time of day, afforded a magnificent view of Earth. It looked surreal, like a flat cutout picture against the void. Ben stared at its great waters and his eyes defocused: he imagined he could see HMS Teazer, a speck on the Indian Ocean, near enough to touch. But his ship had made its voyage to the West Indies two centuries ago and left him behind.

Ben felt his eyelids drooping, but he couldn't afford to sleep. He would only dream of home again, and he didn't feel ready to cope with another disappointment.

'Doctor!'

'Oh, my word!' The Doctor sprang to his feet, shocked out of his contemplation. His first thought was that no one could have entered his room without his knowing it. But there was no point in denying the presence of the bizarre intruder who stood before him in the half-light. The man's skin was pale, his hair dark and scraped back. He wore a neat black suit, topped off by a red-lined cloak. His eyes were bloodshot and white fangs glistened in the corners of his thin-lipped mouth.

'You are needed.' The voice was hushed and throaty.

'By many people, yes,' the Doctor agreed, backing away slowly, 'which is why it would be such a shame if I was harmed.' The vampire followed him around the bed and he was acutely aware that he had nowhere else to go. 'If you're attempting to frighten me, I have to say you're doing an excellent job.' It took another step towards him and the Doctor felt the wall against his back. He raised both forefingers in the shape of a cross, but it was a hopeless gesture.

'Be in room four three eight at fifteen thirty hours,' said the vampire. 'Come alone.' Then it fell silent and cocked its head, as if awaiting a response.

The Doctor frowned, curiosity replacing fear with the immediate danger past. 'Who are you? What are you doing here?'

'Good morning, sir.' The voice had changed; it now sounded as if it belonged to an old-fashioned English butler. 'My name is Thomas and I represent the automated systems of the Hotel Galaxian. How may I assist you?'

The Doctor reached out experimentally and passed his hand straight through the vampire's body. Thomas didn't seem to notice. He simply stood, wearing a patient smile. 'You're a hologram!'

'Indeed, sir. You may summon me from all information points on the station.' He indicated a red 'help' button on the headboard of the Doctor's bed, alongside the controls for the communications system and tea-making facilities.

'But I never pressed that,' the Doctor insisted. Thomas didn't seem to understand, so he elaborated: 'I didn't call you. You came here entirely of your own volition.'

'I assure you such a thing is not possible, sir. May I venture to suggest you brushed against the button without knowing it?'

The Doctor narrowed his eyes. 'And I don't suppose you recall giving me a message about room four three eight at fifteen thirty hours, either?'

'My memory banks have no recollection of the incident, sir.'

'They haven't, eh? One more thing: why do you take the form of a classical vampire? I would hardly call it appropriate.'

Thomas seemed embarrassed. 'My resolution circuits were programmed with this image some months ago, for a children's Hallowe'en party. I'm afraid I have yet to be returned to my default setting. I agree that my appearance is improper and I apologise on behalf of World Corps for any inconvenience this may cause.'

'Yes, thank you Thomas, that will be all.' The Doctor waved the hologram away, distractedly. It fizzled and vanished in an instant and he was left with more than ever to think about.

So his contact was, presumably, alive and well in the Galaxian. But instead of approaching him directly, he had used the computer to arrange a secret rendezvous. It all suggested that this mystery man was in a good deal of trouble.

Or, perhaps, that he was luring the Doctor into an elaborate trap.

CHAPTER 2

THE UNUSUAL SUSPECTS

Ben hammered on the door impatiently. 'Come on, Pol. How long can it take you to get kitted out? We'll be late, you know.'

Polly sighed and took one last look at herself in the dress mirror. The reflected image brought a smile to her face. Geoff Hornby had done her proud, providing an old-fashioned, sumptuous, white ball gown with elaborate lacework. The fit was snug, admittedly – the corset was cruel even to her slim figure – but it was worth some discomfort to look so good. She only regretted that there was no time to do her hair to match.

She swept regally towards the door (teetering on high heels and forced to hoist skirts as she was, it was near impossible to walk any other way) and yanked it open even as Ben was making to knock again. She wasn't disappointed by his reaction. 'You can pop your eyes back into their sockets,' she admonished playfully. 'I thought we were in a hurry.'

'You look a proper duchess in that get-up,' he said admiringly.

'Thanks. You're not half bad yourself. An officer's uniform suits you.' Even so, she couldn't resist adjusting his peaked cap and brushing a piece of fluff from his otherwise immaculate black jacket.

Ben tugged at the collar of his starched shirt uncomfortably. 'I'm not so sure. I keep thinking I'm – I don't know – getting above myself, I suppose.'

'Oh, Ben!' Polly laughed. 'You've even taken off those medals, haven't you?'

'Did you see how many there were? If we're to be sneaking about looking for clues, I don't want to be jangling like a cow with a bell round its neck. Besides, I don't think it's possible to get so many gongs in a lifetime.'

'We are in the future, Ben. Perhaps they're more common now?'

'Yeah, well the costumes aren't very futuristic, are they? This uniform's not much different to the 1966 version.'

'I'll bet it hasn't changed,' teased Polly. 'Your lot never did understand fashion.'

'Ha, ha.'

'Come on, let's find the Doctor.'

'Already tried him,' said Ben. 'He's not in his room.'

'Do you suppose he's down in the bar already?'

'Only one way to find out. Shall we go?' Ben held out his arm, and Polly grinned and took it.

The Interplanetary Bar filled most of Deck B8 (admittedly one of the smaller, lower levels). It was decorated in shades of blue and purple, with varied lighting effects and decorations adding a touch of the bizarre. A patch of green light here, an unchecked rambling plant there, a stuffed alien menace in the corner. The overall effect was surreal, but somehow calming. Ben couldn't imagine the contemporary sounds of the Beatles or Manfred Mann blasting through this place. You were more likely, he considered, to hear whale song.

As in the dining room, one wall blistered outward into space. Ben felt Polly stiffen on his arm as they swept down the short flight of steps from the doors. To her credit, though, she remained outwardly indifferent, determined not to let a phobia beat her. Of course, it helped that their grand entrance elicited a spattering of applause. Even Ben's chest inflated with pride and he thought he might get used to this game after all.

The other players had gathered in a medium-sized alcove, seated on a curved, cushioned bench around a long table. An illuminated but empty fish tank cast white light across them from behind and an inanimate silver humanoid stood, sentry-like, nearby. It was supposed to be a Cyberman, Ben realised, but it bore scant resemblance to the monsters he had fought at the South Pole. It was too metallic and the zip down its front was too obvious.

One man appeared to have elected himself as the welcoming party. He was middle-aged and stout, with a round, ruddy face and sprouting tufts of hair which, Ben thought, made his head resemble a pineapple. Tiny pince-nez spectacles were balanced precariously on his nose; they suited him, although they might have come with the costume. He was wearing a long, blue, velvet jacket, a spotted bow tie and a shirt of bright orange which was almost painful to look at.

'Salutations, darlings!' he boomed in a resonant voice, standing and throwing wide his arms. Polly allowed him to hug her and to plant an affectionate peck on her cheek. Ben kept his distance and held out his hand, which the man pumped vigorously. 'Lord Henry Mace at your service. You may have heard of me. I'm a leading light of the am-dram scene Earthside.'

'Oh, we haven't been to Earth for a… few years,' said Polly. Her diplomatic response seemed good enough for Mace, who proceeded to introduce the other three

23

people at the table.

'These delectable young ladies are Daphne McAllister and Terri… Willis, wasn't it dear? I thought so. And the upstanding young man in the policeman's robes becomes Bryan Melrose, chartered accountant, by day.'

Polly performed the introductions on behalf of herself and Ben, who glanced about the room and wondered if the Doctor was hiding in one of its nooks. The only other person he could see was a man with a thin black beard, dressed in leathers. He was slumped in a corner, ignoring everyone else. He seemed to be engrossed in a paperback detective novel, but his dark glasses must have made it impossible to read in the subdued light.

'I love your costume,' said Daphne McAllister to Polly. 'Did you make it yourself?'

'No, it was supplied for me,' she admitted. 'It does look good, doesn't it? It's a bit awkward, though. I don't know how I'm going to sit down.'

'You must try, dear girl,' said Henry Mace. He beckoned her to take a place beside him. 'I brought along my own apparel for this adventure. I, appropriately, am to portray a thespian, which is no great stretch of my talents, of course.' Polly gathered up copious folds of fabric and manoeuvred herself, with difficulty, into the proffered seat. Ben perched on the edge of the bench, once more uncomfortable among strangers.

'We're supposed to be pop stars - Melodie and Harmonie, the Tuneful Twins. Should be a giggle.' Daphne half stood to show off her blouse, miniskirt and leggings, the patterns of which suggested to Ben that a dozen colours had died in a crash. Terri sported an identical outfit.

'Groovy!' enthused Polly, then, remembering where she was: 'I mean, it's nice.' Terri Willis's grunt indicated that she didn't think so. Bryan Melrose didn't seem to care. His posture was tense and he kept scratching at his throat. His expression was doleful, but this was partly a product of his thin face, long nose and sagging cheeks. His hair was fair and thinning and the bulky, armoured uniform he wore was several sizes too big. He looked as out of place here as Ben felt.

'I hope we don't have to sing though,' said Daphne confidentially. 'I don't think either of us have sung since we were in the school choir together, have we Ter?'

'Ah, musicals! You need only ask, my dear, I've starred in dozens.' Mace's voice was loud and rich, demanding attention. Ben could see he enjoyed being at centre stage. 'Of course, I've had extensive voice training. My tonsils are a finely-honed instrument.' To the amazement of everyone, he burst into a song, about business being business and always aiming to please. Ben didn't recognise the tune – but he scarcely needed to to hear that Mace's baritone voice veered up to a semitone away from each note, and not always in the same direction.

Polly and Daphne looked at each other and struggled to control laughing fits. Terri was less amused. 'When you said an instrument, I didn't think you meant a chainsaw!'

Mace was quietened instantly. 'If you don't wish the benefit of my experience…' he said sniffily.

'How about the benefit of your closed mouth?' suggested Terri with a humourless smile.

Mace sulked, Terri studied her fingernails with forced nonchalance and everyone else shuffled feet and avoided each other's eyes. Daphne broke the tense moment. 'So, you two come from a colony world?' she inquired brightly, addressing Ben.

'That's right,' he said, and quickly stood before she could ask him which one. 'Is the bar open yet? I don't know about you lot, but I ain't half ready for a drink.'

The Doctor had taken a quick inspection tour which ended back on A1, the lowest residential level, on which all the guests appeared to be staying. He had studied the floor plans for long enough to have them more or less memorised. Now he stared out of a corridor window near his room, running through calculations in his head. Even taking into account the refractive qualities of the plastic shielding and a safety margin for his rough estimates of distance, he knew something was amiss.

Two pairs of footsteps approached and, although he remained apparently pensive, he switched some of his attention to the task of eavesdropping on the conversation in progress. One never knew when a stray titbit of information may come in useful.

'- think it's a holiday for me, do you?' cultured female tones were complaining. 'I was supposed to be in Paris this weekend, running the biggest hotel in the World Corps leisure portfolio. Instead, I'm shanghaied to this hole and expected to play manager, receptionist, chief cook and bottle-washer.'

'It's not my fault, Ms Hayes,' protested the more familiar voice of Geoff Hornby. 'I had everything organised until your employers bailed out on me.'

'If you had presided over as many international conventions as I, you would not use the word "organised" in reference to this petty, mismanaged operation.'

The Doctor turned as the pair drew level. Hornby stopped and smiled weakly. Ms Hayes - an upright thirtysomething with tied-up hair and neat, pinstriped jacket and skirt - didn't care to acknowledge his presence. She strode on and Hornby called after her plaintively, 'You will do what you can about those dinners, won't you?' Her reply, while indiscernible, was clearly resentful.

'Ah, the tribulations of management.'

'Aren't you getting into costume?' asked Hornby. 'We'll be starting in a few minutes.'

'Of course,' said the Doctor gently. Hornby hurried on, with the stooped shoulders and urgent gait of the chronically harassed.

As the Doctor fiddled with his keycard reader, a door was flung open at the far end of the corridor. An elderly gentleman emerged, his white hair growing wild about a prominent bald spot. He was wearing a tweed jacket and trousers, and a white shirt tail flapped behind him as he pivoted to shout back into his room. 'Well one of us has got to go down there or we'll jeopardise the whole plan!'

The Doctor shrank back into the shallow alcove provided by his door frame. Somebody must have replied to the man's protestation, although he wasn't close enough to hear. The angry rejoinder, however, was more than audible. 'No, you just sit there and play with your toy. I'll cover for you as usual!' The sound of a ferociously slammed door still echoed even after the man had stomped out of view towards the elevator lobby.

The Doctor eased himself into his room.

Polly could see that Ben was having problems. She

joined him at the circular, central bar, hovering uncertainly before one of several terminals. 'It's a serve-yourself gizmo,' he explained, 'but I can't go asking how to use it; that'd give the game right away.'

Polly sighed. They were both used to the problems caused by the Doctor's insistence on keeping his time-travelling capabilities a secret. They accepted the ruling, though. Apart from anything else, it avoided long explanations. 'You'll also make them suspicious if you take much longer,' she warned. 'You said you were getting these drinks ten minutes ago.'

'And that's another thing: I hope we can charge this lot to our rooms, 'cos I don't even know what kind of money they use these days. For that matter, the Doc had better have some way of paying our bills planned. I don't fancy spending six months on KP duty here.'

'You worry too much. Here, let me try.'

'No need, I've almost cracked it.'

'What does this do?' Polly reached past Ben and stabbed at a red button, labelled HELP. She jumped back, startled, as the menacing figure of a stereotypical movie vampire appeared from nowhere, across the bar.

'Good afternoon, sir, madam. My name is Thomas and I represent the automated systems of the Hotel Galaxian. How may I assist you?'

Ben composed himself and complained, in a slightly aggrieved tone, about the complexities of ordering. As Thomas patiently explained the function of each keypad and the meaning of each symbol, Polly's eyes explored the room. They lighted upon a slowly revolving, reflective globe hanging over a corner; an enlarged Escher-type maze on one wall; a flickering red light above a shocking yellow sign reading DANGER: RADIATION HAZARD. That had to be a joke, didn't it?

Yes, of course it did. Another example of the designer's esoteric tastes.

She was more interested in people. She nudged Ben in the ribs, distracting him from the task of putting the now-departed vampire's tuition into practice. 'Who's the man over there?'

'Oh, him,' said Ben, without interest. 'He was there when we arrived, just reading. Looks like he doesn't want to talk.'

Polly stole another glance at the leather-clad stranger and said, 'He's a bit old to be dressed like a rocker, isn't he? Someone should tell him.'

Ben shrugged and turned his attention back to the terminal. With a grim smile of determination, he pressed the final button. Behind the bar, a hatch opened. Six glasses trundled dutifully out along a conveyor belt, pausing beneath the relevant pumps and optics to be filled. Polly couldn't help but chuckle. 'I wonder if all bars are like that nowadays, or just this one.'

'You've seen the rest of the room,' said Ben drily. 'What do you think?'

The drinks arrived and Ben picked up three. Polly opted for two, mindful of her heels. Better to make a second trip than to ruin this lovely dress. 'I'll go over and talk to him,' she said as they made their way back to the table.

'Who?'

'The rocker.'

'No, leave him alone, Pol. He obviously wants peace and quiet. He's probably sick of listening to "Lord" Henry Mace.'

'Don't be rotten, Ben. You've only just met the man.'

'I've heard enough from him, though. He's like a

child, desperate for attention.'

'You said something similar about the Doctor,' she reminded him. 'Henry Mace is an eccentric, that's all.'

'Pol, the Doctor's what you call eccentric. This guy's a ruddy nutter!'

'How many people are in the hotel at the moment?' the Doctor asked Thomas. He was sitting cross-legged on his bed, recorder poised at his mouth. He often found music conducive to his concentration.

The holographic vampire pursed his lips as if thinking. In reality, the Doctor knew, the information would be provided by a microprocessor far away. Then: 'Twelve, sir,' he answered, 'including your good self.'

'There's no chance of anyone being here without your knowing it? Say, if they didn't arrive through the docking bays?'

'May I remind you that your own mode of transport is unknown to me,' said Thomas politely. 'However, I was aware of your heat signature from the moment of your arrival – and of your identity from the time your booking was registered.'

'There's no fooling you, is there Thomas?'

'I hope not, sir.'

The Doctor blew a low, mournful note on the recorder. 'Except for when it comes to mysterious messages, of course,' he muttered, mostly to himself. 'I don't suppose you could tell me why the stars seem to be out of alignment, either.'

The group in the bar had split into two, with Ben in the middle. To his left, Polly and Bryan Melrose were listening politely to accounts of Mace's past acting triumphs. 'And when I turned around, they were all wearing bowler hats,' he roared with exaggerated humour. 'Bowler hats, I tell you!'

To his right, Daphne and Terri reminisced about their school days together. From what Ben could overhear, Terri was determinedly puncturing her friend's attempts to romanticise the experience. 'Mr Morris was not a "decent old bloke", Daphne, he was a perverted lech. How could you not know about him and Mandy Simpson?'

Ben took a long swig from his pint of bitter beer ('hair of the dog' always did the trick, to his mind), but found his gaze lingering on the two young women through the bottom of the glass. There was no denying that both were extremely attractive. Daphne's was a classical beauty, with full, shoulder-length red hair, glistening eyes and every curve where it should be. Terri, on the other hand, had more severe features, heightened by a harsh application of make-up. Her black tresses were cut short and her eyes were a hard green. Still, Ben thought, she looked the more genuine of the pair – the one with character. He preferred that to Daphne's powder-smoothed skin and mannequin symmetry.

Of course, neither woman could hold a torch to Polly – but Ben harboured no illusions on that score. They were from different sides of life; only friends at all because, amid a barrage of the unfamiliar – including the Doctor, whose very identity could change at the drop of a stovepipe hat – they had only each other to rely on for consistency and understanding. Once the TARDIS returned them to London, 1966 – if it ever did – Polly Wright would be raving straight back up the King's Road with the 'in' crowd, and Ben Jackson would return to barracks alone.

'What do you do in real life, then?'

It took him a moment to realise that Bryan Melrose, having quietly extricated himself from Mace's audience, was addressing him. It was the first time Ben had heard his voice: it was quiet and nasal, as if the owner had a cold.

'I'm a seaman there, too. Not such a high rank, though.' Ben hoped not to have to elaborate. Who knew how much the structure and duties of the merchant navy might have changed in two hundred years? 'How about you? You're an accountant, aren't you?'

Melrose nodded. 'My company sent me on this weekend. They said it was a "character-building exercise". To tell the truth, it isn't my sort of thing.'

'I know how you feel, mate.'

As both men sipped their pints, Ben heard Polly ask, 'So, are you an hereditary peer or were you appointed?'

'Quite right dear,' said Henry Mace, vaguely. Ben was sure he had only pretended to mishear the question. Then he burst into false laughter and banged on the table for attention. 'I must show this to the others. Who do you think this is, everyone?' They all turned to look, with varying degrees of reluctance. Terri's irritated roll of the eyes was particularly pronounced, but Mace didn't seem to notice. He hunched up his shoulders and, in a voice that would have suited a cartoon mouse, he squeaked, 'Ooh, Jessie, the vicar's coming to high tea and my trousers have fallen down again.' Mace found his own impression extraordinarily amusing – but, given the baffled looks that passed among the others, it was just as well that he identified it himself. 'It's my good friend Tom Chuckle, comedian and impresario. Did I tell you about the first time I met Tom?'

'Yes you did,' said Terri pointedly.

Mace looked set to repeat the anecdote anyway, but happily, Geoff Hornby chose that moment to enter. An older, dishevelled-looking man straggled behind him; he smiled faintly to the assembled players and quietly took a seat nearby.

Hornby performed a head count and concluded, 'There's one missing.'

'That would be the Doctor,' volunteered Polly.

Hornby looked at his watch impatiently. 'I'm going to have to get the briefing started.'

'Go on then,' said Ben. 'I'll fill the Doc in on the details when I see him.'

Hornby seemed reluctant, but he agreed. As he shuffled through his notes, Polly leaned towards Ben and whispered, 'You don't suppose he's in trouble, do you?'

'You know the Doctor. At least if we can get this over with quick, we can set about finding him.'

One by one, Hornby asked the players to stand while he introduced them, by both real and assumed names. Ben forgot most of the latter immediately, but found a convenient list in his briefing pack. He fidgeted awkwardly as he was announced to the others as 'Admiral Anchor, a brave and much-decorated sailor on the verge of retirement'. If Hornby noticed the absence of said decorations, he didn't comment.

The latest arrival's name – his real one – was Neville Adler, and he was to portray an absent-minded scientist. 'I must apologise for my lack of costume,' he said, playing nervously with a frayed red handkerchief which he then stuffed untidily into his breast pocket. 'I've only just finished helping my wife with some work. She's upstairs, you know. She asked me to pass on her regrets at being unable to join us.' Ben hid a smirk:

no costume was needed to make this fellow look the part, he thought. Adler hesitated, realised he had run out of things to say, and made to sit down. He collided with the table instead and spilt various drinks across its top.

Once Adler's profuse apologies – and his attempts to mop up the damage with his handkerchief – had died down, Hornby introduced the final player. It was the mysterious man in the leathers and dark glasses. 'This is Ted Matlock. He's playing Vince Throttle, a hi-tech Silicon Demon from the streets of New York. And to make up the numbers, I'll be taking on the role of conscientious student Andrew Bookworm myself.' Hornby had already swapped his ostentatious attire for a conservative pair of cords and a woolly jumper. The pink spectacles were nowhere to be seen either, and Ben wondered how he had managed to read his notes without them.

'But you already know who did it,' protested Daphne. 'Won't it spoil the game?'

'No, no, it won't matter. Anyway, there's the difficult part out of the way. From now on, your briefing packs should tell you all you need to know.' Neville Adler frowned and rummaged through his pockets, finding nothing. 'All you have to do is go and act out your part. Try to remember what your characters are doing here, what their aims are and what secrets they're trying to keep from whom. Enjoy yourselves, but be warned: some time in the next couple of hours' – Hornby lowered his voice for dramatic effect – 'there's going to be a murder!'

The moment was spoilt as the doors behind him were barged open. 'I'm so sorry, I hope I'm not too late,' said the newcomer, buttoning up the front of a plain red dress and scurrying down the steps hastily. A cheap necklace clattered against a prominent chest and golden locks tumbled past a very... familiar face.

Polly put a hand to her mouth to stifle laughter. Mace shouted out 'Bravo!' and Ben covered his eyes in embarrassment.

It was the Doctor.

The players had begun to disperse, ostensibly to go about their characters' business. Polly and Ben joined the Doctor for an impromptu, whispered conference. 'What are you playing at, dressed like that?' Ben wanted to know, to the Doctor's visible dismay.

'Don't you like it? I'm just helping out Mr Hornby with a slight gender imbalance. I got the wig from the TARDIS, but I think it works rather well with the outfit, don't you?' He brushed a stray hair from his face and grinned disarmingly. 'I had to improvise with the bustle though, using coat hangers.' He patted his wire-frame chest and looked comically startled as it dropped to his stomach.

Polly laughed and assured him that he made a most convincing woman, as he struggled to adjust himself. 'Look, what about this mayday?' prompted Ben. 'Have you found anything?'

'Indeed I have,' said the Doctor, suddenly very sober. 'In fact, I have a rendezvous scheduled in a little over half an hour.'

'With who?'

'I don't know yet, Polly. Now, there were ten people here when I arrived, including ourselves. I believe there are twelve in the hotel.'

'Mr Adler said his wife was upstairs.'

'He would be the gentleman in the tweed coat, I

presume. Yes, that would make sense. And the hotel's acting manager, Ms Hayes, would give us an even dozen. So: nobody here we don't know about. At least, not if Thomas is to be trusted.'

'And you don't recognise anyone?' asked Ben.

As the Doctor shook his head, a polite cough took Polly's attention. She turned to find Hornby hovering behind her. 'May I have a quick word in private please, ma'am?'

Ma'am? Of course, she recalled, she was meant to be in character. 'I suppose so, you, erm, common oik.'

She bade farewell to the Doctor and Ben, and Hornby led her out into the elevator lobby. They rounded the corner and pushed through a fire door into the stairwell. 'I need to talk to you,' he whispered, 'but somewhere less public. Can you get away?'

'Erm, yes, I suppose. What for?'

He frowned. 'Well, you know. About last night?' Polly looked blank, so Hornby hissed, 'It's in your briefing pack. We're having an affair!'

'Oh. Right. Of course, yes.'

'Shall we say fifteen minutes then? In the gymnasium on Deck B6?'

'Make it twenty. I have to meet one of those ghastly new pop bands to discuss patronage, but I shall make my excuses and leave early.'

Hornby grinned his approval. 'I'll see you then,' he called, as he hurried off down the stairs. 'Looking forward to it.'

'Quite a range of costumes, isn't there?' the Doctor commented appreciatively. 'Mr Hornby obviously wants this to be a period piece. Now if only he could decide which period…'

He and Ben had retired to a window seat, beneath a dim violet light. The bar was slowly emptying. Ben watched as Ted Matlock left alone, without a word to anyone. Then his attention was drawn to Daphne and Terri, who were engaged in a very public argument. For a second, he wanted to intercede – but they were merely acting.

'Well your songs aren't so great, you know,' shouted Daphne.

'They'd sound better if they were sung properly. I'm keeping this group afloat and you know it!'

'Then go and get yourself a solo career. But don't come back to me when it flops!'

'I might just do that!' Terri turned and stormed out of the bar.

Mace swooped in to comfort Daphne. 'You've done the right thing, darling,' he assured her, raising his voice and glancing around to make sure everyone was listening. As it happened, only Ben and the Doctor remained to hear. 'You have too big a talent to be held down by such petty disputes. May I venture that an association between the two of us could be of mutual benefit in the launching of a new, meteoric career?' He bowed ridiculously low and almost fell over in the process. Daphne burst out laughing.

The Doctor stared out of the window. Ben followed his gaze across the starfield, until it entirely filled his vision and he felt suddenly isolated and very cold and had to look away. 'Do you want me to come to this meeting with you?'

The Doctor shook his head without looking at him. 'The message said to go alone. I think I should honour our friend's wishes for now. Besides, there are more important things for you to do.'

He was glad to hear it. 'What things?'

'I want you to learn as much as you can about the other guests. You can use your motives in the game as a cover for talking to them.'

'I suppose so.' Ben pulled his creased character details from his pocket and skimmed through them. 'I'm supposed to be Adler's brother, for a start. Yeah, I can just see that! Oh, and according to this, I'm engaged to a Miss Lucy Buxom. Who's playing her?'

The Doctor turned to him and smiled demurely. 'Oh, fabulous!' Ben groaned.

'Don't worry, I won't hold you to any promises.' His serious tone underlay the jocularity of his words.

'What is it? What's wrong?'

'Look out of the window, Ben. Tell me what you see.'

'Stars. Lots of them.'

'Do you recognise many?'

He shrugged. 'From Earth, yeah. The navy taught me how to navigate. It's tricky from this angle, though.'

'We're looking towards the Smaller Magellanic Cloud. The problem is, a large proportion of its bodies appear to have shifted. The displacement is barely visible to the naked eye, but it is there.'

Ben didn't know where this was leading. 'So the stars have moved a bit. So what?'

'You don't understand. The nearest of those stars is over a hundred and fifty thousand light years away. A shift large enough to be visible from this distance can hardly be described as "moving a bit". Catastrophic would be nearer the mark.'

'How could such a thing happen?'

'In so consistent a pattern? It couldn't. Which leads me to suspect that our eyes are being fooled. We are seeing an illusion. Somewhere out there, Ben, light rays are being bent around an object and returned to a path just fractionally different from their original one.'

Ben mulled the statement over for a few seconds, then exclaimed, 'There's an invisible ship!'

'Somewhere out there, yes. And I wonder how it might tie in with our little mystery?' The Doctor's eyes defocused as he descended into quiet contemplation. Distractedly, he muttered to himself: 'By the pricking of my thumbs...'

CHAPTER 3

SOMETHING WICKED

Polly arrived early for her character's meeting with Daphne and Terri (or 'Melodie' and 'Harmonie', she reminded herself) and found the door to the Venusian Conference Suite locked. Even as she wondered who could rectify that for her, she heard a thump and a muffled curse from farther down the corridor.

She hurried over, concerned, to where a young, smartly turned-out woman was kneeling to load bags of crisps back into a wooden crate. 'Here, let me give you a hand with those,' she offered. The woman accepted with no more than a mortified smile.

As they hefted the refilled container back on to its base, she spoke for the first time. 'My name's Alison Hayes. I'm in charge of the hotel for the weekend – but I don't recall seeing you before.'

Polly groaned inwardly, sensing another of those awkward situations arising. She introduced herself with forced cheer and the pair shook hands. 'I did see your name on the computer,' Hayes recalled, 'but I have no record of your arrival.'

'Ah yes, we made our own arrangements.'

'Which didn't include a docking bay?'

'It's a sort of tea-mat set-up,' bluffed Polly, hoping she remembered Geoff Hornby's mistaken assumption correctly. She changed the subject quickly. 'Look, I know you must be frightfully busy, but I'm supposed to be using this room in a couple of minutes and it appears to be locked.'

Without saying anything, Hayes managed to look extremely put out by the request. She produced a card from her pocket – similar to the gold ones which gave access to the bedrooms, but in white – and swiped it through the reader by the conference suite's door.

'It must be difficult for you to run this place by yourself,' said Polly sympathetically, hoping to keep on the good side of this woman.

'The computer takes care of most of it. It's the niggling things that keep me busy: planning and programming menus, authorising payments, humping around supplies.' Hayes narrowed her eyes. 'How are you intending to settle your bill, by the way?'

'The Doctor will see you about it,' said Polly hurriedly.

'Company cheque, is it?'

'I doubt it. Anyway, I won't keep you. Thanks for your help, Miss Hayes.' Polly edged her way around the door, beaming broadly.

'It's Ms Hayes, actually.'

'Right enough. Bye, then.' She darted inside the room and was relieved to see, through a glass pane in its door, that Hayes was once more on her way.

'What does Mizz mean?' she wondered.

The Doctor busied himself at the TARDIS console, dashing between controls and displays, taking readings and occasionally pausing to mutter to himself. The complex devices of his people were only confirming his own deductions.

'So there is somebody out there.'

It was a ship of no design he had encountered before. Nor could the TARDIS's extensive databanks match its signature to a known type. What the Doctor's instruments could provide was a vague outline of the

cloaked vessel, which revealed it to be sleek and flat-
nosed and of a not inconsiderable size. It was also
bristling with weaponry. And it was almost certainly
the ship with which the TARDIS had collided on its
incoming journey.

'Which means it approached the station much earlier
than I had assumed,' he mused, idly pulling at his lip.
'Approached it, yet took up a stationary position
beyond. I wonder why.'

Ten minutes later, he emerged into the dining room,
still checking over the device he had hastily cobbled
together. It resembled an old-fashioned fob watch, and
indeed he had attached it to his frock-coat pocket by
way of a chain. In fact, though, it was a remote link to
the TARDIS, with one particular function: in the event
of the mysterious ship drawing closer, an alarm signal
would be transmitted and the Doctor would be
instantly aware of the development. What he could
then do about it was another matter.

Somehow, he had to find out who the ship's
occupants were. And what they were waiting for.

Ben had tried to escape from the Interplanetary Bar,
but was dragged into a conversation with Henry Mace
and Daphne McAllister. The gist of it was that Mace's
out-of-luck actor wanted Ben's character, the Admiral,
to have a word with his fiancée – the Doctor – on his
behalf. Miss Lucy Buxom was apparently a secretary at
a prestigious television network, and Mace believed
she could do both his character and Daphne's some
good. Or something like that. Ben found it difficult to
keep up, particularly when his mind was more
occupied by real-life puzzles. He wondered how he
could possibly find out anything about the hotel's

occupants if they were all too busy playing other people.

Mace, in particular, had launched himself into his role with gusto. 'Darlings,' he orated passionately, 'if you could see the no-hopers who, by the dictates of nepotism, appear on that station. To think this talented young lady and I...' There was more, but Ben tuned it out. It did occur to him that Mace might be doing an excellent job of portraying a terrible actor and a crushing bore; however, as his earlier, out-of-character, performance had been strikingly similar (and not much less studied), Ben doubted it.

It was Daphne who eventually saved him. 'We really do have to be going,' she said. 'We have a meeting with Dame Moneybags and we're already late.'

Mace checked his watch – an elaborate, gold-chain affair – and his eyes widened in horror. 'We must hurry, my dear. We cannot afford to keep the good lady waiting. Worse still, what would happen if your treacherous sister were to keep the appointment in our stead?'

Ben let out a heavy sigh of relief as they bustled out of the room. In the past quarter of an hour, he had learnt precisely nothing. Perhaps a chat with Neville Adler, as he had originally planned, might prove more productive.

The Doctor had suggested that, as the hotel's computer apparently monitored the heat traces of its guests, the hologram Thomas might be able to locate a particular one for him. His finger was poised over one of the red help buttons at the bar when he was startled by what sounded like the discharge of an energy weapon, accompanied by a cry of pain. He froze. Could this be some sound effect devised by Hornby to indicate that his play murder had taken place?

He discarded his theory as, a second later, he heard the piercing scream of Daphne McAllister. Ben left the bar at a run.

The Doctor was crossing the reception area when he heard the muffled sound of the distant shot and, a few seconds later, the scream. As near as he could tell, both came from the direction of the main staircase. He shouldered his way through the access door and scuttled downward, filled with panic at what he might find. He had been expecting trouble since arriving at the Galaxian, but he could never be fully prepared for the pain of innocents or the mindless brutality of humankind. Somebody was in trouble and he was needed to clear up the mess again.

As he passed the door to Deck B4, he almost ran into Neville Adler, who was running desperately in the opposite direction. Adler whimpered and tried to squirm his way past, but the Doctor took a firm hold of his shoulders and stared fiercely into his eyes. 'What is it, man? What's happening down there?'

'It's nothing to do with me,' he squealed. 'They're trying to kill each other and it's not my fault!' Adler made a concerted effort to break free and, this time, the Doctor let him go. He could catch up with him later. He continued his descent and, soon enough, turned a corner to come upon a scene of pandemonium.

At first, it wasn't clear who was fighting whom. There was simply a pile of heaving bodies on the stairs, each struggling to gain an upper position, some crying out at intervals, others appealing frantically for calm. Beyond the seething mass, Daphne cowered against the wall, watching in fear and distaste. Ben hurtled on to the scene from below and, like the Doctor, froze in horror and indecision as he sighted the mêlée.

'This will not do at all. Stop this at once!' the Doctor blustered. 'Oh dear,' he added miserably when his words went unheeded.

Ms Hayes had managed to detach herself, her hair bedraggled and her face red with exertion. A moment ago, she had been shrieking demands that this behaviour cease forthwith, so the Doctor was mildly surprised to see her holding Ted Matlock in a headlock and dragging him behind her. 'Help me to pull this one free,' she yelled to him, and the Doctor made a snap judgement that she was probably doing the right thing.

Ben had come to his own decision and he waded in from the opposite side, tearing people away one by one. 'All right now, come on, let's be having you!'

Matlock struggled for a moment, then allowed himself to be manhandled away from the others. As soon as the Doctor and Hayes let go of him, he turned with a snarl and scrambled up towards the nearest exit door.

By now, their efforts and Ben's had all but brought things to a conclusion. The Doctor, Geoff Hornby, Henry Mace, Alison Hayes, Daphne McAllister and Ben were left standing on the staircase, breathing heavily and avoiding each other's gazes as they all tried to make sense of what had happened. And there was one more: Bryan Melrose was on his hands and knees, obviously in pain. The Doctor saw the ragged gash in his armoured uniform, the livid red burn on his shoulder beneath it and the discarded gun simultaneously.

'What's up? Someone playing the game too seriously?' Terri Willis had arrived, behind Ben.

'Oh, Terri, it was horrible!' sobbed Daphne.

The Doctor stooped to pick up the gun. 'Seriously enough for someone to bring this along, anyway. It's a rather nasty little concentrated-energy weapon.' He turned to Melrose, who had pulled himself into a sitting position, teeth gritted against the pain of his injury. 'You were lucky. If a blast from this had hit you squarely, it would have gone straight through you. As it is, you'll suffer no more than the equivalent of a bad sunburn.'

'It hurts quite enough, thank you.'

'Ah, yes. I wonder if you two ladies would be kind enough to escort our friend here to the medical centre and find him something for his wound.'

'Can't you tell us who did it?' asked Hornby impatiently, as the Doctor helped Melrose to his feet – surreptitiously checking for concealed weapons in the process – and turned him over to Daphne and Terri. 'Who shot you?'

Melrose shrugged, then sucked air through his teeth as the movement proved more painful than he had anticipated. 'Didn't see,' he mumbled. 'Happened too fast. Sorry.'

'Do you believe him?' Ben asked the Doctor sceptically, once Melrose was out of earshot.

'I try not to form opinions until all evidence has been presented. Now, which of you was first on the scene?'

Hornby glanced around at the remaining participants: Hayes, Mace, Ben, the Doctor, and himself. 'I suppose it would be me. I was on the stairs when I heard the gunshot, but by the time I got here, there was already a three-way skirmish between Bryan Melrose, Ted Matlock, and Neville Adler.'

'Adler?' echoed Ben. 'I never saw him.'

'I passed him on my way here,' said the Doctor. 'He was in a terrible state and very keen to get away.' He looked meaningfully at his companion, who nodded his understanding and slipped away.

'I didn't see the gun either,' Hornby continued, 'until just now. The next thing I remember was Daphne screaming and somebody ploughing in behind me.'

'I was merely endeavouring to bring the whole unfortunate episode to a speedy conclusion,' said Mace. 'My initial impression of the fracas was that the four of you were equally culpable.'

'That's not true,' protested Hornby. 'I was trying to separate the other three!'

'Gentlemen, please!' interrupted Hayes stridently. 'After what has occurred already, I don't think we need any more of this unseemly bickering. Not in my hotel!'

'You're right,' said Hornby. 'I think we should all get on with the game. I'm sure this thing has blown over now – it was probably just a few people getting carried away with their roles.'

'I think the best thing we can all do is to remain calm and, above all, cautious.' The Doctor made his way past them, sliding the energy weapon into his inside pocket.

'And where might you be going?' Mace demanded.

'With a bit of luck, to see someone who might shed some light on all of our problems.'

In the elevator lobby, a metal-rimmed hole in the wall was labelled WASTE DISPOSAL. The Doctor put his ear to it and heard the grinding of gears below. Perfect. He retrieved the gun and deftly removed its plasma generation cartridge, which he casually flipped to its doom. He returned the now harmless weapon to his pocket, in the hope of gleaning some clues from it later.

For now, he had an appointment to keep.

Polly was feeling neglected. She had waited in the Venusian Conference Suite for over fifteen minutes, but nobody else had turned up. Still, she had consoled herself, it was probably all part of the game. Once the 'murder' was committed and recriminations were under way, she could at least testify that two people hadn't been where they were supposed to be.

But now it was getting ridiculous. She had arrived at the gymnasium late and so had been doubly surprised not to find Geoff Hornby there. She wandered disconsolately about the wide, open space and idly inspected the sundry grooves in its black, rubbery floor and false-brick walls. So far as she could tell, the gym's apparatus was mostly stored beyond those boundaries. No doubt there was a bank of controls somewhere from which one could direct a vaulting horse to rise to the surface or a set of wall bars to slide forth. She couldn't find it. The only signs of the room's function were the white, yellow and blue pitch markings for a variety of indoor sports.

It did occur to Polly that the others might not be playing the murder game any more, that something might have happened. All in all, then, she was relieved when the door was flung open and a panting Hornby burst in. 'I'm sorry I'm late,' he gasped between hoarse breaths. 'There was a problem.'

'A problem in the game, or really?'

'Really. Look, we'd better do this quick.'

'Do what?'

'The whole scene. The clandestine meeting, the argument, the blackmail thing. There'll be someone else along soon.'

'Oh, if you like.' Polly strove to recall her character details. Then, looking down her nose and reciting pompously as she imagined Dame Natasha Moneybags might, she announced, 'I have decided we should call a halt to our relationship.'

'No, no you can't. I, erm, can't live without you, 'Tasha. If you won't see me again, I'll be forced to tell the newspapers all about us – and about your secret in the loft.'

Polly was thrown off her stride by the speed of it all. 'I don't know what to say,' she confessed, rifling through her briefing pack.

'Don't say anything. Just kill me,' urged Hornby.

'Just what?'

'You're the murderer. For heaven's sake, just kill me and be done with it!'

'I don't remember reading that,' said Polly. She was vaguely disappointed. 'Can't someone else do it?'

'Of course they can't!'

Polly didn't dare argue further: Hornby sounded too stressed to cope with it. She remembered her playful bet with Ben and regretted that she would not be able to join in the game of deduction after all. On the bright side, though, there was still ample opportunity to pit her wits against the other players. Imagine Ben's surprise, in particular, when he learnt of the evil secrets so cleverly hidden beneath her innocent exterior.

'OK,' she said resolutely, 'what do I do?'

'It's a spur-of-the-moment thing,' said Hornby, 'so just

pick up the nearest thing you can use.'

There was silence for a second, as they both looked around the decidedly empty gymnasium.

'Oh no!' Hornby dashed across to a small door, set into one corner, and yanked at it hopelessly. 'I don't believe it! Ms Hayes was supposed to open this storeroom. There are javelins and medicine balls and all sorts in there. Now what are we left with?'

'Perhaps we can improvise,' suggested Polly. 'Have you got a pen or something?'

'It's hardly the same thing, is it?'

'Well, maybe you can just lie down dead and, when someone finds you, tell them to pretend you've got a javelin through your chest. I mean, it wouldn't really be there anyway, would it?'

Hornby's reluctance to do this was demonstrated by his renewed attack upon the door. Finally, he turned back to Polly and spread his arms in weary defeat. 'Look, you'd better get out of here. We're behind schedule already and I worked out the plot details so any one of three people could walk in at any second. If they find the two of us together, this'll go down as the fastest murder game on record.'

'What about you? What are you going to do?'

'I'll improvise. If it comes to it, I'll pretend to have strangle marks on my neck or something. Now go!'

Polly went, pausing at the door to assure Hornby that, if she came across Ms Hayes, she would send her along with her keycard.

She rode down in the elevator towards the Interplanetary Bar. Her plan now was to find 'Melodie' and 'Harmonie'. She could claim to have come straight from their abortive meeting, and berate the pair for their unreliability. It was a credible explanation of her whereabouts, she thought.

But the only person in the bar was Henry Mace, who sat sullenly in one corner and sipped at an unidentifiable green cocktail. Polly primed herself to behave in character anyway. One alibi was as good as another, she supposed.

'Excuse me, my man – I am looking for those dreadful young ladies who call themselves "the Tuneful Twins". I intend to give them a piece of my mind.'

Mace's reply was unusually subdued. 'If you mean Daphne and Terri, they have taken friend Melrose to the sickbay.'

'Why? What's happened?'

Mace took a long sip from his drink. 'Mr Hornby's murder game,' he intoned, 'has become a tad too realistic for my liking.'

Ben had summoned Thomas from a terminal in the corridor. The hologram had been extremely obliging, locating Neville Adler for him in a matter of seconds and advising Ben that he had retired to his room. He even provided the room number and the additional information that his wife was there too. So much the better, thought Ben. Nobody had yet seen the elusive Dorothy Adler, so the chance to meet her was an unexpected bonus.

Their room, it turned out, was not far from Ben's own. As he reached it, he heard voices from within and he pressed his ear to the door in an attempt to hear what was being said. The words were still indistinct and he felt like an unprincipled snoop for doing it, so he withdrew and rapped smartly on the wood panelling instead.

He had to knock again before the door was opened.

Neville Adler peered at him short-sightedly, as if he had expected somebody else. He was nervous and unsteady on his feet. 'If this is about what happened on the stairs, I was simply caught up in a fist fight between hooligans. I have had to come up here to recover my wits.'

'It's not about the fight, Mr Adler,' Ben promised. The older man had clearly forgotten him, so he introduced himself again. 'Ben Jackson – or Admiral Anchor, I suppose I should say. I'm involved in the game. I believe we're playing brothers.'

Adler's face cleared and he relaxed his tensed shoulders. 'Ah yes, I remember now. I do apologise, my boy, but this has been a hectic day all told. You heard about the incident, I take it?'

'I was there for the end of it.'

'Dreadful business! And it has given me quite a headache, I can tell you. So if you wouldn't mind –'

'Forgetting your manners, Neville?' interrupted a reproving female voice. 'Why don't you invite the poor lad in?'

Adler looked surprised by the instruction, but he shrugged, took a step back and ushered Ben past him obediently.

The hotel room was of the same basic design as Ben's, but it was larger to accommodate a double bed. The Adlers had made it their own, with pink towels neatly hung across rails, lilac-scented air-freshener globes strewn about and potted plants wherever Ben looked. He was no botanist and couldn't identify the many assorted species; however, the scatterings of dry leaves beneath them assured him that, unlike the Galaxian's own flora, they were perfectly real.

Mrs Adler greeted him with a smile. She was about

the same age as Neville, Ben decided – mid-fifties? – although, in contrast to his shambolic appearance, she was as neat as could be. Her full, black hair was untouched by age – or dyed? – and held in place by a series of pink clips. Her face was square and craggy, as if badly sculpted, but she had made a considerable effort to soften its contours with make-up. Too much effort, in fact. She wore a loose-fitting pink tracksuit and an intricate gold-weave necklace which seemed out of place against her casual clothing.

'Do take a seat,' she twittered, 'and you must excuse my having to work while we converse. "The latest blockbuster", you know.' She said it with enough self-mockery not to sound pompous. Ben noticed a small grey case lying open on the table before her. It looked like a pocket diary or something, but closer inspection showed that its lower section held a keyboard. He suppressed incredulous laughter: computers seemed to get smaller wherever he went.

'You're writing a book, then?' he asked as he pulled up a chair.

'One of many, dear. It's our profession. We are crime writers.' Dorothy's husband was about to sit on the bed, but she interrupted him: 'No, Neville, offer our guest a drink first.'

Neville slumped across to the vending machine in the corner. 'Tea or coffee, my boy?'

'Tea please,' said Ben. 'White, no sugar.' He would have preferred a beer, but knew better than to ask. He was well used to politely drinking unwanted tea anyway, due to the frequency with which Polly served it in the TARDIS.

Dorothy was typing at a fair speed. She paused to ask, 'Neville, what's a better word for "old-fashioned"?'

'"Archaic"?'

She chewed her lip for a moment, then decided: 'I'll use "antediluvian".'

'I've told her to leave it for a few days,' Neville confided as he fetched Ben's tea over. He had forgotten the milk, so he had to return for it. 'We're ahead of deadline after all, and we could do with a short break.'

Ben opened his mouth to comment, but Dorothy beat him to it. She spoke without glancing up from her work. 'This is something of a busman's holiday though, dear. It was Neville's suggestion: he wanted the experience of being a real-life detective, so we could enrich the characterisation of our own creation.'

'I do think it's important to be able to fully identify with a point of view, Dorothy dearest.'

'Of course, I was reluctant – and when I saw how few people had enrolled for the game, I decided my time would best be spent forging ahead with the new work.'

'What's the book about?'

The couple exchanged a glance. 'Just the usual,' said Neville. 'A detective novel. It's, ah… uhm…'

'We can't tell you, dear,' said Dorothy apologetically. 'Not until it's published, you understand.'

'Anyway, my boy,' said Neville, 'what is it you wanted to talk to me about?'

'Well, I'm not sure really. It's just, with us playing brothers, I thought we should chat.'

'Yes, yes. Quite. The game is continuing, then?'

'To be honest, I don't know.' Ben sensed an opportunity to get some information. 'Bryan Melrose was shot, you know.'

Dorothy's hand flew to her mouth in shock. 'You never mentioned it to me, Neville. Is the poor man all right?'

'He was grazed, but nothing worse,' Ben assured her.

Neville turned away, as if ashamed. 'That's how it all began. The other man, Matlock, came out of nowhere and started firing. Melrose tackled him. I got dragged into it and, next thing I knew, there were arms and legs everywhere.'

'How perfectly horrid!' exclaimed Dorothy. Then she turned to Ben and smiled sweetly. 'Biscuit, dear?'

Ben declined and took a large mouthful of his tea. 'I'm afraid I'll have to be going, Mrs Adler. Other people to see. Thanks for the hospitality, though.'

'Our pleasure, dear. I hope we'll see you again before you leave. Such a polite young gentleman. Not like so many these days.'

Despite his best efforts, it took Ben another five minutes to escape from their hospitality. First Mace and now the Adlers, he thought ruefully as he emerged into the corridor and made for the lifts. At least he had found out about the shooting – that was, if Neville could be believed. But why shouldn't he be? Ben's impression of the couple was of a pair of kindly old folk, nothing more; a little cloying, maybe, but harmless.

He had just reached the elevator lobby when the lights went out. He glanced up automatically – but before he had time to worry unduly, the brief power failure was over. Ben frowned and wondered what could have caused it. And it was in that moment of speculation that he failed to hear the soft tread of footsteps behind him. Until it was too late. Something heavy hit the back of his head and coloured fireworks exploded behind his eyelids. For an instant, Ben entertained the notion of staying on his feet and whirling around to confront his attacker.

He remembered his brave plan, with bitter irony, when he eventually woke up.

Polly almost yelped with fright as the bar was plunged into darkness. She stopped herself in time, and was relieved to find she could see again, although her heart was hammering against her ribcage.

Daphne had arrived unnoticed, and she too was concerned. 'What was it?' she called from the doorway. 'What happened?'

'No need to worry, my darlings,' boomed Mace. Sensing Polly's unease, he squeezed her hand reassuringly. His skin felt clammy and she wished he hadn't so presumed. 'I'm sure it was no more than a brief aberration in the generators.'

'I'm sure,' agreed Polly, smiling thinly and trying to sound confident.

'And how is our young Mr Melrose?' Mace inquired, as Daphne joined them.

'He's fine. He's gone upstairs to get changed and he'll be meeting us here later.'

Polly tried to take an interest in the conversation, but her eyes were drawn to the window and its black panorama. Well might Henry Mace make light of his 'brief aberration in the generators' – but when all was said and done, it was those generators that kept them up here, wasn't it?

The Doctor was sitting impatiently in room 438, having arrived early in the hope of catching somebody off guard. It was too late now. He had spent ten minutes searching for traps and bugs; five more idly blowing into his recorder. He had retrieved the instrument on his way here, along with his coat.

Wearing this over his red dress, and having disposed of the unreliable coat hangers, he felt at least semi-respectable. But his meeting, apparently, had been cancelled. Someone had been here – the bedclothes were rumpled and the door had been left unlocked – but there was no sign of life now.

Another ten minutes passed before he decided enough was enough. He left the room, walking cautiously along the corridor and checking regularly over his shoulder in case an attack was yet to come. On this empty upper level, though, nothing stirred.

He stood before the rank of four elevators in the lobby and heard the rumbling of machinery below as he pressed the call button. Perhaps the fight on the stairs had frightened off his contact, he speculated. Perhaps the thing to do now was to go back to his own room and wait for another message.

The doors to the right-hand lift swished open and the Doctor automatically took a step towards them. He froze on the threshold, realising that the cubicle beyond was occupied.

Ted Matlock lay unmoving, crumpled against the far, mirrored, wall. The Doctor smelt burnt flesh and he knew before he knelt to examine the man that he was dead.

He cast his eye about the inside of the lift, but saw no obvious cause for such an accident. As the doors closed and the downward journey began, he searched the pockets of Matlock's leather jacket for anything that might offer a clue. He found only a paperback novel. It was entitled The Murder Game and it was written by Neville and Dorothy Adler.

The doors opened again and a familiar pricking sensation on the Doctor's neck told him he was being observed. A lifetime of being caught in such compromising positions had prepared him for what would happen next. He turned to face the horrified Alison Hayes and put on his most sheepish, childlike simper.

CHAPTER 4

WHODUNNIT?

'OK, stand up slowly with your hands where I can see them. Don't make any sudden movements.'

The Doctor's faint smile drained into his stomach as Alison Hayes produced a compact white gun and pointed it towards his head. Her aim was unwavering, her expression resolute, and he had the definite feeling that she had done this before. She even took the precaution of blocking the lift doors with one foot, denying him an easy escape.

He raised both hands and carefully stood. 'I know what this must look like,' he said, his tone heavily persuasive, 'but I can assure you, I discovered the body myself only a few seconds ago.' As Hayes's eyes flickered downward, he added, 'And yes, I'm very much afraid he is dead. He's been electrocuted.'

'Save it for later. We're taking a walk down to the main bar. I'll feel safer when there are a few more people about.'

'Tell me, Ms Hayes, do hand-held energy weapons come as standard issue for hoteliers these days?'

'Move!'

He was frustrated now, and angry that such illogical suspicions were delaying his investigation of a serious crime. 'Why don't you engage your brain?' he spluttered. 'If you think I murdered this man, then where is my weapon? If we were in the lift together, why is there no sign of a struggle?'

Hayes seemed to listen to some of his words, at least.

61

'All right,' she said, 'out here, hands against the wall. We'll see if you're carrying or not.'

With bad grace, the Doctor did as he was bidden. Hayes patted down his legs and arms, then felt inside his frock coat. To his alarm, she produced the gun with which Bryan Melrose had been shot. He had forgotten it was there. 'Well look at it,' he insisted, aware of his own voice sounding quite flustered. 'You can see I've removed the cartridge. It's useless.'

'Perhaps. But it might not have been two minutes ago.' Hayes threw her find to one side, well out of the Doctor's reach, and began the arduous task of sorting through his outer pockets. From the left one, she produced a screwdriver, a bag of jelly babies and a clockwork frog, which was actually a unit of currency in the Alpha Mardis systems. She struggled with a child's yo-yo, which had become wedged into a hole in the lining, and the Doctor snaked down a hand to assist her.

'You can put that straight back where it was,' Hayes grunted. But he had already half turned and was working on the problem with one hand inside the pocket and one outside.

The yo-yo, eventually, came free into Hayes's grasp. By this time, of course, the Doctor was holding her gun.

Hayes took a step back and tensed as if ready to defend herself, unarmed or not. The Doctor inspected the bothersome implement, paying her no heed. 'Well, this is interesting. It appears to be the same model as the one you've just found. It's not the murder weapon, though. If Mr Matlock was shot at all, it was with something that packed an electrical charge.' He handed the gun back to its nonplussed owner, who hefted it less certainly now their roles had been made indistinct.

'I think our first task is to remove Mr Matlock to a more dignified resting place, don't you? Then we should follow your suggestion and gather everyone in the bar.'

Hayes warily agreed and returned her gun to its concealed shirt holster. By now, however, the corpse had disappeared behind sliding doors and had been conveyed automatically to a lower level. It took almost ten minutes of calling up elevators and hoping for the right one to arrive before they recovered it.

The first thing to return was Ben's sense of smell. Hardly surprising, he thought, wrinkling his nose to stave off a strong, unpleasant antiseptic odour. He opened his eyes grudgingly and recoiled from a fierce blast of light which threatened to scorch his retinas. A few seconds later, a more cautious peep revealed a ceiling-mounted disc in which a white bulb glowed, actually quite dimly.

Something wet caressed his forehead, for which he was grateful. He hadn't realised how much his skull hurt. A stabbing sensation was only just beginning to kick in with full force. He wanted to close his eyes again, to let trickles of cold water lull him back into sleep. But, as memory resurfaced, a proper sense of urgency asserted itself and he had to know what his situation was.

'Where am I?' he asked. His voice was dry and the words came out in a rasp.

'Not telling you.'

'Why not?'

'Because it's such a clichéd question. Do you come round from being knocked unconscious often?'

'OK then,' said Ben. 'What year was the Battle of Trafalgar?'

'1805.' A face hove into view, but by this time Ben had placed the voice and knew he was talking to Terri Willis. 'And you're in the hotel's medical centre. In case you don't remember, someone clouted you over the back of the head. I was in my room when I heard you cry out.'

'I cried out? I don't remember.'

'Believe me, you did. I found you unconscious in the lobby.'

'Did you see anyone else?'

'Not a soul. Just one big bruise, with you attached to it. Can you sit up? I've got a pill here. It should help ease the pain.'

Ben washed down a small white tablet with a plastic tumbler of water. He tried to think back to the events leading up to his enforced period of sleep, but his memories contained no clue to the identity of his attacker. He had not been paying attention to his surroundings, he realised; too busy mulling over his conversation with the Adlers. The power cut had distracted him further so that he had not the vaguest impression of how his foe looked, sounded or smelt. Nor did he know where he had come from. One of the bedrooms? Or had he been waiting in the shadows of the corridor? Not from the lifts, Ben was sure – he would have heard him. But it wasn't even beyond the bounds of possibility that Neville or Dorothy might have followed him from their room. He just didn't know.

'Someone left a message while you were out,' said Terri. 'The hologram, Thomas. He said we're to go to the Interplanetary Bar as soon as possible. It sounded like there was a meeting there.'

Ben's interest was piqued. 'Do you suppose

something else has happened? Hey, maybe that's why I was conked! Maybe someone didn't want me to see them.' He tried to stand up, but his rubbery legs betrayed him and he crashed back on to the bed.

'Could be,' said Terri, 'but we'll have to find out later. For the time being, you're not fit to go anywhere.'

Thomas's message had not been delivered to Polly, Daphne and Mace, as they were in the bar already. They learnt of it from Bryan Melrose, who was the first of the other guests to arrive. He had changed out of his costume and into a sober grey suit and thin red tie, in which he looked more at ease. He rubbed his shoulder occasionally, but there was otherwise no sign of the grotesque injury which Daphne had described to Polly. She assumed the medical equipment of the future was advanced enough to render such mishaps inconsequential.

'I take it everyone received the same summons as I?' The question came from Neville Adler, who shambled into the room with a sense of indecisive urgency. A few nods and grunts convinced him this was the case. 'Does anybody know what it's about?' He offered up a weak, apologetic smile. 'It's my wife, you see. Once the muse takes her, she cannot be interrupted – and she absolutely won't come downstairs until she is assured this is nothing trivial.'

'We are all, figuratively speaking, in the dark,' proclaimed Mace, 'although perhaps something has arisen in connection with a certain contretemps not forty-five minutes since.' The abashed look which passed between Adler and Melrose was not lost on Polly.

'Do you suppose it might have something to do with

the lights going out?' she asked. She pushed the insidious idea that the station might be in trouble to the back of her mind.

'It might very well do, Polly,' said the Doctor, breezing on to the scene with Alison Hayes in tow. 'In situations like this, it's often best not to believe too readily in coincidence.'

'Situations like what?' Neville Adler wanted to know.

'Yes, what's going on?' Mace pitched in, redundantly.

The Doctor interlaced his fingers and managed to appear unhappy, contrite and worried all at the same time. 'Thank you all for coming, ladies and gentlemen. I expect you're all wondering why Ms Hayes and I asked Thomas to assemble you here.' He coughed nervously. 'Well, I regret to inform you there has been a death in the hotel.'

His proclamation was greeted by silence.

Then Mace struck up: 'Is that all, dear fellow? Confound it, we were led to believe something serious had occurred.'

He was thinking of the murder game, of course, though the Doctor's incredulous expression suggested he hadn't yet realised it. Part of Polly hoped Mace was right, but she knew in the pit of her stomach that her travelling companion was not merely play-acting. Besides which, he had discarded his costume in favour of his customary frock coat, shirt and baggy trousers. The game was well and truly over.

Hayes cleared her throat to draw attention. 'Approximately fifteen minutes ago, the Doctor here discovered the body of Ted Matlock in one of the elevators. The cause of death appears to have been electrocution. It may have been accidental, but we have yet to find evidence to suggest so. At this stage, we cannot rule out foul play.'

'You're saying he was murdered?' Daphne asked, eyes round with disbelief.

'It's possible,' said the Doctor.

'It's virtually certain,' Hayes corrected him.

'I say,' said Neville, 'are you sure this isn't part of the game?'

'I'm sure of one thing, and one thing only: somebody in this hotel is a killer.' A tangible sense of fear and discomfort rippled across Hayes's audience. Polly wrapped her arms about herself and stared at the others, one by one. Hayes. Mace. Adler. Daphne. Melrose. She had just been getting to know each of them, but suddenly they didn't feel like the same people any more. They were suspects, not to be trusted. Chances were, one or more of them had committed the ultimate sin and were capable of doing so again.

'Well surely suspicion must fall on those not present,' said Mace, his voice a little higher than normal. If he had been embarrassed by his earlier misunderstanding, it had not long silenced him. 'The perpetrator of the deed is probably even now making his getaway. Where is our esteemed host, for instance? Or the Jackson boy?'

'Ben wouldn't have anything to do with this,' insisted Polly.

'Indeed? And whose word do we have for that, young lady? Yours? You arrived with Jackson, if I remember. Late and unannounced.'

'That doesn't mean anything. Anyway, there are others missing.'

'Mrs Adler for one,' observed Hayes.

Neville took her point. 'I'd better call our room and

get her down here. There's a communications console outside, yes?'

'Terri hasn't arrived either,' said Daphne. 'Oh, I hope nothing's happened to her.'

'It's a large hotel,' said the Doctor soothingly. 'I think we should give everyone a few minutes longer before we start to panic.'

'And don't worry about the culprit escaping,' said Hayes. 'I've instructed Thomas to seal off the docking bays until I say otherwise. Nobody is leaving until my investigation is concluded!'

'That is outrageous!' Mace thundered, leaping to his feet. 'I am an innocent citizen. You have no right to keep me here against my will!'

'I have business meetings to attend,' piped up Melrose, less stridently.

'Then I suggest we get to the bottom of this unpleasant business as quickly as possible. First, I want to know where everybody was at the time of the murder.'

'Which,' the Doctor reminded her, 'we are yet to establish. I wonder, did anyone see Mr Matlock at all after the, erm, gathering on the stairs?' Apparently, nobody had. 'Ah, how unfortunate. In which case, we can only narrow the time of death down to a period of about thirty minutes.'

'Unless we assume the power flicker was connected,' said Hayes. 'If Matlock was electrocuted, he might have short-circuited the Galaxian's systems in the process.'

The Doctor shook his head. 'As I said, it's a large hotel. If our friend had taken enough volts to cause a stationwide drain of such magnitude, there would have been no corpse left to discover.'

There was a cold, reflective silence then, broken only

by Neville Adler's return and his quiet affirmation that Dorothy was en route.

'So?' prompted Hayes, eventually. 'Who's going to start?'

Nobody else seemed keen, so Polly volunteered. 'I was in the gym with Geoff Hornby, playing the game. When I left him, I came straight down here.'

'In the lift?' Mace challenged.

'Well, yes. But not in the one where... I mean, I never saw... Oh, to think I might have come across the... the...' The Doctor rushed to Polly's side and put a reassuring arm about her shoulders. She didn't know what disturbed her more: the thought of Ted Matlock's corpse tumbling through a door to land at her feet or the idea that Mace, at least, considered her under suspicion. Not that she could blame him. Why should he be any less wary of a stranger than she was?

'I went directly to my room,' said Neville. 'Dorothy was already there and neither of us left until we were summoned. I can vouch for Jackson too – for most of the time, anyway. And Miss Wright is correct, he is a very well-mannered young man.'

'I left the medical centre with Mr Melrose and came straight here,' claimed Daphne. 'He went up to his room to change.' Bryan Melrose nodded his agreement to her version of events.

'What I would like to know, Ms Hayes,' said Mace, 'is where you and this Doctor fellow were. It seems rather suspicious to me that the corpse should be discovered by the one man who hasn't even given us his real name – and another from the group of latecomers, to boot. Well? How about it, Doc? Perhaps you'd like to start by telling us how you came to be in the Galaxian in the first place!'

'How dare you!' snapped Polly.'The Doctor's trying to help us – and we won't get to the truth by hurling unfounded accusations.'

'It seems to me your party is at the centre of everything,' Mace contested. 'We don't even know where one of you is – and I might add, Ms Hayes, that it's no use you shutting off the docking bays when this lot have their own means of coming and going. Their accomplice could be light years away with the evidence by now!'

'He has a point, Doctor,' said Hayes.

But Mace was no longer interested in explanations. 'And we'd all like to know where you've been, dear lady, sneaking around the hotel on your own all day. And where are the rest of the staff your organisation promised, hmmm? Hmmm?'

'Are you trying to imply something?'

'And how about Mr Adler here? He gets involved in a fight in which somebody is shot, and then disappears. Have any of us seen his mysterious wife yet? No! Perhaps she's lying dead upstairs too. I wouldn't put it past him to have killed her in cold blood. I wouldn't put it past any of you. I'm surrounded by murderers and liars!'

'You're getting hysterical!' said Hayes, sternly.

'And I resent your insinuation,' Neville blustered. 'Where exactly were you when the lights went out, anyway, Mr Mace?'

'Lord Mace. It's Lord Henry Mace! And I don't have to stay here a second longer listening to this. I'm going to barricade myself into my room – and I'm not coming out until the police arrive!'

So saying, Mace ran for the door, his attempts at haste rendered haphazard by his not inconsiderable bulk and his paranoid insistence on checking over his shoulders constantly. He actually screamed as he ran into Geoff Hornby on the threshold. He shoved him out of the way and scuttled on by, out of sight.

'Oh dear,' was the Doctor's only comment.

'What's going on?' asked Hornby. 'I've been lying in the gym for ages, waiting to be discovered. Is nobody playing this game?'

'For what it's worth,' said Polly quietly, 'Mace was alone in the bar when I got here. Of us all, he probably has the weakest alibi.'

'And the best chance,' said Hayes, 'to commit murder.'

Ben gazed impatiently around the drab grey walls of the medical centre, finding only brief diversion in the arrays of coloured liquids and bottled pills lined up on shelves behind glass. His guess was that they were for display purposes only. The hotel's computer probably dispensed medication as required, preventing abuse of supplies.

'I feel ready to try standing again.'

'You probably aren't. Just give it a few more minutes.'

Ben scowled, but didn't argue. He felt overpoweringly hot, so he struggled out of his admiral's jacket, pulled off his tie and undid his top shirt button. The skin of his throat breathed gratefully.

'I wish I'd had time to get rid of my costume too,' said Terri, examining her multicoloured blouse ruefully. 'I was halfway out of the stupid thing when I was distracted by you.' Ben tried to ignore the mental image conjured up by Terri's description. 'I don't know where Hornby found it, but I'll bet he was the only person under sixty in the shop.'

'I didn't like to say anything, but well, it does look

sort of like an accident in a paint factory.'

Terri laughed. '"Factory"? Where do you get this quaint language of yours from?'

Her teasing made Ben feel acutely uncomfortable. 'I guess I'm just an old-fashioned guy,' he said stiffly, and hoped she would leave it there. She didn't – and what she said next left him feeling hotter than when he had been wearing his jacket.

'I think it's cute,' said Terri. And it wasn't just the fact that she had said it. It was her tone of voice and the way she looked directly at him, as if it was not just an innocuous comment; as if his reaction meant everything. Ben wanted to give her a casual reply, but he was too tongue-tied. He froze and, as he stared into her eyes, he saw no trace of mockery. Only a sparkle which could have meant anything. Or which could have been a product of his own imagination. He wasn't used to handling situations like this.

So, all in all, Ben was quite glad when Henry Mace chose that moment to burst in, stop dead and cry out at the top of his voice.

'I wouldn't worry too much, Polly,' said the Doctor. 'Our murderer operates in darkness and clearly doesn't wish to be exposed. So long as we are not alone, there should be no danger. We can't even be sure he or she will strike again.' The Doctor was talking to his companion, but she only received one-third of his attention. He was also surveying the other guests over steepled fingers.

Hornby seemed to be in shock, as if the whole situation was his fault for organising the game. Daphne was comforting him and drawing comfort from him. They had locked arms and they spoke to each other in subdued voices. Dorothy Adler had arrived some minutes ago and she reacted to the developments with indignation, as if she blamed Hornby too. She sat beside her husband, but there was no contact and little dialogue between them. Melrose bore the full brunt of Dorothy's opinions, reacting with autonomic nods and murmurs.

Beyond them all, Alison Hayes was alone. Just watching. Her eyes met the Doctor's and he wondered what was going on behind her shrewd gaze. She was probably wondering the same thing about him.

Dorothy rose and turned to her husband. 'Come on Neville,' she said, as if ordering a pup to heel. 'We're going back to our room.'

The Doctor hurriedly placed himself between them and the door. 'I don't think that's a good idea. We should stick together for the present, for safety's sake.'

'There's really no need,' said Dorothy brusquely. 'Neville and I will feel quite safe locked into our room with each other for company. We can also put our time to productive use, continuing our writing instead of waiting here for a maniac to reveal himself.'

'She's made up her mind,' offered Neville unhelpfully.

The Doctor grudgingly turned aside, but Dorothy didn't wait for him. She pushed on, a rudely pointed elbow hastening his departure from her path. Neville gave him a wider berth and shrugged apologetically as he scampered by.

Melrose was next. 'I do take your point,' he told the Doctor timorously, 'but at the moment, I think I'd benefit most from a quiet few minutes in bed. The exertions of the day are beginning to take their toll. I'll lock my door.' He rubbed at his shoulder, as if to reinforce his point, as he too left.

The Doctor sighed heavily. It occurred to him that he had lost his prime suspects. The fight earlier had reportedly been started by Melrose, Matlock, and Neville Adler. Now one was dead and the others had found excuses to avoid his scrutiny. Only five people, including himself and Polly, remained in the bar. And another problem loomed.

'I'm starting to worry about Ben,' said Polly.

'He is taking his time, I suppose,' said the Doctor, anxiously.

'And Terri,' said Daphne.

'Why don't we call up Thomas?' He led them to the bar and pressed one of the red help buttons. Polly flinched at the sudden appearance of the holographic vampire, his aspect all the more alarming because he had materialised in a patch of crimson light.

'Mr Jackson and Ms Willis,' said Thomas, when Polly's question was put to him, 'are both located in the medical centre on Deck B3.'

'The medical centre?' gasped Daphne. 'Is something wrong?'

'I am only able to tell you, madam, that they are both moving. As is the room's third occupant, Lord Henry Mace.'

It was enough for Polly. 'I'm going up there!' she announced.

'Not on your own,' the Doctor warned.

'I want to go too,' said Daphne. He nodded his assent and the two girls rushed off. Halfway to the door, Polly stumbled, looked down at her impractical shoes in exasperation and kicked them off without heed of where they landed. She hoisted her awkward skirts and hurried after Daphne, barefoot.

'Where's Ms Hayes?' asked Hornby, suddenly. The

Doctor glanced around and saw, to his chagrin, that the World Corps representative had absented herself. So much for sticking together, he thought.

'And then,' he intoned gloomily, 'there were two. Or three, if you include artificial life forms. Which gives me an idea.'

'Shouldn't we have gone with them?' asked Hornby.

'No, I don't think that was necessary.' He rummaged through his pockets and produced a screwdriver. 'Hmmm, not very sophisticated, but it will have to do.'

'What have you got in mind?'

'A small reprogramming job on our friend here,' said the Doctor. He indicated Thomas, who gave him a quizzical look in return. 'And then we can both do what we came here for in the first place.' Hornby looked confused, so he clarified: 'Solve a murder mystery!'

'What are you doing here?' squeaked Mace, backing up towards the door and accidentally knocking it so it slammed shut behind him. He cowered against it. 'Skulking in corners, plotting in the dark. If you come near me, I shall scream!'

'You just did,' said Terri.

'Come on mate, what's your problem?' Ben levered himself off the bed, wanting to be ready if this lunatic tried something.

Mace misinterpreted the action and his eyes widened in fear. 'What are you doing? Get back, get back!'

'Are you accusing us of something, or what?' asked Ben, becoming irritated by the newcomer's behaviour. He felt dizzy and leaned against a wall for support – and, in his vulnerable moment, Mace cannoned into him, propelling them both into the sheet of glass across the shelves. It vibrated furiously and Ben thought it must shatter. Instead, a whooping alarm siren went up. The impact made him feel sick and he groaned as a black tunnel reduced his field of vision.

Mace had the advantage, but he fought like a two-year-old, hands flailing, legs thrashing. Ben closed his eyes and fought back waves of nausea. He braced both arms beneath the considerable weight of Mace's flabby body and pushed as hard he could. His foe collapsed on to the bed and Ben dived after him, one arm across his throat, pinning him down. The bottom legs of the bed gave way and they slid towards the floor in a heap. Still Mace squirmed, bawling and screaming. Ben was perturbed to see tears streaming down his cheeks. His face was beetroot-red with anger and exertion, though his tiny spectacles clung against all reason to his face. Ben released his grip, uncertainly, and was suddenly aware of Terri's presence beside him. She was holding a chair above her head.

'No!' he shouted. Then, more calmly: 'No, I think the fight's gone out of him now.'

Terri looked down at the blubbering mess that was Henry Mace and with, Ben thought, a little reluctance, she lowered her makeshift weapon. 'Are you going to explain what the hell this is about?' she demanded.

The tantrum appeared to be over, but Mace was petulant as ever. 'You tell me. We're all supposed to be in the main bar, but where do I find you two? Hiding away, concocting dastardly deeds -'

'Getting medical attention,' Terri finished for him. 'In the medical centre, believe it or not.'

'So why aren't you in the bar?' Ben challenged. He massaged the tender lump on the back of his head and wished for the alarm to stop shrieking.

Mace scrambled back to his feet, but kept his

distance. 'Shut up, shut up! Stop trying to catch me out.'

'I only asked -'

'Don't question me! You're saying I killed him and I didn't - I was nowhere near, I'm completely innocent. I'm just after something for a headache, and who can blame me? The things I've had to put up with!'

'Whoa, hold on a minute there. You killed who?'

'No, no!' screamed Mace tearfully, and Ben tensed lest he attack again. 'You're trying to twist everything I say. You did it and I'm going to tell everyone. You're not getting me!' He had managed to edge his way back towards the door and now he turned, grabbed for the handle, missed, grabbed again and eventually stumbled out of the room and blundered away, screaming, 'Help, help! Murder!'

'I think we'd better find out what's going on,' said Ben. 'Do you suppose there's really been a death? Mace can't have been acting, can he? I think he's genuinely upset. And frightened.'

'I think he's a genuine cretin,' said Terri.

Polly and Daphne had chosen to use the stairs. It had lengthened their journey time, but they both agreed they couldn't face climbing into a lift. Not yet. They walked mostly in silence, but as they emerged on to Deck B3, Daphne stopped Polly and confided in her. 'I'm worried,' she said, 'about Terri.'

'I'm sure she'll be OK,' said Polly, although she was harbouring similar fears about Ben. 'Thomas said they were both moving, which has to be a good sign.'

'It's not that. I'm worried about what she might have done.'

'What do you mean?' Polly didn't want to hear this.

She tried to assure herself that the anxious twinge in her chest was ill-founded. 'I thought you two were old friends.'

'We were. I mean, we are. But… oh, I've got to tell somebody this… I haven't seen Terri in ages. I mean, I hadn't, until she contacted me a fortnight ago. It was her who suggested coming here, a sort of reunion for us. She said she had a good job now and could afford to rent a private shuttle and everything. She's never told me what line of business she's in, though. In fact, she's been a bit secretive about a few things. I just don't know what she's been up to for the past few years.'

'But surely you don't think she's capable of murder?' As much as anything, Polly was trying to convince herself.

'No!' said Daphne, with certainty. Then, wavering: 'Oh, I don't know. I just can't imagine it.'

'Well, then.'

'But we were supposed to take Mr Melrose to the medical centre together and she dashed off saying she had to get changed or something. I haven't seen her since. Oh Polly, tell me I'm being stupid for even thinking this.'

Polly wanted to oblige, but found she couldn't. Instead, she grimly opined that they should find their two friends as quickly as possible, and put both their minds at rest. She hoped.

But as they approached the corridor that housed the medical centre, they both heard the alarm siren and Polly's heart fluttered. They didn't exchange words. They simply ran, until Polly flung open a door to reveal what was obviously the scene of a protracted struggle. The bed had collapsed, white sheets strewn about the floor. A chair was upturned and a jagged crack scarred a glass partition, behind which a number of bottles had been disturbed and lay bleeding rainbow colours into their shelves.

Of Ben and Terri, there was no sign.

CHAPTER 5

IN THE DARK

The Doctor had dismantled one of the information points. A tangle of colour-coded wires trailed over the side of the bar and across the carpet into a spaghetti junction. He sat cross-legged before it, twisting and poking with hands and screwdriver, emitting the occasional 'hmm' of introspection and 'ahh' of discovery.

Thomas wasn't pleased. 'I must remind you again, sir,' he said, hands squirming with anxiety, 'it is against hotel rules for guests to interfere with World Corps equipment. I really have to ask you to desist.'

The Doctor didn't respond. Despite his human mannerisms, Thomas was only a manifestation of the computer, after all, acting out a series of predetermined routines. As a hologram, he didn't even have the option of attempting physical restraint.

He found what he was looking for: a blue wire, which he traced with eyes and fingers through the electrical web and back to the gutted terminal. He reached into its innards and, with surgical precision, extracted a tiny circuit board. It strained against its multicoloured leash as he gingerly separated it from the mass and laid it out on the bar top. It was too much for Thomas, who moved on to the next level of programmed disincentives. 'I shall have to report this breach to Ms Hayes,' he decided. He shimmered and was gone.

The Doctor's lower lip bulged with disappointment. 'Oh, I didn't know he could do that. I must have triggered a warning system.'

'Do you think she'll try to stop you?' asked Hornby. He was leaning against the bar, a respectful distance away, from which position he had been watching and keeping a welcome silence. Until now.

'I really don't know. It all depends, I imagine, on what she has to hide. There's certainly something.'

'What are you trying to do, exactly?'

The Doctor took a deep breath. He was used to being distracted from vital work by the necessity to give explanations, and he had developed the art of being concise. 'I'm hoping to bypass certain restrictions to make our vampire friend more useful.' He searched his clothing for an eyeglass and, finding one, screwed it into place. He pored over the circuit board until he found a certain nodule, then thrust the end of his screwdriver into it, destroying it while being careful not to harm its immediate neighbours. He straightened up with a satisfied smile, let the eyeglass fall into his hand, and deftly yanked free a green wire. 'There, that should do it.'

Thomas rematerialised and the Doctor hid the wire behind his back, feeling irrationally guilty like a schoolboy caught with a catapult. 'I have spoken to Ms Hayes,' he said stiffly, 'and she does not seem to object to your behaviour.'

'Splendid!' said the Doctor, clapping his hands together and grinning. 'In which case, there's just one minor alteration left to carry out. But Thomas, it will mean your being unable to actualise for a few minutes.' Thomas scowled, but seemed to have no oral response in his databanks to suit the announcement.

The Doctor hesitated, hands poised over the terminal. 'Before you go off line, though,' he said thoughtfully, 'I wonder if you could do me one favour. I'd like a quick rundown on the current whereabouts of everybody in the hotel.'

Thomas looked as if the request was a severe imposition on his time (which surely couldn't have been part of his programming), but he acceded to it anyway. 'As you know, sir, yourself and Mr Hornby are in the Interplanetary Bar.'

'Yes, yes,' said the Doctor, making circling motions with his hand to move him on.

'Mr Melrose and Mr and Mrs Adler are in their respective bedrooms. Ms McAllister and Ms Wright are in the medical centre on Deck B3. Ms Willis and Mr Jackson are currently in an elevator, heading downward and just passing B6.'

'Crossed paths,' observed the Doctor with a rueful sigh.

'Ms Hayes is in a corridor in the main administration section on Deck B3. Lord Mace is in the perimeter corridor of A4.'

'A4? That's an upper accommodation level, isn't it?'

'Which we aren't using,' Hornby pointed out, though the Doctor already knew. 'What's he doing up there?'

'I could not give you such information, sir, even if I had the means to collect it.'

'He could just be hiding,' mused the Doctor, 'if he is as confused and upset as he pretends to be.'

'I'll have some questions next time I see him,' promised Hornby.

'Well, in the meantime, there's no use worrying. So long as Henry Mace is alone, he can't come to any harm. Or cause any, I hope.'

Thomas's refined tones echoed eerily about the

medical centre, though Polly could see no speakers. 'I regret to inform you that I am currently engaged elsewhere. I will, however, be at your service as soon as I am able. If you wish to cancel your request for my assistance, please press the help button again.'

Polly clenched her fists, fighting a sense of impotence. 'He would be busy now, when we need to find Ben. And Terri,' she added, as a polite afterthought.

'I think we should go back to the bar,' said Daphne. She was trying to sound confident, but it was clear to Polly that her nerves were on edge. 'Chances are, they've gone down there and we've missed them. Especially if they took the lifts.'

'You're probably right, I know. I just don't fancy wasting time on another wild-goose chase, at least until Thomas has pointed us in the right direction.' Polly looked around expectantly, as if the vampire would pop into view at any second. He didn't. 'I wish we knew how long he was going to be.'

There seemed to be nothing else to say then, so they waited in silence for one minute. Two. Two and a half. Then Polly's ears pricked up at the sound of careful footsteps behind the door. Daphne had heard them too. They stared at each other, but both were paralysed by the suspicion of imagined devilry and could do nothing as the chilling sound came closer. And drew level. And receded, as whoever it was shuffled by, unmindful of their proximity.

Daphne let out a breath and laughed giddily and voicelessly, a hand over her heart. Polly's fear receded faster, to be replaced by a steadfast determination. She leapt to the door, pulled it open and peered around its frame. She was just in time to catch the back of a tweed jacket as its owner disappeared around a corner.

'I think it was Neville Adler,' she reported, 'but what's he doing down here?'

'He said he was going to his room.'

'Precisely. Come on, let's follow him.'

'Are you sure?'

'Come on!'

Polly ran down the corridor, Daphne trailing more reluctantly behind. She didn't catch sight of her quarry again, but an educated guess at the first junction took them back into the lobby. The grinding of gears and the location display above one elevator revealed that it had just left. 'What now?' asked Daphne.

'We see where he goes.' Polly watched as levels B2 and B1 flashed by on the indicator, until it settled on D. 'The docking bays.'

'He might not be getting out there.'

'Why else would the lift have stopped? I can't imagine it was summoned there.'

'We should tell Ms Hayes,' Daphne suggested.

'No. Let's get up there and see what he does.'

'What about Terri and Ben?'

'If we can find out what's going on in this place, we'll stand a better chance of helping them. If they need helping.' They made for the stair door, around the corner. As they slipped through it, Polly's dress caught on the handle and she became entangled. She grunted in despair and spent the next few seconds freeing herself. 'I'm going to have to get out of this costume,' she decided. 'Come on, the bedrooms are four floors up. I think we should take the lift after all.'

Daphne shrugged, seeming to know better by now than to argue when Polly had the bit between her teeth. But as they turned the corner again, they were just in time to see another set of elevator doors sliding shut. And, as they watched apprehensively, another passenger was deposited on the station's centremost level.

Daphne asked the question that burnt in both their chests. 'Who on earth was down here with us?'

Ben and Terri had returned to the Interplanetary Bar and were exasperated to learn they had missed their own search party. On the assumption that Polly and Daphne would come back here, they decided it best to wait and to let the Doctor and Hornby update them on events during their absence. Ben was disturbed to learn of Matlock's murder but, truth to tell, he was quietly relieved that the fate of which Mace had spoken had not befallen one of his friends. He recounted his own experiences and was able to tell the Doctor something he didn't know: that, according to Neville Adler, it was Matlock who had shot Bryan Melrose.

The Doctor quietly absorbed this information and Ben could almost see his mind ticking over as he slotted it into the appropriate section of an abstract jigsaw puzzle. He half expected him to regurgitate the known facts in the form of a brilliant solution, but the picture was clearly not yet complete. Instead, he resumed his tinkering with the entrails of the information terminal. Then, with a triumphant cry of 'Aha!', he jumped to his feet and stabbed at the help button to summon Thomas.

The vampire wore a perturbed expression as he appeared. 'I assume, given my resumed existence, that you have concluded your alterations, sir'

'Indeed. Now, if you please -'

'In which case, sir, I have an outstanding request to attend to. Your young friends in the medical centre. I will return shortly.'

'Blimey, Doc,' said Ben, as Thomas took his leave, 'he's getting a bit sniffy, ain't he?'

'I'm afraid I may have inadvertently upset him.'

'I don't think he wanted to be customised,' said Hornby.

'What have you done to him, anyway?'

The hologram returned before the Doctor could answer. 'The young ladies appear to have left, sir.'

'I thought they might have. Now Thomas, as you may have noticed, I've made a couple of improvements to your operating system. Well, I think they're improvements.'

The hologram looked thoughtful for a second then, seeming to barely believe his own words, he said, 'I have an increased datapool.'

'Quite right. I've removed certain fail-safes which prevented you from drawing information from the World Corps computers on Earth.'

'It is quite a… liberating sensation.'

'And, given the number of deliberate gateways and secret back doors between computers in this day and age, I imagine you can access pretty much every major system on the planet. Am I right?'

'You are, sir. But may I mention that some of this data is confidential in nature?'

'Do you want to ask Ms Hayes's permission to proceed?'

Thomas gave a long-suffering sigh; a very human reaction, Ben thought, particularly to the Doctor. 'What do you wish to know?'

The Doctor clasped his hands together and wore an eager smile. 'I think some background details on the hotel's current occupants might prove interesting.'

Polly felt more comfortable in jeans and flat shoes, although butterflies frolicked in her abdomen as she and Daphne approached the stairwell again. The docking level, with its occupants known and unknown, was only one flight down.

'Do you trust the Doctor?' asked Daphne as they walked, and Polly initially thought it a strange question. Still, her partner had trusted her enough to open up about Terri.

'Implicitly,' she said. 'We've been in difficult situations before and he's always done the right thing.

'Difficult?'

Polly smiled. 'More frightening than this, even. It's the Doctor's nature to find trouble. He doesn't cause it though, and I don't think he looks for it. He's a tourist really, always eager to find something new and exciting.' She pursed her lips as she thought about her companion. She hadn't known him for long really, though they had been through much together. It was hard to pin down his nature in words: it was nebulous and prone to sudden change. 'Sometimes,' she considered, 'I think he's frightened of becoming jaded. I think he keeps Ben and me with him to share in our fresh sense of wonder.' She gave a short laugh. 'I can't imagine why else he'd put up with us, always asking questions and getting him into fixes.'

'And Ben?' Daphne prompted.

'Oh, he's just… well, Ben. He's solid. Reliable.' She left it there, because she didn't know what else to say. She felt as if she was holding something back, but she wasn't sure what. All she did know was that the act of calling Ben Jackson to mind had caused her to break out in a fond smile. Of familiarity, or something more? Either way, the smile faded as they reached the door to the docking level. 'I'm not sure I want to do this,' confessed Daphne.

'We won't be doing anything,' Polly assured her, although she was nervous too. 'Just watching – seeing who's down here and what they're up to, so we can report back to the Doctor. Besides, I don't think we'll have trouble outrunning Neville Adler if he sees us.' Daphne smiled bravely and, thankfully, didn't mention Neville's anonymous colleague.

Despite her display of courage, Polly's fingers lingered over the handle. Then she told herself not to be so silly, pushed it down decisively, shouldered the door open, and stepped out into darkness.

'I have collated the information,' Thomas reported.

The Doctor scrambled to his feet and stuffed his recorder back into his pocket. 'Excellent! I expected it to take much longer. You must have a very efficient processor, Thomas.' It was news to Ben. To him, the minutes of silent waiting had appeared to last for ever. Still, he supposed, his companion had a better idea of the complexities involved in the operation.

The Doctor rubbed his hands together, gleeful at the prospect of getting to work on the mystery. 'Now, where shall we start?'

'I want to find out about Mace,' said Ben as he, Hornby and Terri gathered around eagerly.

'No, let's ask about Matlock first,' said Hornby. 'We might find out why someone wanted to kill him, or at least why he shot Melrose.'

'Hmmm. We'll take them as they come I think, Thomas.'

'Very well, sir. McAllister, Daphne. Date of birth: third of October 2113. Pre-school education –'

'A simple overview will do.'

Thomas looked offended. 'This is a simple overview, sir.'

'Just tell us of any criminal record, memberships of organisations, anomalies in the records...'

'Financial problems,' suggested Hornby. 'Infamous relatives.'

'Hey, who do you think she is?' protested Terri. 'Dick Turpin reincarnated?'

'That kind of thing, Thomas,' said the Doctor. 'Anything odd.'

'Ms McAllister has a sound financial history and no notably deviant relatives or associates on file,' said Thomas, tartly. 'She has no criminal record and has only been affiliated to the Girl Guides and the St John Ambulance Brigade. There are no obvious anomalies in her computerised records.'

'Who's next?'

'Willis, Terri.'

The subject in question started as if she had been poked in the back with a live wire. 'You're checking on me?'

'I did ask Thomas to research everybody,' the Doctor assured her. 'You aren't being singled out.'

'Did you include yourself?'

'Ah... well, no.'

'I did, however,' said Thomas smugly, 'take the liberty of scanning for both you and your associates in the course of my investigations. My findings were quite fascinating.'

The Doctor looked appalled, and Ben sympathised. All the same, there were so many things he didn't know himself – so many questions he had run through his mind on sleepless nights – and he couldn't help but wonder what Thomas had learnt.

'Let's hear them,' said Terri.

Thomas cleared his throat theatrically and began. 'Of Mr Jackson and Ms Wright, I found no mention at all. Normally, this would suggest they were born on one of the six colony worlds which do not maintain computerised links to Earth – or, more likely, that their identities are false. However, in light of certain discrepancies in the Doctor's own records, I extended my research to a much earlier time than logic would usually dictate.'

Ben squirmed, feeling uncomfortable in the spotlight and guilty because he had as good as wished this on his friend. Terri looked at him quizzically, but he ignored her in favour of his highly polished black shoes. 'What are you saying?' she prompted.

'In census records from 1942 on, I found references to a Ben Jackson and a Polly Wright, born in close proximity to each other. Both in London, England, in fact. Their descendants would currently be –'

'That's enough, Thomas!' the Doctor snapped. 'If you know this much, you must at least have hypothesised that Ben, Polly, and I are time-travellers. To reveal Ben's own future to him would be an act of criminal irresponsibility.'

Ben could manage only one word. 'Descendants?' It felt weird. It felt wrong. It felt scary. And it forced home the realisation that, on the planet below, the uncertainties of his future had been cast in unyielding time and relegated to an immutable past. Ben Jackson and the next few generations of his family were dead, buried and forgotten; a cluster of brief entries in historical records. He felt small and lonely and insignificant and, suddenly, he knew what the expression about someone walking over your grave meant. Perhaps someone had. And he ached to know one more thing too: had Thomas meant to imply that his descendants and Polly's were one and the same? It wasn't possible, was it? He wanted to ask, but he didn't dare form the words. He felt detached and numb.

Hornby and Terri had excitedly chattered their way through a hundred and one questions about time travel, which the Doctor had fended off as best he could. Ben hardly listened, at least not until Thomas spoke again. 'This does allow much information to, ah, fall into place as it were. Your mentions in UNIT files, particularly.'

'I know nothing of such an organisation,' said the Doctor coldly. 'Not yet.'

'Indeed not, sir. Perhaps we should move on.'

'I think it would be a very good idea.'

Thomas smiled – at the Doctor's discomfort, Ben could have sworn. 'Willis, Terri. It may interest you to know that I can find no mention of her in records dated after 2132.'

'Four years ago,' Hornby supplied (to Ben's relief, as he had quite forgotten the year).

'And in case you're wondering,' said Terri, 'it's none of your business. Any of you!'

'It could be,' said the Doctor, 'if you made an enemy of Ted Matlock during that time.'

'Or if you're not Terri Willis at all!' said Hornby.

'Oh, talk sense! Daphne vouches for me, doesn't she? And your bit of snooping has proved she's the same sweet, innocent virgin she's always been.' The Doctor regarded her through half-closed eyes, over steepled fingers, but said no more. Instead, he nodded to Thomas to continue.

'Hayes, Alison. No remarkable entries. In fact, I found very little at all. The same applies to Neville and Dorothy Adler. They are prolific writers of crime fiction – I came across many references to their work. However, they clearly use professional pseudonyms, and I have been unable to learn their true identities. By cross-referencing the accounts records of their publishing company with its book lists, I could produce a list of possibilities. I regret to say, however, it would not be a short one.'

'I did wonder about them,' the Doctor confessed. '"Adler" was the name of one of my old friend Conan Doyle's fictional characters.'

'Irene Adler,' Hornby recalled, his face lighting up at the realisation. 'Sherlock Holmes said she was the one person who had outwitted him. I can imagine Dorothy wanting to take her name: she's always seemed a bit self-important.'

'But why check in here under pen names?' Ben asked.

'I wouldn't be surprised if she just wanted to announce who she was,' said Hornby. 'How many times has she mentioned her book today?'

'We might come back to them,' said the Doctor. 'Who's next?'

'I have no more information, sir.'

He seemed taken aback. 'No more? You must have. What about Matlock? And Melrose?'

'As I said, sir, there is no more data. I can find no record of those people on Earth's computers.'

'Or of Henry Mace!' Ben realised.

'Nor,' said Thomas meaningfully, 'of Geoffrey Hornby.'

Hornby held up his hands before him, nervously, as if to show he had nothing to hide. 'This isn't what it seems. I can explain.'

All eyes turned towards the game's erstwhile organiser. But, all of a sudden, Ben wasn't interested in hearing what he had to say, as something far more urgent had occurred to him. 'Here, just a minute. I thought that thing' – he indicated Thomas – 'said Polly and Daphne were on their way here, ages ago. So where are they?'

Polly stood and trembled as she waited for her eyes to adjust to the gloom, hearing no more than Daphne's breathing at her shoulder. She jumped, terrified, as the fire door swung shut behind them with the least audible of clicks. Robbed of the square of light from the stairwell, she felt isolated and vulnerable. 'Why aren't the lights on?' Daphne whispered. Polly didn't know, but she hoped it was simply that Ms Hayes had shut down the entire level in sealing off the docking bay doors. The alternative – that somebody was planning deeds best done in darkness – was too worrying to contemplate, for now.

She was standing on carpet. From the cool, open feel of this deck, she hadn't expected that. It made sense though, she supposed: World Corps would want their clients' first impression of the Galaxian to be as good as possible. Some details were becoming clearer, as if surfacing through black mist. She was on a wide, curved balcony. A few feet to her right, the concave outer wall of the station was studded with circular doors. Polly had travelled with the Doctor long enough to recognise them as airlocks. She could only make out the nearest three. To her more immediate left, a white railing was interrupted by a short flight of downward-leading steps. The lower tier of the deck was stacked high with boxes and crates, and she could see just the beginnings of a labyrinthine path through them. Beyond the cargo, she imagined, there would be more airlocks: the tradesmen's entrances, as they would have been called in her time.

Her first instinct was to go down the steps. She felt exposed on this raised area, too visible despite the darkness. But Daphne was already meandering towards the right. Polly tapped her on the shoulder and gestured downward, but she shook her head. 'Our ship's behind one of these doors. I just want to find it.'

Polly couldn't see the point of such a course, but she could identify with the fear that made Daphne choose to pursue it. She said nothing, only followed as her companion tiptoed towards the third door and rested both hands on the circular, spoked wheel of the opening mechanism. She took a deep breath and turned it. It moved a fraction of an inch, then stopped. Daphne tried again, but to no avail. She gave up finally and whispered in a tearful voice, 'We're locked out, just like Ms Hayes said. We're trapped.'

'Don't panic. Please, don't panic. We're no worse off than we thought we were. At least we're still together. We're safe.'

'I know. Thank you, Polly.' They joined hands instinctively.

'Come on. I think we should go down among the crates. Then we can sneak about for a bit without being seen.' Daphne nodded, and Polly led her gently towards the steps.

They descended furtively, mindful that they were now treading on metal, on which the slightest clatter could give them away. At the bottom, Polly chose a random path and moved quickly, feeling a need to get under cover as soon as possible. In part of her mind, she knew she was also trying to cheat her own fear; to plunge into the unknown before emotions could check her.

Visibility here was worse than she had hoped. There seemed hardly a sight line unblocked by wood or plastic. The smell of old sawdust was in her nostrils and she hoped to goodness she wouldn't sneeze. Every so often, both women froze at the sound of footsteps. But they were some way distant and they echoed so as to make it impossible to pinpoint their source. Polly and Daphne could be sure of only one thing: they were not alone.

They made their way deeper into the cubic forest, apprehension slowing their pace by degrees. More than once, Polly thought she had seen somebody in the deceptive shadows. They took long pauses, listening carefully, and it was during one of these that Daphne asked, 'Do you know the way back?'

'More or less, yes, I think so.' Polly wasn't stupid. She had realised how easy it would be to get lost and she had tried as best she could to keep their heading broadly consistent. 'We need to go that way,' she said. She had meant to point, but found herself describing a vague arc instead. 'So long as we keep straight on, though, we should find the wall whichever direction we head in. We can follow it round to the steps.' Daphne nodded and seemed happier.

And then they heard a furious scamper of footsteps. A cry of alarm, in a male voice. The discharge of an energy weapon. A strangulated scream – perhaps the same voice. A thud.

Daphne let go of Polly's hand and screamed. Polly barely managed to stop herself from following suit. Not that it would have made a difference.

More footsteps. They sounded close ahead now. And Daphne had drawn attention to their presence. Instinctively, Polly ducked behind a crate, trying to envelop herself in its shadow. She made a grab for her friend, but missed. Daphne panicked and ran. She was lost to Polly's sight in a second, her footsteps and whimpers sure to draw pursuit. Then Polly's heartbeat drowned out all other sounds. Ghastly silhouettes reared up around her, convincing her that she couldn't just wait to be captured. She decided to do the unexpected: to sneak around to where she thought the sounds had come from. In her fear, though, she stumbled into a box and stifled a cry as a sharp pain stabbed through her knee.

The footsteps turned towards her. She thought they came from behind now, cutting her off from the exit, and she limped away from them as fast as she could, no longer caring where she went. Her toe caught something lumpy and unexpected and she pitched forward, her fall broken by something soft and misshapen. It took her a second to realise it was a person. A second longer to recover her senses and to see that Neville Adler was dead, a horrific burn seared into his chest. His face was set in a determined rictus: he had seen his fate coming and had fought it. It had claimed him all the same.

Polly couldn't help herself then. She screamed, long and loud.

And a hand was clamped across her mouth from behind. Another pressed the muzzle of a gun into her temple. Her unknown captor didn't need to speak to tell her silence was required. When she stopped straining her vocal chords, the hand was removed but the gun stayed. She didn't resist as one arm was twisted behind her back. She was propelled across the deck with a series of rough pushes. They seemed to be headed in a definite direction, but she didn't think it was back to the steps.

Elevator doors slid open for them. It wasn't a passenger lift, with the mirrored back wall that would have been useful right now. It was larger but dingy, decked out in dulled silver. A service lift. She was herded into it and her arm was released as her captor pressed a destination button, out of her sight. From a long way away, Daphne cried out her name. Polly didn't dare answer, nor to turn her head to even see whose prisoner she had become.

Adler had probably turned his head.

'Ms McAllister,' said Thomas, 'is currently located on the docking level. Ms Wright is in the main service lift, which has just stopped on Deck B1.'

'What the heck are they doing there?' cried Ben.

The Doctor had the slightly sick feeling that often accompanied such tidings. He had brought Ben and Polly here; he was responsible for their welfare. He couldn't bear it if something were to happen to either of them.

Ben was all for heading out of the bar right away, and Hornby and Terri would probably have followed him. But the Doctor knew that, in the words of an old acquaintance of his, preparation was half the battle. Much as he needed to be with Polly, he also had to find out the full extent of her situation. 'I want another location check, Thomas. Tell me where everybody is. As quickly as possible, please.'

'I take it you wish me to exclude this current gathering?'

'Yes, yes, get on with it.'

'Very well, sir. Mr Melrose and the Adlers are still in their rooms. Lord Mace is still on Deck A4 and appears to be wandering quite aimlessly. Ms McAllister is on the docking level, as you already know. Ms Wright, on the other hand, has emerged into a kitchen on Deck B1 – which, I might add, is not currently in use.'

'And Ms Hayes?' the Doctor prompted.

'Ms Hayes,' said Thomas, 'is with Ms Wright.'

CHAPTER 6

EXPLOSIVE REVELATIONS

The Doctor had insisted on taking the stairs. It may be quicker, he had said, than waiting for a lift, which would in any case give warning of their arrival. Seven floors up, Ben decided he had made the wrong choice. He considered himself a fit man, but even he was running short of breath, and poor Geoff Hornby was lagging well behind. Ben was surprised to see that Terri Willis coped with the exertion almost as well as the Doctor himself. He wondered vaguely if the TARDIS had a gymnasium, in which he could get himself back into shape, working off the effects of time in barracks and too much booze. In his new, unchosen profession, it could save his life.

The Doctor stopped at the door to Deck B1. 'Geoffrey, you're with me. Ben, you take Terri up to the docking level and find Daphne. Come on, Mr Hornby, this is an emergency!'

Hornby huffed and puffed his way up the final few steps, as Ben took the next flight three at a time. He would rather have gone after Polly, but orders were orders and there was no time for debate. Besides, the Doctor was the one person he could trust to look after her better than he would himself.

The service lift had gone downward, probably no more than a level or so, and Polly had been bundled out into a large, empty room where at least the light was better. A heavy push sent her tripping across a tiled floor and she put out her hands to avoid a collision with a work bench. Its surface was grey and disinfected, pitted with a million thin scars. It had been used as a chopping board. They were in a kitchen, Polly realised, although instinct told her it hadn't been used in some time.

Her captor hadn't followed her, choosing to remain at the lift entrance instead. The gun was no longer pressed to her temple, the warmth of breathing no longer on her neck. 'You can turn around now,' said a confident female voice, but Polly hesitated before doing so. She had seen too many films in which the villain had only revealed himself because he was confident of the victim's subsequent inability to divulge such information.

She swallowed, fought to unravel the knot in her guts and turned slowly. She found herself facing Alison Hayes. The World Corps representative was grim-faced and, Polly noticed miserably, still very much armed. The gun was trained on her head. 'I'm sorry you had to stumble across the unpleasantness downstairs,' said Hayes. 'Sorry because it's forced me to make this move sooner than I had planned.'

'Just let me go. I won't tell what I know, I promise.'

'A transparent lie. But don't worry yet, I might not kill you.'

Polly felt her legs shaking and she wanted to sit down. She fought to remain still. She was terrified of giving this woman a reason to shoot. 'What do you want?' she asked, her voice catching.

'Information.'

'Is that what you tried to get from the others?' Hayes frowned as if she didn't understand. 'Are you killing people until you find what you want?' Polly challenged. She leaned back against the bench for support and her nervous hands found a drawer.

'Hard as it may be to believe in your current situation, I didn't kill Ted Matlock.'

'But you did kill Neville Adler?'

'I had reasons.'

Polly wanted to spit out something to the effect that there were no reasons, no justification, for cold-blooded murder. It was what the Doctor would have done. He would have shamed Hayes with the truth of her actions, made her see what a monumental evil she had committed – and if, at the end of his lecture, she had unrepentantly continued along the same misguided course, then at least he would have tried. And then he would have stopped her. Polly didn't have the Doctor's courage. But the thought of him inspired her, and her fingers worked away behind her back to coax the drawer open.

'You're wasting your time,' said Hayes quietly. 'There is no cutlery in there. Do you think I wouldn't have checked before I brought you down here? And do you think, in any case, that a knife would be a match for my weapon? You saw what it did to Adler, I assume.'

'What is it you want from me?' Polly demanded, forcing out the question between barely contained tears of fear and frustration.

'I want to know about you and your friends.'

'What about us?'

'You can start by telling me why you're here.'

'We're travellers.'

'Don't lie to me again!'

'I swear, it's the truth!'

'You're either Matlock's contacts or you're working for the sharks. Which is it?'

'I don't know what you mean.'

'What is your connection to Ted Matlock?'

'We'd never heard of him before we came here. I didn't even speak to him before he... he...'

'So you're working for the sharks!'

'What sharks? Look, what are you talking about?'

Hayes was angered by Polly's desperate protestations. She closed the gap between them and jammed the gun painfully into her prisoner's thorax. 'I'll give you one last chance to tell the truth,' she threatened, her eyes fire, her voice ice. But Polly was struck dumb and could only stare at her, her own gaze wide and damp.

Suddenly, Hayes cocked her head, withdrew the gun and whispered fiercely, 'Someone's coming!' Polly hadn't heard a thing, but the words brought a momentary hope to her heart. She turned to look at the main doors, at the other end of the kitchen. But if she had had it in mind to scream or shout for help, she was foiled. Hayes clamped two fingers on to her left shoulder, at the base of her neck, and expertly manipulated a cluster of nerves. Without warning, Polly lost the use of her muscles. A second later, halfway to the floor, her senses followed.

The Doctor led Hornby across most of Deck B1 before they found the kitchen. Fortunately, his memory of the Galaxian's layout had proved true and they proceeded more or less directly to their destination.

He flung open the door and pouted in disappointment as he saw no evidence that the room beyond was occupied. The light was barely adequate and rows of workbenches formed a maze of nooks and shadows. Too many hiding places, he thought. He put a finger to his lips and motioned to Hornby that they should proceed around the room in opposite directions. They moved as silently as they could, the Doctor wincing each time Hornby's shoes scuffed against tiles. He peered beneath table tops and into corners, alert for an ambush. But, by the time he rejoined his colleague at the far end of the room, before the service lift, he was convinced of its emptiness.

'Could we be in the wrong place?' Hornby whispered.

The Doctor shook his head. 'No, this is definitely where Thomas said they were. They must have moved on. Which, at least, suggests Polly is alive.'

'Perhaps Ms Hayes heard us coming.'

'If so, she can't have gone far.'

'Can't we ask Thomas to locate them again?'

'If we can find an information point, yes. There isn't one here.' He scoured the kitchen with his eyes, and allowed them to rest on an innocuous grey door which Hornby must have passed without noticing. A glass panel was inscribed with the words PRIVATE – STAFF ONLY, on the far side. The letters were reversed to his viewpoint. The Doctor concentrated, trying to bring the floor plans back to mind. He succeeded and felt a sly smile tugging at his mouth. 'I've been here before. Come on, Geoff. This way, I think.'

His decisive action was halted by the whirring of engines and the realisation that the service lift was in motion. Hornby shrank away as if expecting something nasty to leap through its doors. The Doctor steadied him with a hand on his arm. 'It's stopped. It was coming down towards us, but it stopped on the level above this one.'

'The docking level!'

'Quite. Now, who do you think might have business there?' Hornby shook his head. 'Come on, Geoff, put those brains to work. Try to assemble a few pieces, make deductions.'

'You make it sound like the murder game!'

'Didn't you intend for the game to be as realistic as possible?'

'No! Well, yes. I didn't think. I won't be organising another. To make light of death, to turn all this into entertainment... it's amoral. The real thing's too horrific!'

'You won't obliterate a basic organic fascination with death, just by closing your eyes to it. Use it. Forget the human element, wrong as it may seem. Treat it as a puzzle and use the skills you've acquired to solve it. Work out who's done what, their aims, and how they might achieve them, and you can predict the future. You can prevent further atrocities.'

'I can't!'

'There's time enough for mourning when the danger is over. It's too late for Matlock, but you can help someone else.'

'Like Polly?'

The Doctor gave him an encouraging smile. In response, his shoulders straightened a little and he nodded thoughtfully. Perhaps the pep talk would have a lasting effect. Perhaps not. It might at least get Hornby through the next few minutes. 'Come on,' said the Doctor, shepherding his newest pupil towards the door. 'We've work to do.'

Ben collided with Daphne, who careened through the door to the docking level as if an army of Daleks was after her. She whimpered and thrashed as Ben held her wrists and attempted to calm her down. Terri shouted at her, trying to get across the fact of her identity. After a few seconds, the realisation hit home and Daphne ceased her struggles. She collapsed into Ben's arms and sobbed and was, for a minute or so, totally incoherent. Terri patted her between the shoulders, brushed red hair back from her face and whispered assurances. As Daphne began to compose herself, Ben pushed her away gently, feeling inexplicably guilty for their close contact. He couldn't meet Terri's eyes.

'What's wrong? What happened in there?'

'Where's Polly?'

Daphne answered Ben's question first. 'I don't know. There was a shot. I heard her scream, it was horrible!'

A chasm of fear gaped open in Ben's stomach. 'She was shot?'

'No, no, the shot was earlier. Before we were split up.'

'I'm going to find her!'

Terri stopped Ben halfway through the door. 'She's not up here. We know she went downstairs, remember?'

She was right. The idea of Polly being in danger had clouded his reasoning. All he could think of was finding her, but it would be easier to do so if he followed the Doctor's course. 'You two'll be all right without me, won't you?' he asked.

Daphne didn't say anything, but Terri smiled and nodded a confirmation. 'I'll take her to the bar,' she said. It was all Ben needed to hear.

His responsibilities discharged, he bolted down the stairs and to the rescue of his best friend. Five minutes later, he came to a breathless halt in one of Deck B1's interminable corridors and finally accepted that he was well and truly lost.

The Doctor was back on familiar ground. The dining

room was still and quiet, as the kitchen had been – but the sight of the TARDIS, nestled in its corner by the trellis, was enough to fill him with confidence. Yet he had to remind himself sternly that he could still be in peril.

'There's a terminal there,' said Hornby, pointing over to the main doors. He made for it, but the Doctor yanked him back.

'I suggest you think before you act. There's only one other exit from this room. If Hayes and Polly did indeed come through here -'

'They'd be long gone, surely?'

He shook his head. 'That door would have taken them out into the main corridor. We would have seen them.'

'Unless they sneaked past while we were in the kitchen.'

'I have very sharp hearing,' said the Doctor pointedly. 'Not that I would need it.' He raised his voice deliberately and added, to the room in general, 'It's difficult to be furtive when you're keeping a reluctant prisoner – conscious or not! It might be advisable, Ms Hayes, to come into the open. We can talk.'

His words were swallowed by silence. It did occur to him that his guess had been wrong. More likely, though, Hayes was indeed here somewhere. In hiding. Playing games.

'Very well,' he said. 'I shall come to you.'

He kept Hornby to his side and a short way behind, as they made their way across the room. There was no need for silence now that he'd announced their presence so comprehensively. But they had to be vigilant. The Doctor couldn't imagine their quarry would simply wait to be uncovered.

When he did find someone, however, it wasn't Hayes.

Rather, it was Polly's crumpled body, lying beneath a table. His hearts sank and he couldn't help but let out a short, fearful wail. He sprinted towards her, and was drenched in relief to find her breathing and apparently uninjured. 'She's all right,' he reported to the inquisitive Hornby. He reached under the table, supported Polly's head on his arm and tapped her cheeks in an effort to revive her. She groaned and stirred. 'Hayes must have rendered her unconscious so she could make her own getaway,' he deduced.

'Sorry, but no,' said Alison Hayes. The Doctor spun around awkwardly on his haunches and wailed again, this time in dismay. Hornby collapsed against the table leg next to him, his face rigid. Hayes's gun had them both covered and the Doctor raised his hands slowly.

'Well,' said Hayes, 'this is turning into quite a party.'

Ben found a map of the level on one wall, but his own impatience and worry thwarted his initial attempts to decipher it. He had to start again, forcing himself to take his time and to pay more attention. He unwound a little when he found the kitchen. But, to his dismay, he couldn't work out his own position relative to it. The corridor he stood in was a monotonous stretch of patterned wallpaper and featureless, nameless doors. He tried the nearest, in the hope of finding clues behind it. It opened easily and Ben saw, with mounting unease, that its lock was damaged. Somebody had forced an entry.

He found himself looking into a tiny storeroom, fluorescent lighting tubes and cleaning equipment heaped untidily on its shelves. And someone else was looking out. Bryan Melrose crouched in the gloom, riveted by Ben's unexpected arrival, tense but frozen like a startled rabbit not knowing whether, or which way, to jump.

'What are you doing here?' cried Ben. Then he saw the answer to his own question.

Sitting before Melrose was a blue plastic box, from which a pair of silver terminals grew like shorn horns. Melrose was caught with a wire in his hand; his guilt could hardly have been plainer. Ben had no doubt that he was priming the device, perhaps linking its protrusions to complete a circuit. It was the clock, though, that gave the game away, its white face cradled in a nest of wiring, its red second hand ticking off the moments to disaster.

It was a bomb.

Ben's reaction was instinctive, born of a keenly honed sense of self-preservation. He threw himself at Melrose, lifting him bodily and flinging him across the room, to where he could do no harm. 'What do you think -' he spluttered, but the rest was knocked out of him as Melrose counterattacked. His wiry frame was stronger than it looked. Ben was slammed back into a metal shelf, which spilt tins of polish about him. Melrose's hands went for his throat. Ben experienced a twinge of panic as he saw the set of the man's jaw and the insane light in his eyes and considered, for the first time, the possibility that he might actually be homicidal. Matlock had shot Melrose, he recalled. Could the motive for the latter man's murder have been as simple as revenge?

He fought back determinedly, seizing Melrose's wrists and forcing him away. Melrose kicked out, finding Ben's shin, and Ben let go of him and landed a solid punch to his head. He was staggered, and Ben closed in and hit him again, in the stomach this time. Melrose doubled up, winded, and Ben floored him with a good old-fashioned sock to the jaw. He stood over his collapsed foe, breathing heavily. 'Are you going to tell me what we're fighting about, or do you want some more?' he challenged.

But Melrose wasn't finished. A cluster of brooms leaned against the shelving next to him, and he snatched one and swung it like a cudgel. He didn't have the distance or leverage to make it effective; Ben caught the handle easily and wrested it from his grasp. But Melrose used the distraction to scramble past his legs and make for the door. Ben caught hold of his suit jacket, but Melrose shed it and fended him off with a flurry of kicks and punches. He cursed as the businessman slipped free and ran. He pursued him into the corridor and quickly gained ground. He almost caught him, as Melrose stopped to yank open a door. Ben didn't pause to read the engraved golden plaque by its side. The brief chase was almost at an end. He jumped over the threshold. And didn't land.

In front of him, Melrose spun into the distance. Ben's own momentum carried him forward, in the wrong direction. The wall receded behind him, ever further out of reach. Blackness closed in all around and he caught his breath in sheer terror.

His panicking mind tried to deny what his senses were confirming: that Melrose had opened a door directly into space, which Ben had leapt through with no protection whatsoever. He measured his remaining life in seconds.

The Doctor raised himself into a standing position, which wasn't an easy task with his hands held over his head and his gaze rooted to Hayes's gun. Her grim expression was accentuated by shadows; her back was to the bubbled observation wall and she was framed by the cosmos. He kept talking, on the basis – learnt through experience – that most villains wouldn't kill him without having the last word first. 'Well, here we are again, Ms Hayes. I hope you'll think very hard before pulling the trigger. Ending a life is a big responsibility, you know. You can't go back and undo things if you regret it.'

'Be quiet!'

'In fact, most modern weapons have a stun setting to cover just such an eventuality. You ought to consider it.'

'Be quiet, I said. All I want to hear from you is a few answers to a few questions. Your friend here wasn't very helpful.' Hayes nodded towards the semiconscious Polly, beneath the table. Geoff Hornby still cowered beside her, taking partial cover behind the Doctor's legs.

He feigned disappointment. 'Oh, wasn't she? How very odd. Polly's usually so cooperative.' His voice hardened and he snapped, 'Perhaps she didn't appreciate being taken hostage and threatened.'

'And I don't appreciate being subjected to your prattle! Now, tell me: how did you get here?'

'To the dining room?' he asked, with deliberate obtuseness.

'To the Galaxian,' said Hayes frostily.

The Doctor sighed. Honesty, he decided, might be the best policy. 'You're looking at it,' he said, indicating the TARDIS.

'The box? Be serious!'

'I am. That "box" is really the outer plasmic shell of a dimension-spanning vessel. How else do you think it came to be here? It isn't part of the decor, you know.' Hayes said nothing, and the Doctor smiled. 'But of course you don't know, do you? Because you've never set foot inside this hotel before. You're no more a World Corps representative than I am.'

'Not much of a deduction under the circumstances.'

'Granted. And it's just as easy to see you were working with Ted Matlock – unless you both brought the same model of weapon here by coincidence. You're a government agent, aren't you?'

'You are on a roll. You're almost right, anyway. And you?'

'Oh, I just like to help.' The Doctor lowered his hands tentatively, and Hayes didn't seem to mind unduly. 'I came here in response to a distress signal. The caller knew my name, but didn't leave his own. I was supposed to meet him in a room upstairs, but he didn't turn up. On my way back to the game, I found Matlock's body. I haven't been contacted since. Now I don't like to make unfounded assumptions, but one possibility does stand out. Was it Matlock who summoned me?'

Hayes lowered her gun and shook her head ruefully. 'Actually, that would have been my second question.'

Ben reached out towards the doorway, but sent himself into a lateral spin instead. The aftereffects of two attacks upon him and a ghost of the previous night churned his stomach and forced a groan from his lips. His lungs heaved and, to his surprise, sucked in fresh air. His startled mind reassessed his situation. He could see, now he looked for it, a transparent barrier holding back the vacuum. He had stumbled into a blister on the side of the hotel: an antigravity chamber, spanning several levels and designed to offer the experience of spacewalking to the thrill-seeker without the attendant fatal complications.

His relief soon turned to annoyance as he realised what Melrose had done. He had certainly acted deliberately in luring his pursuer into here. Although seeming off balance himself, there was no doubting he was more familiar with such an environment than was the castaway sailor. He circled Ben with practised thrusts of his legs and arms, and Ben scowled at him and tried to mimic his movements. He attained some degree of control over his attitude, but couldn't halt his steady outward drift. Melrose, on the other hand, was drawing closer to the exit. It was like a macabre, slow-motion dance, but Melrose performed a graceful waltz while Ben had tripped over his own feet halfway through the Twist.

He fumbled in his pocket and pulled out one of Hornby's wretched medals. It was as good as anything. He hurled it, as viciously as he could, across the chamber. Unimpeded by the tug of gravity, it should at least sting and distract. He was spun by his own action, though, and propelled ever faster in the wrong direction. He didn't see Melrose again for several seconds, but when he did he noticed with satisfaction that his automatic reaction to the medal's hitting him had knocked him off course. He was still nearer to their shared goal, but Ben had now been gently halted by the outer wall, and he used it to steady himself. He hunched into a ball, placed the soles of his feet on the surface and put all the power of his leg muscles into one good kick, straightening himself out to point like an arrow towards the door. It didn't quite work, and he floundered like a cat in water as the room performed more somersaults around him. But at least he was heading in vaguely the right direction. He gritted his teeth and bore the sickly discomfort until he was bobbing against the near wall, some way below his target. By this time, Melrose had gone.

Fortunately, someone had had the foresight to provide ladders for the novice. Ben hauled himself determinedly on to each plastic rung, and finally collapsed through the welcoming portal, grateful for the pressure of reasserted gravity despite the commensurate sinking of his stomach. He didn't have the luxury of waiting to readjust. He pushed himself to his feet, feeling bizarrely quite heavy, and raced back to the storeroom, hoping to the heavens that he'd guessed wrongly about Melrose's intentions. He hadn't.

Whether Melrose hadn't had the lead Ben imagined, or had been exhausted, or had taken longer to get used to being back on ground, he didn't know. Whatever the reason, the storeroom door was still closing as he skidded around the final corner. Spurred on by the diminishing gap between them, he crossed the distance in seconds and kicked the door so hard that it smashed against a shelf and toppled two tins of paint. Ben took Melrose by surprise all over again. He didn't pause for thought this time, just put his full body weight into the urgent task of separating man from bomb before it was too late.

Melrose went down hard and Ben all but fell on top of him. His exertions were beginning to tell: his limbs felt as if they were carved from lead. Still, he could keep his enemy pinned to the floor. Melrose's attempts to topple him were weak too, and in vain. 'You've got to let me go. You don't understand.'

'Oh, talking to me now are you?'

'The explosive device,' he gasped. Pools of sweat shone on his forehead and cheeks. 'I wasn't priming it.'

'No?'

'I set the thing hours ago. I came back to defuse it. No time now.'

Ben felt suddenly cold. He suspected some kind of a trick, but the desperation in Melrose's voice convinced him otherwise. 'Please – let me go!'

The clock stood poised at one minute to midnight, a spindly finger beginning the slow, painful trip across the final, fateful division. The second hand had already entered the last quadrant of its journey. They had less than fifteen seconds.

Polly surfaced from an unusually deep sleep, to find the Doctor's voice in her ears. 'Then how did Matlock know about me?'

'Some Earth agency must have details of you and your ship on file.'

'Not to my knowledge. But, oh, I suppose I could leave a frequency to contact me on at some point in my future. I do have some experience of dealing with alien incursions. I just wish I was going to realise that a message intended for me then could intercept me now. How can I be about to be so short-sighted!'

'You're really earning my confidence here, you know.'

Polly's neck was stiff from lying in an awkward position, and her head felt stuffed with cotton wool. She tried to blink away tiredness, as her hearing focused in and out of the conversation in progress.

'The agency I work for has ties to the European government, and that's all you need to know.' The speaker was Alison Hayes. As Polly's faculties returned, memories of her captivity flooded back. The Doctor must have come to her rescue. Or was he a prisoner himself?

'You mean you don't have official sanction for your mission?' the Doctor challenged.

'What I mean is, I'm a freelance operative. My employers can deny all knowledge of me if things go wrong. It's part of the deal.'

'They must be paying you a lot of money.'

'What does money have to do with anything?'

Polly thought about feigning sleep a while longer, to be ready to spring a surprise on Hayes if an opportunity came. Sprawled as she was, though, she was in no position to do anything, even if her muscles hadn't been throbbing so. She ached to stretch her limbs. More importantly, she wanted to see what was happening.

She hauled herself out from beneath the table with difficulty. Geoff Hornby was crouched by one leg, and he graciously offered a hand and helped her to stand. He stayed by her side and let her lean on him. She had, in turn, given him the courage to come out of hiding and face the situation. They lined up next to the Doctor and faced Hayes, nervously but with determination. She took a pace backward and regarded them with suspicion.

'Hello, Doctor,' said Polly, weakly.

'Hello, Polly,' he said, his malleable features brimming with affection. 'Are you all right now? You had us worried. I was just having a chat with your friend here. I think we're about to reach an understanding.'

'Has she told you how she killed Neville Adler yet?'

His expression changed suddenly, like clouds shutting out the light of a summer's day. His tone became hard and accusatory. 'Did your employers tell you to do that?'

'It was necessary.'

'It's rarely necessary to commit cold-blooded murder, Ms Hayes!'

'She mentioned sharks, too. She thought we were working for some.'

117

'Well?' the Doctor challenged.

Hayes shrugged. 'You may as well know. Certain people have come to the Galaxian with the express intention of meeting, and doing business with, the Selachians.'

'Selachians?'

'Who are they, Doctor?' Polly already knew it wasn't good news. Her companion had sounded utterly appalled.

'One of the most ferocious, warmongering, totally paranoid races in this quadrant of the galaxy.' His audible dismay was deepened by a sudden realisation. 'And it's almost certainly their spacecraft which is holding a fixed position just a short way beyond this station.'

Ben wasted vital seconds thinking of nothing, so jumbled was his mind. His reflexes finally kicked in at about the same time as Melrose's; they wasted vital seconds trying to stand and becoming entangled, each holding the other back. They went for the door simultaneously too. Neither gave ground and they squeezed through side by side, popping into the corridor like corks from the same champagne bottle. Ben saw hope at last, as a clear path stretched ahead. Panic measures kicked in and both men ran for their lives. There was no time to do anything else.

The final seconds of the countdown lasted for ever, but that was scant comfort to someone who felt as if he was wading through thick syrup, expecting a fast and bloody death.

For all his efforts, Ben was barely a hundred yards from the storeroom when the bomb was detonated.

CHAPTER 7

PICKING UP THE PIECES

Ben's first, fleeting impression was of a ball of fire at his back. He screamed his throat raw as a gust of hot air hit him like a physical push from a giant's hand. Combined with his own survival instinct to dive for cover, it sent him several feet through the air and almost made him black out on landing. He lay face down, hyperventilating, his besieged thoughts slowly receiving the message that things weren't as bad as he had imagined. He was alive, for a start.

He rolled on to his back and raised his head to look. The storeroom door had been blown off its hinges and lay mangled against the far wall. Beyond this, he could see few signs of damage. His panting was mixed with giddy laughter, which soon turned into a painful coughing fit. He managed to get up on to his hands and knees and he tried to breathe deeply, to bring his respiratory system under control. For some reason, air eluded him. He became aware of Melrose, equally wretched, lying by his side, his throat rasping as his chest undulated like an overworked pump. He would have a few questions for him, he thought. For one thing, he had expected a much bigger blast. What was the point of engineering such a small one, in an unpopulated area?

Even as Ben worked out the answer to that for himself, his senses supplied the evidence to confirm his awful theory. An increasingly fierce wind whistled by him; the hotel's air supply was being gulped voraciously into the storeroom. He should have seen it earlier. The room, he realised, had an outer wall. And it had been holed.

Ben wanted to struggle, but he was too tired and the pressure too great. He collapsed back on to his stomach and felt himself being pulled against his will, his fingernails leaving grooves in the carpet, his legs kicking idly in the vain hope of finding purchase where there was none. He was being dragged towards his doom.

It was with delirious relief that he looked up through streaming eyes to see a thick white bulkhead, falling across the corridor to seal off the afflicted area. Too slow, though. Ben ran the risk of being caught on the wrong side of it. He closed his eyes and worked his protesting muscles as hard as he could, scrambling to gain traction and to resist the irresistible suction just long enough for the emergency systems to do their work.

The pull lessened, but didn't ease off totally. Ben heard a groan, but he had to wipe away tears with his shirt-sleeve before he could see what had happened. The bulkhead had dropped as far as it was able. It had stopped in deference to the presence of Bryan Melrose's body beneath it. The so-called accountant was trapped, his head and shoulders on the near side, his legs out of sight beyond. He cried out and pounded his fists on the floor, but did nothing useful. And, before Ben could react, he heard the determined thump of another barrier slamming into position behind him, to safeguard the rest of the station.

He was well and truly trapped. And his air supply was still being evacuated into space.

'You mean the Selachians are outside?' Hayes asked the Doctor.

'You mean you didn't know?'

'I knew they were involved, of course I did. But there was no sign of their actual presence. I assumed they were far away.'

'Not far enough.' The Doctor tried to keep calm, but he knew fear was showing in his eyes. His voice had a shrill edge and he caught himself entwining his fingers nervously. As if he didn't have enough problems, without Selachians as well. 'I think,' he said to Hayes, 'you'd better start talking. I need to know what's going on.' She opened her mouth to obey – but then another problem landed squarely into his lap.

'Oh, no!'

No one else had noticed it yet. The Doctor ignored the inquisitive looks of Polly, Hayes and Hornby to concentrate on the task of confirming his unpleasant hypothesis. He stood with legs apart and distributed his weight evenly between each foot. His balance was still off. Something was definitely amiss.

'What is it, Doctor?' Polly's apprehension had grown to too high a level to restrain.

'Can't you feel it?' No, of course she couldn't; none of them could. 'The station's moving.'

'That's impossible!' asserted Hayes.

'I'm afraid not. The gyroscopic systems are doing a good job of hiding it, but we are in motion.'

As if to confirm his statement, Thomas appeared unbidden, for the second time in the Doctor's experience. He addressed Hayes this time, his computer imaging system actually lining his face with worry. 'I am sorry to disturb you, madam, but given the absence of personnel in the engineering section, I

121

thought you should hear my tidings.'

'What is it, Thomas?'

'An explosive device has been detonated on this deck, madam. The hull has been breached.'

The Doctor nodded. The news was certainly consistent with his own observations. 'Has the area been sealed off?'

'It has, sir.'

'But we've been knocked out of orbit, haven't we?'

'Indeed. And might I remark that, without technical staff to correct our current drift -'

'We'll go flying off into deep space!' Hornby cried.

'Oh, I don't think so,' said the Doctor.

'You don't?'

'No. I believe we're heading for a bumpy landing on Earth – though not before we've all been burnt to a crisp on re-entry.'

'In a little under ten minutes, sir,' Thomas confirmed graciously.

The Doctor leapt into a flurry of action, grabbing Hayes by the wrist and pulling her to the door. 'Come on, Ms Hayes, we've a rescue mission to organise.' Halfway, something more urgent occurred to him. He stopped, rifled through his pockets and tossed the TARDIS key to a dismayed Polly. 'Ask Thomas to find Ben and send him here. And as many of the others as he can manage. If the worst happens…'

She nodded dumbly. The Doctor could see that she wanted to say something, but there was no time to wait for her to find the words. He forced a smile and a heartening wink, then rejoined the impatient Hayes and left at a run.

'Work with me!' Ben shouted through clenched teeth.

'This is to save both our lives.' He and Melrose had hold of each other's forearms, and Ben had planted a foot against the partly closed bulkhead to give himself leverage. He pulled for all he was worth, but Melrose was no use, finding nothing on the far side to push against. Ben was still buffeted by the fatal gale of his own impending death, and a terrible burning at the back of his throat made him all too aware of his diminishing supply of oxygen. He was winning the battle, but barely. Melrose was emerging, inch by painfully slow inch, from beneath the shutter. Ben couldn't afford to slacken off. If he allowed his aching arms even a fraction of a second's respite, then all his work would be undone instantaneously.

When the seemingly eternal struggle ended, it ended suddenly. As soon as Melrose's feet were clear, the bulkhead hit the ground and the opposing force to Ben's efforts was abruptly cut off. He pulled Melrose a good few yards along the corridor and they fell, entangled, gasping hoarsely in the rarefied atmosphere. The computer saw that its second bulkhead was no longer needed and it lifted it, allowing a gentle breeze of sweet air to waft in. Ben gulped it in gratefully and was in no hurry to move. Melrose was actually crying.

A few minutes later, Thomas appeared beside them and announced that Ms Wright had requested their presence in the dining room on B1. When pressed, he admitted it was 'something of an emergency situation'. Ben collected himself and stood shakily. He removed Melrose's tie and bound the unprotesting man's hands behind his back with three different knots. 'That'll do for the time being. I'm not letting you out of my sight after this.' He hauled his prisoner to his feet and wondered where he might find a map of the level, now that the nearest one was in the sealed-off area. He should have asked Thomas for directions, he realised. Still, there was only one direction he could take from this point.

Ben had barely taken three steps along the corridor when the hotel suddenly tipped on to its side. He hit the wall and Melrose landed on top of him, knocking the breath from his body.

Their ordeal wasn't over yet.

The Doctor was becoming frantic with the realisation that, this time, he might be too late to save everybody. First, he had found that the affected area of the station lay neatly across his path, a stubborn bulkhead barring his way. He had changed course in mid-step, taking the long way around towards the stairs. Alison Hayes kept pace beside him, silently. Precious time was lost.

Now, even as he started down the final flight towards B10, the main engineering deck in the bowels of the station, the whole thing tilted and he was thrown off his feet. He tried to adjust to the new attitude of the floor, to continue his desperate race, but the Galaxian had been thrown into a haphazard spin and he couldn't predict in which direction he would be flung from one second to the next.

The Doctor was skilled at keeping track of time, but just at the moment he almost wished he wasn't. The Galaxian, he predicted, would hit the atmosphere within the next one to two minutes. Even if he could reach the main thruster and gyroscope controls, he would almost certainly not have time to prevent its destruction now. He kept trying until the end, anyway. He clung on to a banister until the plunging station attempted to throw him where he wanted to go. He went with the motion, but was unable to control it fully. He smacked painfully into the metal door at the staircase's end and held on to its handle doggedly, fearful of being lodged from his improved position.

Then, just like that, the floor eased back into a horizontal plane. The Doctor clung on for a second more, in case the respite was but an illusion. He concluded, thankfully, that it wasn't.

'What's happened?' Hayes asked. She had taken the worst of it: her neat suit was torn, her legs bruised and her hazel hair tossed into disarray. She didn't complain.

'I don't know how, but the gyroscopic systems seem to have come back on line.'

'By themselves?'

'I very much doubt it.' The Doctor flung open the door and rushed through into the engineering section. He was only mildly surprised to see that nobody was present. He was at the very bottom of the station, in a small, almost circular room which afforded magnificent views of space in all directions but the one behind him, leading to the stairwell. Earth loomed ominously large at his left-hand side. No elevators came down as far as this.

Clunky grey instrument banks were ranged about the walls, leaving only a tiny space in the centre for three operators' chairs. The Doctor took one of these and, working out the consoles' functions switch by switch, punched up a status report. Hayes sat beside him and made a few more hesitant checks of her own.

'It looks like it was only a small bomb.'

'You only need a small bomb to cripple a space station.'

'Hey, someone's hacked into these systems!'

'An extremely skilled programmer,' the Doctor mused.

'Whoever it is, we have them to thank for saving our lives. They've stabilised the hotel and have gone some way towards reversing its downward spiral. They've bought us a few minutes, at least.'

'They've left now, though,' Hayes reported.

'They withdrew as soon as I touched a control. They don't want to be identified.'

'But who could do all this?'

'Actually, it's not an entirely unexpected development. Where did you, erm, find Neville Adler?' Forced though he was to work with her, the Doctor had not forgotten Hayes's unexplained crime. For now, however, more urgent matters demanded his attention.

'The docking level,' she said stiffly.

'But, according to Thomas, he went straight to his room after leaving the bar, and stayed there until after you had taken Polly to the kitchen.'

'He's mistaken.'

'Ah, but Thomas doesn't make mistakes. At least, not according to Thomas. And yet, your friend Matlock used him to send a message to me, without his being aware of it later.'

'So he's not infallible.'

'Indeed. At least, not against a computer expert.' The Doctor had been setting controls throughout their conversation; he now eased a lever forward, causing manoeuvring thrusters to fire at a precise angle and affecting a gentle change of course. Satisfied by the results, he flexed his fingers and proceeded to the next stage of his rescue plan. 'The question is,' he muttered as he worked, 'how many more lies have the computers been programmed to tell? And by whom?'

Polly had ridden out the storm with Geoff Hornby in

the dining room. At her suggestion, they had held on to the TARDIS: it slid a little whenever the floor was angled away from its corner but, to their relief, it was too heavy to be overturned. That hadn't stopped the furniture from flying their way, though, and Polly had spent most of the preceding five minutes letting loose scream after scream as she was assaulted by a never-ending volley of tables and chairs. In the end, she had suffered no more injury than a bruised shin, and when the shaking finally stopped she was able to count herself lucky.

Hornby was relatively unscathed too, although he had lost one of his contact lenses. They spent some time on hands and knees, feeling in the carpet, but could not find it. 'Never mind,' he said with a sigh. 'It was a disposable one anyway. It's just that I haven't brought any more.' He removed the other lens, pulled a soft, thin case from his pocket and produced his pink-framed spectacles from within.

'You mean you just throw them away? It must cost a fortune!'

He looked at her strangely. 'You really are from 1942, aren't you?'

'From 1966,' she corrected him primly, the reminder of her long-gone birthdate illogically making her feel ancient.

Polly's spirits were lifted by the arrival of Ben, who marched Bryan Melrose before him like a prisoner. Melrose's hands were tied behind his back, and Polly wondered what had occurred in her absence. They exchanged expressions of relief at each other's continued health and, as Ben forced Melrose to sit on a chair and used his own belt to bind one of its legs to his, Polly called up Thomas to ask if there had been any developments.

'We are not out of danger yet, madam,' he reported, 'but my earlier estimate of the time remaining to us no longer applies.'

'You mean the Doctor's bought us some breathing space?' Ben called over.

'We do appear to have been granted a reprieve, sir, but I have no knowledge of how this was accomplished.'

'Looks like there was no need to send out the alarm after all,' said Hornby. But Polly was quietly glad that they had done. She felt much safer with Ben here.

'Maybe not,' said Ben, looking at Hornby suspiciously, 'but I can't say I'm happy with the Doc leaving you and Pol together. If I'm not mistaken, you haven't explained why you gave us a false name yet.'

'We did talk about it,' said Polly. She too had been apprehensive when the Doctor and Hayes had left, but it had clearly been preying on Hornby's mind too and he had been quick to set things aright.

'I never said I wouldn't tell you my real one. It's Smith. John Smith. "Geoff Hornby" is a professional pseudonym. If I'm trying to make people think my games are exciting, I don't want to put them off with a dull name.'

Polly giggled. 'I thought it usually happened the other way round.'

'Not that I expected any game to be this frantic. It's not what I had in mind at all.'

'OK, I believe you,' said Ben.

'You can check with Thomas if you like, there'll be plenty of records under my real name Earthside. I'd have told the Doctor right away if I'd known what he was doing.'

'I believe you,' Ben reiterated. With the immediate danger past, Hornby had regained his habit of talking rather too much. In an obvious attempt to change the subject, he turned to Polly and asked, 'Did Thomas tell everyone to come here?'

She nodded. 'If the worst came to the worst, the Doctor wanted us to evacuate in the TARDIS... er, his ship.'

'Good. We could do with getting everyone together anyway.'

'If they all turn up, this time.'

'We've got a few things to sort out.' Ben glared at Melrose meaningfully. 'Starting with why this fellow tried to blast us all to smithereens.'

'I've done as much as I can,' said the Doctor, sitting back and regarding the instruments despondently.

'We're not out of danger?'

'Not entirely, no. We acted too late. We've been ensnared by Earth's gravitational pull. I've done my best, but the thrusters don't have the power to break completely free. I've taken us into a fresh orbit, but it's a decaying one.'

'How long have we got?'

'Just over two hours. Happily, I've been able to arrange for the station to crash-land into the middle of the Atlantic Ocean. What fragments of it remain, anyway.' They had not needed this additional complication, he thought – especially since, like so many things, it could have been avoided. Sometimes he felt humankind was incapable of doing anything without him. It was unfair, perhaps, but his irritation needed an outlet. 'None of this should have happened,' he snapped. 'If World Corps had sent the necessary staff to implement basic safety precautions and checks, we wouldn't have come so close to a pointless tragedy. Our lives wouldn't be at risk now!'

'We can still evacuate,' Hayes pointed out defensively.

'Past the Selachians?'

'Anyway, why blame me? You know I'm not connected to World Corps.'

'But your organisation forced them to cancel their shuttle, am I right? They didn't want too many innocents getting in the way of whatever your mission here is.'

Hayes looked as if she was about to argue; instead, her face fell and she shrugged resignedly. 'I don't know,' she confessed. 'But yes, I imagine you're right. This was Matlock's play. I was his deep-cover backup, in case things went wrong. That's why I wasn't sure about you. Matlock said help might be arriving, but he didn't name names. I was told things strictly on a need-to-know basis.'

'Typical military bureaucracy!' the Doctor said scathingly. 'So wrapped up in your own petty secrecy that you spend all your time second-guessing each other, chasing each other's tails. I think you "need to know" right now, don't you Ms Hayes? Only there's no one around to tell you any more.' She set her jaw into a determined sulk and the Doctor saw that he was beginning to lose her. He softened his tone and leaned forward, giving her his most persuasive stare. 'I think I need to know too, since I seem to have drawn the job of picking up the pieces of your operation.'

Hayes nodded. 'Granted,' she said.

'Then tell me.'

She drew a deep breath and was about to start when, much to the Doctor's frustration, they were interrupted again. This time, it was by a mechanical chirruping sound from inside his own coat. He dug into his breast pocket and produced the fob-watch alarm system. A flick of his thumb silenced it and he stared into its blank face with a profound sense of dismay.

'Not good news?'

'Not good, but predictable. The Selachians want something in this hotel. They've just seen it blasted off course and almost destroyed. Their own sensors have probably warned them that it's on its way down. I'd say they're getting impatient.'

Hayes turned pale. 'They're on their way, aren't they?'

'I'm afraid they are.' The Doctor returned the device to his pocket and tried to be optimistic. 'However, docking with this station in its current orbit, without being dragged into the atmosphere alongside it, is a precision task. I'd say we have some time. If you know what they're after, it would be very helpful indeed.'

Hayes nodded and swallowed. 'I'll make it quick.'

'You may as well come clean,' said Ben. 'You were caught red-handed!'

Polly was tiring of this. Ben had put his questions to Melrose repeatedly, but had had no satisfaction. His captive had simply glowered at him and said nothing.

'I don't understand,' said Hornby. 'You had no way of leaving the station. You would have been committing suicide!'

'Come on, mate,' said Ben, his exasperation showing. 'I just saved your life back there. I think I'm entitled to something.'

'Keep very still,' interrupted a commanding voice from the doorway into the kitchen, 'and move back against the wall. I mean, don't keep very still. Keep your hands still. Put them in the air, in fact. But move your feet towards the wall, slowly. Then keep very still!'

Everyone turned to look at Henry Mace, looking more ridiculous than ever as he hefted a small red, tubular fire extinguisher in one hand and aimed it like a gun with the other. No one made to comply with his requests. 'I'm warning you all,' he said, sounding as far from confident as was possible. He actually backed away himself. 'I'm not afraid to use this and I won't be held responsible for the consequences if you make me. Now do as I demand!'

'Or he'll scream until he's sick,' said Terri Willis. To Mace's alarm – which he displayed with grotesque exaggeration – she brushed past him from the kitchen and strolled into the restaurant without a backwards glance. Daphne followed, rather more reluctantly and giving Mace as wide a berth as possible. 'I see the gang's all here.'

'Just four unaccounted for now,' said Ben.

He didn't know about Neville Adler's death yet, Polly realised. 'It's, erm, three actually,' she ventured.

'Shut up!' screamed Mace. 'Stop talking, all of you, and do as I say!' He fiddled with the extinguisher and managed to drop it. Foam billowed out of its nozzle and he screamed and let go of that too. It thrashed about like an enraged snake and sprayed floor, walls, but especially Mace with white suds. Ben ran over and expertly brought the device under control. Mace sulked and joined the others reluctantly, brushing foam from his hair. He made an attempt to regain his dignity, perhaps not realising that it was too late. 'You've managed to convince me of your good faith. I was simply worried – understandably so – by your summons. Your intention could have been to lure me into a pernicious trap.'

'Speaking of which,' said Terri, 'why don't you shut yours?'

'Good idea,' said Ben, raising his voice authoritatively and addressing the whole group. 'We'll never get anywhere at this rate. We need to work through this problem in a logical, ordered fashion.'

They all listened, and Polly felt a fierce glow of pride in her best friend. Inclined to shyness he may be; awkward in unfamiliar social circles, certainly. But, given a job to do, he would stick to it and perform it to the best of his ability. He was well suited to taking charge, infrequently though he tried it. In a situation like this, there was only one person she would rather have giving orders.

Her warm feeling of pleasure faded instantly, however, as Terri went to Ben's side and linked her arm with his. 'Perhaps we should start by recapping what we know,' she suggested. 'Some of us have missed things – like why we did the big nosedive, for example.'

Ben agreed, too readily for Polly's liking. It was insane, she told herself. He was allowed to have friends, wasn't he? Girl friends, even. Still, she couldn't help but feel that he should have shrugged off Terri's unsolicited – and far too affectionate, in her mind – touch and offer of support. He didn't. Polly felt a pang of something in her chest, inexplicable but hurtful all the same. She knew what it wasn't: it couldn't, she told herself, be jealousy. A more absurd idea could scarcely be imagined.

'The explosion would be a good place to start,' said Ben, directing attention towards Melrose. 'This man has admitted to planting the bomb, but he won't tell me why. He was also, let me remind you, shot by Matlock just before he died. Perhaps, between us, we can persuade him to give us a few answers.' His words, ostensibly meant for everyone, were directed at the recalcitrant Melrose himself. They had no effect. The prisoner turned away with a dismissive snort.

'And he claimed to have been in his room, unaccompanied, at the time of the murder!' added Mace, his tone suggesting that this confirmed the suspect's guilt beyond doubt.

'In fact,' recalled Hornby, 'the computer told us he was in his room twenty minutes ago, but he couldn't have been. He must have gimmicked it somehow.'

'Oh, this is all so horrid!' Daphne shuddered in fear and disgust and wrapped her arms about herself.

'Think what you like,' snarled Melrose.

'You hear him?' bellowed Mace. 'He won't deny it. He's practically admitting his culpability. Call Ms Hayes. Alert the police. The sooner this miscreant is led away in handcuffs, the sooner we can leave this godforsaken place and continue about our law-abiding business!'

'No,' said Polly. 'It might not be as simple as that.'

'And why not, pray tell?'

'For a start,' said Ben doubtfully, 'Melrose was actually defusing the bomb when I found him. I don't know why.'

'There's something else.' Polly hesitated and looked to Geoff Hornby for support. He knew what she was going to say, and he smiled his encouragement. 'There's something I've got to tell you. It's about Alison Hayes – and Neville Adler.'

'There's no need, thank you Polly.' She brightened at the welcome sound of the Doctor's voice. He strode in through the main entrance from the corridor, a bedraggled Hayes at his side. 'Ms Hayes can tell you all

134

about the incident herself, and more. Can't you, Ms Hayes?' She forced an obliging smile and Polly grinned inwardly as it became obvious which of the pair was in charge now.

'Pay attention please, everybody,' said the Doctor. 'We have a great deal to get through and not very much time.'

The Doctor rubbed his hands together nervously as he faced his attentive audience. It was always difficult to break this sort of news. He had to put across the seriousness of the situation, while retaining confidence in his own ability to help everyone through it.

Ben started him off with a question. 'Is the hotel out of danger?'

'I'm afraid not, Ben. However, we are more stable than we were. We have almost two hours before we have to worry again, which gives us time to resolve our problems and evacuate.'

'Why can't we all leave now, in the TARDIS?' asked Polly. 'We can sort out the murder and everything later, when we're safe.'

'Hear, hear!' struck up Mace. 'But what's a TARDIS?'

'We'd need to find Dorothy Adler,' Hornby reminded them both. 'She isn't here.'

'We also have to prevent more needless deaths,' said the Doctor. 'Perhaps many hundreds of thousands.' His announcement had the desired effect: an uneasy ripple spread through the group and their interest was renewed. 'We are shortly to be boarded by an alien race known as the Selachians.' He could see from their reactions that all but Ben had heard of them. Nor had they heard anything good. 'They want something from this station. They have been waiting for quite some time to get it, and they've run out of patience.'

'The cloaked ship!' Ben recalled, striving to keep up. 'But why wait so long to move in?'

'Because the original plan was for a human agent to do their work for them surreptitiously. They wouldn't have had to show their faces at all. But he failed – didn't you, Mr Melrose? Don't bother to deny it, I heard enough as I came in to know that you set the bomb which almost killed us all. And several more like it, I imagine.' Melrose's shamefaced reaction confirmed the Doctor's theory. He continued with more confidence. 'Because it wasn't enough for the Selachians just to get their hands on the merchandise. They wanted to be rid of anyone who might have even heard of it. So you rigged the Galaxian to explode once you were clear. Only you never got clear, did you, Mr Melrose? Matlock was exposed as a government agent, putting a spoke in your plans. You had no choice but to disarm your own explosives, to buy yourself time to complete your task and flee.'

'What I don't understand,' said Daphne timorously, 'is what these Selachian things can possibly want with us.'

'That,' said the Doctor, 'I will leave to Ms Hayes to explain.'

Alison Hayes stepped forward, not without a show of reluctance. It had taken the Doctor some time, on their way here, to convince her that everyone else should hear what she had to say. In the end, she had come round to his way of thinking. Most people did, eventually.

'Simply put,' she announced into an expectant hush, 'the Selachians are after the most incredible weapon ever conceived.'

CHAPTER 8

THE WEAPON

The Doctor climbed on to one of the few remaining upright tables and sat with his knees against his chest. He had heard Hayes's story before, but he listened again with one ear while trying to fit the facts with what he already knew and simultaneously planning a course of action.

'It begins with Neville and Dorothy Adler,' said Hayes, 'except that those aren't their real names.'

'We know,' chipped in Hornby, eager to show off what clues he had already gathered. 'Thomas looked them up. They're using pen names.'

'Someone else's pen names,' Hayes corrected. 'The "Adlers" who booked into this hotel were not writers. They weren't even a couple. But they were clever enough to realise someone might check their backgrounds. What better way to avoid suspicion than to choose names which won't appear in Earth records, but which have a cast-iron excuse for not doing so attached to them?'

The Doctor felt in his jacket for Matlock's book, The Murder Game, by Neville and Dorothy Adler. He riffled through its pages, but found nothing about the authors. Perhaps Matlock had hoped to catch the pair out with details of what they claimed to be their work. Perhaps he had just taken a fancy to it. They would never know now.

'Our "Neville and Dorothy" are scientists, working in weapons research and development for a covert organisation with government ties. They came up with something. I don't know the details; all I do know is what I've passed on to you.'

'That it's the most incredible weapon conceived,' the Doctor muttered. Hayes glanced at him, but he fell silent.

'It's supposedly infallible,' she continued. 'Once it targets you, you're dead. It doesn't miss. It was the result of many years' intensive work by the Adlers and their team, and a great deal of funding. But, once it was developed, they received a better offer. The Adlers were known for their computer skills: they purged the organisation's systems of all data pertaining to the weapon, without anyone noticing. Then they took the blueprints and fled. They dropped out of sight for months, although several agents – Matlock and I included – were retained to track them down. At last, Matlock found them here and called me in to assist him.'

Hornby sat down heavily and looked stunned. 'Did anyone actually come here to play my game?'

'The Adlers certainly didn't. They used your event as cover. They intended to sell the weapon to the Selachians and, by meeting their agent – Melrose – up here, they saved him the bother of having to go through Earth customs. They hired a shuttle and registered for the murder game. They expected the Galaxian to be teeming with players, in the midst of whom the handover could be made without arousing suspicion. Matlock would have acted to stop them earlier, but part of his brief was to retrieve the blueprints. The Adlers had split them into two computer files, contained on separate disks. They hid one each, so neither could be forced into surrendering both. Matlock was waiting for the handover itself to make his move. He contacted the Doctor and his friends because, if things went wrong, they at least had experience of extraterrestrial threats.' The Doctor didn't miss the astonished look on Terri Willis's face. She turned to Ben, clearly seeing him in a new light. The sailor pretended not to notice.

'As near as I can tell,' said Hayes, 'Matlock's cover was blown shortly after the game began. He probably saw Melrose and Neville Adler discussing arrangements, but got too close and gave himself away. Melrose, I imagine, attacked him. Matlock shot back. We know what happened next.'

'And what did you do?' asked Polly tartly.

Hayes sighed. This, the Doctor knew, would be the most difficult part for her. She deserved the discomfort.

'I had to act fast. Matlock was dead and I didn't know half of what he knew. I kept tabs on the Adlers. I already knew they'd hacked into the computer system and that neither they nor Melrose were necessarily where Thomas thought they were. I followed Neville around Deck B3 – almost running into you and Ms McAllister as you came out of the medical centre – and eventually up to the docking level. I assumed the deal had been done, and he was collecting his disk. But he was more wily than he seemed. It was dark up there and difficult to manoeuvre. He heard me coming and challenged me.'

'So you killed him!' said Polly. She made no attempt to conceal her disgust and the Doctor was proud of her.

'I had no choice. Many more would have died if those disks had got into the wrong hands. They still might. If I'd let Neville go, he would have told Dorothy and Melrose about me – and you saw what one or all of them did to Matlock. As far as I was concerned, it was him or me.' She paused and glared at each of them in turn, as if defying them to condemn her. They didn't, and her face softened. She turned back to Polly. 'At the time, I didn't know who the Selachians had sent. When your party arrived so mysteriously, you became my prime suspects. You stumbled across Neville's body and, if you'd only turned around, you would have seen me too. I couldn't take the chance. Before I let you go, I had to find out whose side you were on.'

'And if the Doctor hadn't arrived and convinced you, would you have killed me?'

'I'm sorry. The stakes were too high.'

It was time, the Doctor thought, to intercede again. He slid off the table and took charge of the meeting. 'Our problem now is this: the Selachians seem to have given up on Melrose here. They're on their way to finish the job themselves. We could, as Polly said, evacuate. However, we would be leaving behind the possibility of the Selachians finding the disks before the hotel is destroyed. We can't afford to let that happen.'

'What's the plan?' Ben asked, impatient as always.

'My plan,' said Hayes grimly, 'is to find out who murdered my partner.' She strode towards Melrose, produced her gun and levelled it coolly at his temple. 'And whatever else this collaborator knows!'

The Doctor leapt over, knocked her arm aside and smartly plucked the gun from her hand before she knew what was happening. He yanked out its plasma cartridge and tossed the weapon to one side. It skittered across the floor and came to rest against a table leg. The Doctor and Hayes scowled at each other.

'Where's Mace?' asked Daphne, suddenly.

They all looked around, hopelessly. The would-be

thespian was no longer present. 'He's done a runner!' exclaimed Ben.

'He must have sidled away while we were talking,' said Hornby.

'But why?'

'There could be many reasons, Polly,' said the Doctor. 'Perhaps he's more involved in our difficulties than we've imagined. Or perhaps he simply panicked.'

'He's always seemed unpredictable,' said Daphne. 'He scares me.'

'You can predict one thing about him,' said Ben sourly. 'He'll always cause trouble!'

'It does add to our burdens,' the Doctor conceded. 'Now, what I suggest is this. Geoff and Daphne, I want you to find Dorothy. Start with her room: Thomas places her there, although he may be wrong of course. I want her brought here, ready to evacuate – and if you can persuade her to bring one or both of the disks with her, so much the better. Polly, I'd like you to accompany Ms Hayes on a search for Neville's disk.' His companion wasn't comfortable with the idea, but he needed someone to keep an eye on the government agent. The Doctor's first priority might be to keep the secrets of the weapon from the Selachians, but his second had to be to keep them from Hayes's employers. 'Don't worry – she is on our side for all her, ah, excesses. Besides, she's no longer armed. I'm sure you can handle her.' Hayes didn't appreciate the sentiment, but Polly glowed visibly with pride and chose not to contest her assignment.

'I'll return to the engineering section and do what I can to keep the Selachians from docking. I doubt I'll be able to achieve more than a short delay, though – so Ben and Terri, your job is to see what you can do on the docking level. Seal the airlocks if you can; otherwise, stack crates in front of them. Whatever you can think of. Between us, we need to buy as much time as we can for the other two groups to do their jobs.'

'But even if you keep the aliens at bay, we'll still crash!' Hornby pointed out.

'Quite right. So, whatever you're doing and however successful you've been, I want every one of you back here in precisely one hour. Not a second later, mind. I will not place any more lives at risk. And if anyone does find Henry Mace, please pass that on to him.'

'Why here?' asked Daphne. 'How can we escape from here?'

'We can. Just trust me. All ready? Good. Let's get to work!'

As his six colleagues filed out of the dining room, the Doctor turned to Thomas. The hologram had been listening to the conversation with polite interest and waiting to be addressed or dismissed. 'I'd like you to stay here and keep an eye on Melrose,' he said. 'If he moves, I want to be informed immediately.' He turned to give the sullen prisoner a meaningful look, and added, 'Not that he should, if he wants me to save his miserable hide as well.'

Hayes stabbed at the elevator call button. Daphne was pouring out details of her experience on the docking level to Hornby, shaking as she recalled those terrible events. Ben was watching Terri, who was scrutinising Hayes's every move in turn. Polly took him by the shoulder and pulled him furtively aside.

'Will you be all right with her?'

'With Terri? Sure, she's OK.'

'How do you know? What makes you think she's not the murderer?'

142

'She can't be,' said Ben. 'She found me after I was knocked out –'

'You were knocked out?' He hadn't had the chance to mention it to Polly before. 'How? When?'

'About the time of the murder. It was Terri who found me.'

'Where?'

'Near the bedrooms.'

'Near the lifts?'

'Well, yeah.'

Polly seized on the admission. 'But Matlock was killed in the lifts! It could easily have been her.'

'So why wake me up and let me see her? No Pol, it doesn't make sense. For my money, it was Melrose who did it. It's all but proved.'

'I don't like it, all the same.'

Terri chose that moment to wander over, much to Ben's discomfort. 'What are you two whispering about?' she asked, not unpleasantly.

Polly took Ben's arm and gripped it tightly. 'Just reminiscing,' she lied. 'We're very good friends, you know.'

'Yes,' said Terri smoothly, 'I thought that was all you were.'

Polly glared at her and Ben was startled to see a shadow of what he could only imagine was jealousy falling across her face. His stomach cartwheeled and he felt as if his world had turned upside down. Then the logical part of his brain reasserted itself. He was simply mistaken, it assured him. There was no need to panic; less need to make a fool of himself.

An elevator arrived and Hayes ushered Daphne and Hornby into it and sent them on their way. 'The four of us can get the next one,' she said. 'We're all going to

143

the same place.'

'We are?' It was news to Ben.

'To start with, yes. I still think Adler must have intended to retrieve his disk from the docking level. Ms Wright and I will begin our search there.'

Polly smirked at Terri.

The Doctor had taken a brief diversion into the equipment stores of the TARDIS. He returned to the dining room laden down with components, some of which he hoped to be able to wire in to the hotel's systems.

Bryan Melrose was straining at his bonds. The Doctor shook his head and tutted to himself. He deposited his burden on the floor and checked Ben's knots. They were holding well. 'I really don't think you'll escape, you know,' he said. 'And if you did, what then? You must know how the Selachians feel about being let down. If you run to them, they're most likely to kill you.'

He was only confirming Melrose's fears, and the haunted look in the accountant's eyes proved it. He continued, more sympathetically, 'The best you can hope for is imprisonment on Earth. If you help me, you might get a lighter sentence – although murder is a grave offence.'

'I didn't kill Matlock.'

The Doctor smiled. He was talking at last. 'Then who did?'

The words came tumbling out over each other. 'The rest of what you said was right. I came here to get the disks and to oversee a credit transfer. Neville found out about Matlock and refused to complete the transaction until he was dealt with. I had the explosives to see to, I was too busy to get involved. I swear I didn't know what they were going to do. Did they look capable of murder?'

'A hollow plea, coming from someone who intended to kill us all.

'That was different. The Selachians wanted to be sole owners of the weapon. They didn't want anyone else to have access to the technology. I was just following orders. You can't defy the Selachians! Do you think I wanted this job?'

'No, I don't expect you did,' said the Doctor sharply, 'but you carried it out to the best of your ability.'

Melrose hung his head and said no more. The Doctor retrieved his equipment and left, his admonishment hanging in the air. He thought about Melrose's confession and wondered if it could be truthful. He had placed the blame in the Adlers' laps, but they had a perfect alibi: Ben had been with them both at the time of the murder. Melrose could have been lying, but he had seemed too genuinely scared for his life – and his claim to have been preoccupied with the disarming of his explosives rang true. So the Adlers had meant to deal with Matlock, permanently or otherwise. Had someone beaten them to it? Someone like Alison Hayes, whom the Doctor had just sent off with Polly? Or Terri Willis, who was accompanying Ben? Or Geoff Hornby or Daphne McAllister? Or Lord Henry Mace, who was unaccounted for?

The Doctor couldn't shake the feeling that he had missed something.

Hayes strode out of the elevator and flipped open a panel in the wall opposite. She worked confidently, even in the gloom. Clearly, Polly thought, she had researched her undercover role thoroughly. She had probably memorised every nut and bolt in the Galaxian's construction.

A second later, full lighting was restored to the docking level. 'Just for now,' said Hayes. 'As soon as our work's finished, I'll shut everything down again. If the pumps in the airlocks don't have power, the Selachians won't be able to equalise the pressure. They'll have to force open the doors, which should delay them.'

'For a couple of minutes,' said Terri. Polly didn't like her tone. These Selachians, whatever they were – these sharks, as Hayes had called them – were evidently strong. She fought the urge to ask about them: it was probably best not to know. With luck, she would be far away in the safety of the TARDIS when they arrived.

They emerged on to the carpeted balcony, and Ben looked over the railing on to the cargo deck. 'There's an awful lot of doors,' he observed unhappily. They could see right across to the far hull, and the sight of so many airlocks – so many potential entrances to the hotel – was dispiriting. 'How do we know which one they'll go for?'

'We don't,' said Hayes. 'My advice is to seal off this level altogether. There are only three ways on to it, and I can cut power to the passenger and service lifts once Ms Wright and I have finished our search and are clear.'

'We're left with the stairs then,' said Terri. 'Come on Ben, let's see if any of these crates are full. We can drag them outside and pile them against the door.'

The quartet hurried down a flight of steps to the lower tier. Ben and Terri stopped to examine the nearest boxes, but Hayes rushed on. Polly followed, with a reluctant glance back over her shoulder. She didn't like the idea of leaving her travelling partner with his new friend. But if there was a reason for her irrational resentment, she didn't know what it was – or didn't want to admit it.

'Give us a shout if you find a fork-lift truck in there,' Terri called after them. Her voice already seemed distant.

'Where are we going?' Polly asked, as they ploughed on deeper into the labyrinth. It didn't look as scary in the improved light, but Polly would still have found it impossible to navigate her way through. She admired her colleague's sure-footedness.

'To where I disturbed Adler,' Hayes answered. 'He'd already crossed most of the deck, so the disk can't be too far from where he was.'

And still is, Polly realised with an ice-cold shudder.

Ben and Terri had found an inordinately heavy box which, according to its label, contained sachets of dehydrated soup. They manhandled it up on to the balcony, one step at a time, and along to the stair door. It would be the first brick in their makeshift barrier. Ben hoped they could find enough other 'bricks' to keep the enemy at bay. A great many of the crates, they had discovered, were empty. Presumably, the hotel was working through what supplies it had, with no ships arriving to deliver more or to take away the 'empties'. It brought home to him the fact of the Galaxian's death, the slow process of which had begun long before this latest threat. Soon, it would be no more than a memory. Like his own home; like his life.

The crate went through the door, not without difficulty. They dropped it, relieved, and girded themselves to go through the process again. 'So,' Terri said, as they snatched a moment's rest, 'what about these alien menaces you're supposed to have fought?'

'Oh, it's more the Doctor's line than mine.' Ben could feel his cheeks colouring. Terri watched intently, hanging on his every word, looking faintly amused. 'Wherever he goes, he seems to land us in trouble. Take this place, for instance. I help out, sure, but I'd be in a right pickle without him. I couldn't even see through the Adlers, and I was in their room talking to them.'

'We all thought they were harmless. They played their parts well.'

'I couldn't believe it when Hayes said who they really were. Hey, you don't suppose she was lying, do you? No, I don't suppose so. The Doctor believed her, anyway.'

'What about the alien menaces?' Terri prompted.

'Well,' said Ben reluctantly, 'when I met the Doc, he was fighting these War Machine things in London. Then there were the Daleks, the Cybermen, the -'

'Hold on a minute.'

'What?'

'Come on Ben, any schoolkid could have made this up! Everyone's heard of the Cybermen since they attacked the moon in twenty-whatever-it-was, but they've been wiped out. And Daleks - they're just legends! You'll be telling me next you've been to Mars and met the green men.'

'Don't be stupid!' said Ben hotly.

'Erm, no - I mean, there really are green men on Mars.'

'There are? Well we haven't come across those. But who do you think stopped the Cybermen from taking over Earth in 1986?'

'Well it didn't make the newspapers.'

'And you ask the colonists on Vulcan about Daleks. They won't be talking about legends, believe me.'

Terri laughed. 'Vulcan itself is practically a legend, Ben. But OK, I'm convinced. So, what's next for you? More time-hopping? Back to the twentieth century?'

Ben shrugged. 'Wherever the TARDIS takes us. Don't tell him I said so, but the Doctor can't fly the thing for toffee. I'm trying to learn myself, but it's not easy.'

'Do you really want to go home? It'd be dull compared to Daleks and Cybermen, I'll bet.'

Ben shrugged but didn't answer. It wasn't as if the thought hadn't occurred to him. Much as he yearned for familiarity, he knew that his own primitive era could never feel the same after all he had seen and done. To find himself back on the ground, with the wonders of a universe denied him for ever after; to throw away such experiences just because he felt homesick. He and Polly had never pressed the Doctor about getting them back to 1966. Ben had just assumed it would happen one day, and he had left the timing to fate and to the TARDIS's erratic sense of direction. It had saved him from having to plan for the future himself – to take a decision which he found difficult.

'I can't travel for ever.'

'But you don't have to stop back where you started.' Terri laid a hand on Ben's and his heart fluttered in his chest. She had planted an idea in his mind which had never before had a place there. His rational side spoke to him of an isolated life, lonely, out of time, a stranger in an unfamiliar world. His emotional side, not usually unleashed, discarded such problems and spoke of an exotic new home and new discoveries, anchored by a new stability. If he was honest with himself, he already knew the former impulse would win the day. But at this moment, it pleased him to dally with the latter. Especially because that dalliance involved Terri. They were looking into each other's eyes and their lips were slowly drawn to each other's like magnets, closing in slow motion.

And, in his mind's eye, he saw Polly. Her arms were folded and she was wearing an expression of disapproval.

He pulled back from the moment, self-consciously, and Terri turned away too so he couldn't see her face. 'There's no time for, erm, this,' he muttered lamely, making for the door and studiously ignoring her. 'We've still got work to do. We'll… talk later.'

Once more, the Doctor sat at the controls in the engineering section. His task, this time, was not quite so urgent – but the consequences of failure were no less grave. He had never met the Selachians before, but he had heard talk of them. Even the humans of this time knew of the deadly shark creatures. For a period of several decades during the twenty-first century, they had made their presence felt to every spacefaring civilisation in the galaxy. Some had felt it more keenly than others. The Doctor had once seen an entire world devastated, many of its people slain, all because it had something the Selachians wanted: a great weapon. He wouldn't let history repeat itself, even on this smaller scale. Not if he could help it.

With the addition of his own components, the systems were performing with unprecedented efficiency. The Galaxian had no real defences, but he could override the protocols that would extend a docking tube to even the most hostile of arrivals. It was a stopgap measure, but it was better than nothing. After that, it was up to Ben to delay the invaders further, and to the others to find the disks and get back to the

TARDIS before the unthinkable occurred.

Polly regarded the spread-eagled corpse of Neville Adler through half-closed eyes, fighting a strong repulsion which brought bile to her throat. She didn't want to look, but she didn't want Hayes to think she was squeamish either. 'Shouldn't we move him to somewhere more dignified?' she asked. It seemed only right, although touching the cold, mutilated sack of meat was the last thing she wanted to do. She remembered how it had felt when she had fallen on top of it an hour before, in the dark, and she was almost physically sick.

'What's the point?' asked Hayes, without compassion. 'He'll get a "dignified" cremation soon. His ashes will be scattered across Earth's oceans. It's more than he deserves: some people would pay good money for that kind of a sendoff.'

Polly didn't agree with her cold-hearted attitude, but the only alternative was to drag the corpse – and Matlock's too – to the TARDIS for proper burial elsewhere, and she couldn't have coped with such a horrible chore even if they'd had the time. She resolved to put it out of her mind. 'What do we do, then? Look in the crates?'

'Just check if any have been prised open. And make sure you're thorough. You know how small disks are.' Polly didn't, but now wasn't the time to mention it. 'Adler might have only pulled out a couple of nails and slipped it through the gap. We'll start here and make our way towards the service lift.'

'What if he was carrying it?'

'What?'

'What if Neville Adler had the disk on him? Did you search him?'

'I didn't have time,' Hayes said pointedly. 'If you recall, I was interrupted. Anyway, I was watching him. If he had retrieved it, I would have seen.'

'It was dark.'

'Yes, I did notice,' said Hayes, heavy on the sarcasm.

Polly wasn't prepared to let the matter drop. 'And what if he had it with him already? He wandered around another deck before coming up here, didn't he? It sounds to me like he wasn't retrieving the disk at all, but looking for a place to hide it.'

Hayes stuck to her guns, but she no longer seemed as sure. 'He was just trying to throw pursuers off the scent. Why would he have the disk? He wouldn't have risked keeping it with him since his arrival, and anyway we know he refused to fetch it for Melrose.'

'But what if he did have it, all the same? It must be worth checking.'

'Are you going to do it then?'

Polly shook her head, more quickly than she had intended. Hayes tutted, defeated, and knelt down by the body. She peeled its tweed jacket back from the sticky mess of its chest and felt inside its pockets. Polly looked away and fixed her gaze upon a box label.

'I've searched him,' announced Hayes finally, 'and he has no disk. Are you satisfied?'

Then, suddenly, a figure leapt from cover and cannoned into Hayes from behind. Polly was taken by surprise and given no chance to shout a warning. Hayes was slammed into a pile of crates, which teetered and fell. Polly yelped and leapt out of the path of the cascade. Dust rose and her eyes teared as it caught in her throat. She was coughing uncontrollably, but she stumbled forward anyway. She registered only dimly that Hayes was on the floor. Her attacker held her down and raised one hand above her head. There was little doubt in Polly's mind that she was about to deliver a killing blow.

Adrenaline powered her actions now. She grabbed hold of the assailant's arm beneath the wrist and wrenched it downwards, eliciting a cry. The woman backed into her, using her bulk to force Polly up against another stack of crates and to loosen her grip. She squirmed around to face her, and Polly saw with horror that she was holding a long kitchen knife. Only now did her panic-stricken brain register her foe's identity. It was Dorothy Adler, and tears were flowing down her cheeks, leaving black rivulets in her thick make-up.

'You murderers!' she screamed. 'Murderers, murderers!'

The sharp edge of the knife glinted in the light as she held it poised. Then she drove the blade forward and directly towards Polly's racing heart.

A series of chimes pinged through the small room. The Doctor ignored them; he was busy checking his work for unaffordable errors. By the time he had done so, the communications system was more insistent than ever. It wouldn't do to keep his callers waiting longer, he decided reluctantly. They might try more severe ways of attracting his attention. He accepted the transmission, which was broadcast on audio frequencies only.

There was no introduction, no preamble. 'We request permission to dock. Your automatic systems do not appear to be functioning.' The Doctor smiled to himself at the transparent deception. The Selachians didn't wish to reveal their true natures, but the voice of their representative could hardly be mistaken for human. It was low and flat, and many of its consonants were

153

indistinguishable from each other. The aliens may have learnt the language, but without lips they couldn't speak it convincingly.

'Galaxian to incoming craft,' he broadcast, tongue in cheek. 'Our apologies for the delay. We are experiencing technical difficulties. Stand by.'

This tactic bought him no more than two minutes before they contacted him again. 'Our mission is urgent. We must insist upon immediate access to your station.'

'You could have at least shown a bit of patience,' he muttered to himself. He sent: 'Not possible at this time, repeat not possible. Please stand by. We will attend to your request as soon as our systems are back on line.'

This time, it wasn't good enough. The Selachian ship dropped its cloaking field and rippled startlingly into view through the right-hand portal. Despite himself, the Doctor drew a sharp intake of breath. It was even larger than he had imagined: a perfectly streamlined black cruiser, powered by a row of gravity harnessing discs along its flat underside (the very state-of-the-art for clean, quick take-offs and landings) to demonstrate that it was a product of an advanced civilisation. White teeth were painted in a broad snarl across its snub nose and the ship resembled a gigantic, hungry shark itself.

'We represent the Selachian Empire,' the cold voice hissed. 'If you do not allow us to dock immediately, we will atomise your puny station and every piece of filthy human plankton aboard!'

CHAPTER 9

ATTACH OF THE HILLER SHARHS

The Doctor didn't respond to the Selachian's threat. So long as it waited for an answer, perhaps imagining how it had set the hotel's occupants to panicking, he was earning valuable time.

Of course, it didn't wait long. 'You have ten seconds to agree to our demands and to extend docking facilities to our warcraft. You will do so if you place value on your miserable life.'

He decided to call its bluff. 'I don't imagine my life would be worth much anyway, if I was to accede to the Selachians.'

A pause. Then: 'If you obey us, you will be allowed to keep your life. Refuse and you will perish.'

'My, don't we have a nice line in pithy dialogue?' the Doctor scoffed.

'Very well. You have sealed your death warrant.'

The implacable pronouncement sent a thrill of fear through his hearts. 'No, wait!' he cried, but the aliens had broken contact. His gaze shot to the black ship, framed against the stars. A thin protuberance was extended from the base of its nose, almost too small to see from this distance. From this, suddenly, a focused spray of black plasma erupted, its edges rippled by purple fire. It was aimed upward and the hotel trembled as the beam struck its unseen target.

'Oh dear,' the Doctor wailed. 'Oh dear, oh dear.' He felt quite sick. He held his breath as he punched up damage reports and was relieved to find only the topmost deck affected. The powerful weapon had boiled it away, so quickly and comprehensively that the gyroscope had registered only a slight bump and had compensated handsomely. Had the Selachians aimed at the station's other end – this end – they would have crippled those same systems and sent it down in flames. Not that the Doctor would have been alive to care.

He hailed the warcraft, stabbing at the controls with all the fury engendered by his foes' reckless stupidity. 'Yes?' acknowledged the voice of their radio operator, tersely.

'That wasn't very clever, was it?' the Doctor blustered. He knew it was the wrong tack to take and he made himself calm down. 'We've found out what you're after, you know, and you're doing your cause no good. The disks are hidden. For all I know, you might just have incinerated them yourself.'

He listened for an answer, but received only static. After a few seconds, he cut the link and settled back with a smile of satisfaction. He had given them something to think about.

The brief tremor stole Dorothy Adler's footing. She fell backwards, her arms flailing, and the knife pulled up short of Polly's chest. Released from the paralysing terror of impending death, Polly found her voice and screamed. Her attacker regained her balance and charged again, but by now Hayes had recovered. She leapt on the scientist from behind, slipping one arm about her throat and disarming her with the other hand. Dorothy whimpered and struggled, but she was unskilled in combat and Hayes had all the leverage anyway. She flipped Dorothy over on to her back, and

Polly winced as she slammed into the floor and the fight was knocked out of her. Hayes retrieved the fallen knife and brandished it triumphantly.

'You killed my husband, you bitch!' The words were choked out through tears.

'Don't try it on with me, love,' spat Hayes. 'I know who you are and I know you would have killed him yourself if he'd got in your way. You thought you'd make a nice tidy sum, didn't you, selling your world out to the Selachians?'

Dorothy clamped her mouth shut and glared at her captor hatefully.

'What do you think made the hotel shake?' Polly asked, ending the resultant silence.

Hayes didn't seem concerned. 'Slight glitch in the gyroscope, minor asteroid strike. I don't know.'

'Don't you think we should find out?'

'If it was important, we'd know about it, believe me. We'd be burning up as we plummeted towards a crash-landing on Earth, for a start.' Polly was not much comforted, but Hayes wasn't about to waste time on unfounded fears. 'We'd better get searching. We've still got our deceased friend's disk to find. Unless Dorothy here wants to tell us where to look.'

'Drop dead!' snarled Dorothy.

'She doesn't know,' said Hayes. 'I didn't think so.'

Ben and Terri were talking again, after a long time spent working in silence with awkward memories hovering between them. The first words had been said after the tremor, when each had inquired after the other's consequent health. Ben had dropped his end of a crate on to his foot and Terri had fussed over him for a while although he had sworn he was unharmed really. They sat side by side on the steps between the two tiers of the docking level and Ben massaged his bruised toes.

'We should be getting back to work,' said Terri, after a while. She sounded regretful.

'Just give me a minute. I'll get my shoes back on.'

'How many more crates do you think we'll need?'

Ben shrugged. To him, it seemed they had struggled on to the main staircase with ample – but one of the navy's favourite mottos was 'better safe than sorry'. 'We'll carry on till our hour's up, I suppose. The more weight we can put behind that door, the better. Are they strong, these Selachians?'

'You don't know?'

'I wouldn't be asking if I did,' he said, a little shortly.

'OK. It's just that they're well-known planetside. They've had a lot of coverage recently, so I assumed you'd have heard of them. They're not in the Daleks' and Cybermen's league, but they are a more immediate threat.'

'They've been to Earth?'

'They sent a few delegations,' said Terri, 'to corporations and governments and the like. They've done a few deals.'

'What for?'

'Weapons, mostly. They seem to be after all the technology they can find. It was only when reports started coming back from the colony worlds that we found out what they were doing with it.'

'Someone must have had an inkling. You don't go buying up all the guns you can get if you don't intend to use them.'

'They said it was for self-defence – and you know what big business is like. No one wanted to know the worst of it, because they were making a fat profit. Then the Selachians had a falling out with the rulers of Terra Alpha and, well…'

Ben didn't need to hear the rest. He could imagine it only too well. 'And still people like the Adlers deal with them.'

'Of course. Their business is designing and selling weapons. The Selachians provide a lucrative market.'

'And never mind who they kill!'

'It's how some people earn a living. If they didn't, they reason, the customers would just go elsewhere. Or, in the Selachians' case, they'd take what they want by force. You couldn't stop them.'

'You could try.'

'The rulers of Terra Alpha tried. Besides, the professional weapons dealer can always find excuses to distance himself from bloodshed. Governments shake their heads and tut, but in the end they take no real action. Too many of them are involved up to their armpits anyway. It's the way it works – the nature of the game they're in.'

'The murder game,' Ben muttered darkly.

'We all have jobs to do,' said Terri. She stood up and went to find their next crate, leaving Ben to wonder what she had meant.

The Doctor was beginning to feel uneasy. Ten minutes had passed and the Selachians hadn't been in contact since their initial threat had backfired. It didn't seem in keeping with their impatient natures and he felt sure they must be planning something. He resisted the temptation to hail them again and waited. Soon enough, his worst suspicions were confirmed.

He hadn't seen the portal opening in the warcraft's

side. It was a circle of black against black and the ship, after all, was orientated towards the Galaxian's central docking level some distance above him. The Doctor sat bolt upright, however, as he saw what emerged from the aperture.

The remote figures were clad in golden armour, which must have been sealed against the vacuum. They were humanoid, squat and bulky, with preposterously large fins extending from the backs of their armour and tapering to a sharp point. There were two of them, linking short, thick arms and bound by cords to their starting position. One held some sort of portable manoeuvring thruster which it fired, with an orange flash, at intervals. It propelled the creatures forward with unnerving speed, and the practised, synchronised strokes of their free arms kept them balanced and headed in the right direction. Towards the station.

The Doctor watched, spellbound, until they drew too close to the airlocks to be seen from this lower deck. The Selachians' technology – second-hand, no doubt, plundered mercilessly from its originators – was far more advanced than he had hoped. He hadn't delayed them for half as long as he had wanted. His friends weren't planning to evacuate for almost forty minutes yet, and the invaders were on their doorstep already.

The Doctor left the engineering section at a sprint and bounded up the stairs towards the docking level. His only hope now was to help Ben and Terri with their part of the operation, and to pray that they might have more success.

Polly was beginning to despair. She had checked every crate in the vicinity and was now checking some for the second time, feeling around their edges but failing to find any open. The discovery that some were empty and could be lifted, revealing perfect hiding places between them and the boxes below, depressed her further. Neville Adler could have concealed his disk anywhere.

Hayes's pace, too, was beginning to slacken. She stayed close to Dorothy – who remained on the floor and said nothing – leaving Polly to search further afield. When the prisoner showed signs of movement, which wasn't often, she was invariably stilled by a growled threat.

'This is no good,' said Polly finally. 'Perhaps we should think again. Time's running out, and we don't even know for sure if the disk is on this level.'

'What other clues do we have? We can't just give up and leave it to the Selachians.'

'How would they find it? If it's here at all, it's well hidden. They won't be able to search the whole place before the hotel crashes.'

'We don't know what technology they have,' Hayes argued. 'They might just walk in, turn on a detector and go straight to both disks. They might even be able to save the Galaxian and search it at their leisure. Keep looking. I'd feel a lot more comfortable if we could take the things with us.'

And, of course, her employers were expecting the disks' return, Polly thought sourly. Hayes represented everything that she found objectionable about authority figures: the expectation that others would follow orders blindly, without knowing or believing in the reasons for them. Polly had felt safer partnered with Daphne: she might have been overly nervous and little use in a pinch, but she was trustworthy.

'Come on,' Hayes ordered, 'get back to it!' Polly was about to issue a stinging rejoinder, but a monumental crash suddenly echoed about the deck. It came from some distance away, but it was still loud enough to make her leap for cover. In the aftermath, cold sweat bathed her face and she was acutely aware of the accelerated pulse in her neck.

'What was it?' she whispered urgently.

'At a guess, the sound of Selachians ripping an outer airlock door from its hinges.'

Dorothy leered up at them. 'How does it feel to lose control, dear?' Hayes kicked her in the ribs and she yelped.

'We've still got time.' Hayes sounded as if she was trying to convince herself. 'They'll have to weld the outer door back on before they can break through the inner, else they'll lose all air from the station.'A thought occurred to her and her eyes widened in alarm. 'Assuming, of course, that's not what they're planning. Come on, we're getting out of here. All three of us.'

She tried to lift Dorothy, but the older woman resisted. She thrashed and kicked and even snapped at Hayes's fingers with her teeth. Polly lent a hand and, between them, they hoisted their prisoner to her feet. She remained uncooperative, and it felt as if they were dragging a dead weight along with them.

'Just a minute,' said Polly, 'where are we going?'

'Service lift.'

'What about Ben? We've got to tell him.'

'I rather think he'll have heard for himself.'

The proximity and volume of the crash caused Ben and Terri to drop another crate, although this time both managed to get out of its way before it hit. 'I think we've just run out of time,' said Terri.

'I think you're right.' They turned as one and raced back to the stairs. Halfway, Ben remembered something. He doubled back, until he reached the fuse box – or whatever it was – opposite the elevators. It was still hanging open, and he pressed down on an inviting red switch. To his considerable pleasure, the lights across the docking level dimmed. Hayes had mentioned before that the loss of power would delay the Selachians' access.

He hurried to rejoin Terri as quickly as he could, feeling his way along the balcony rail. Beyond the outward-opening door, the mini-landing formed by the turn of the staircase was crowded with the wooden fruits of their labour. More boxes were balanced haphazardly on steps, teetering over the rail or leaning against walls. Galvanised to new, speedier efforts, they hefted them one by one and slid them into position. As their barricade formed, the Doctor skidded on to the scene and announced breathlessly, 'They're here!'

'We had sort of noticed,' said Terri.

He was dismayed. 'Oh no, they've broken into the airlock already?' Ben nodded. The Doctor took charge instantly, leaping about and waving his arms, animated by urgency. 'Ben, try placing a layer of boxes in a row back to the wall. Make sure they're all packed with something solid: the Selachians will have to physically crush them to get the door open.'

'What do you think I'm doing already?'

'Terri, I'll take over from you. I want you to get to an information point and call Thomas. No, wait a minute, I told him to stay in the dining room. Oh, dear… Go and find him; tell him to contact the others. We haven't got as much time as I hoped. They must get back to the

TARDIS immediately. Ben and I will join you there as soon as we can.' Terri looked as if she was about to protest, but the Doctor manhandled her away from the crates and set to work himself. She hesitated for a moment. Then, after exchanging a helpless look with Ben, she hurried away.

Polly and Hayes stepped out of the lift on Deck A1, Hayes pushing Dorothy before her. She marched her prisoner along until she found a wall panel similar to the one downstairs. She inspected the circuitry within and, a few seconds later, gripped a handful of wires and yanked them hard. They came loose with a sputtering eruption of yellow sparks. 'One circuit broken,' she announced. 'That's all the elevators out of action. If your friends do their job right, the Selachians should be confined to the docking level for a while.'

'Thank goodness,' said Polly.

'Don't look too pleased. There may be a disk down there, remember?'

'Oh. So what are we going to do?'

'Find the other. We can keep them from getting the full blueprints, at least.' Hayes turned to Dorothy Adler, but the scientist shook her head and backed away.

'You won't be getting anything from me.'

Hayes smiled and produced Dorothy's own knife from her pocket. 'I'll get something, all right. Information or guts, it's your choice.'

Dorothy turned and ran with slow, ponderous steps. It was a futile effort and she was caught within seconds. She whimpered as Hayes twisted an arm behind her back and grabbed a tuft of black hair, sending a pink clip clattering to the floor. She pulled Dorothy's head back and laid the sharp edge of the knife against her oesophagus.

'Now, lady, you're going to tell me where your disk is or I'll cut you a new mouth!' Dorothy swore at her. Enraged, Hayes relaxed her grip, spun the woman around and slapped her across the face. Polly winced at the ferocity of the blow. Dorothy cried out and crumpled. Kneeling, she rubbed her reddened cheek and glared up at Hayes with eyes that still burnt defiantly.

'There's no need for this,' protested Polly. 'You won't get anywhere by torturing her.'

'And what do you suggest?'

'Some common sense.' She addressed Dorothy: 'Listen, you – I don't know what you think's going to happen here, but if you expect those Selachian things to rescue you, forget it. They had the hotel mined. That's right – Bryan Melrose planted bombs all over it. He was going to take the disks and kill anyone who might know of them.'

She was getting somewhere. Hayes could see it too, and she joined in. 'Especially you and your so-called husband. I don't know how much money they offered you, love, but they weren't intending to let you spend it. Look, I know you helped us out of our spin before – but what do you suppose caused it? One of Melrose's explosives, that's what. He tried to deactivate them when you delayed the transaction, but he didn't manage to finish.'

'If the Selachians get the disks, they'll kill you,' said Polly. 'They've already proved it.'

'And if they don't get the disks, they'll certainly kill you!' said Hayes. 'Like it or not, miss, we're your only hope.'

'Finished, and with time to spare.' The Doctor inspected the makeshift barricade happily. He produced a handkerchief and dabbed at his perspiring brow.

'Yeah, but how much time?' asked Ben cynically. With the task completed, his body was indulging its own aches and weariness from the last half-hour of intensive labour. He lowered himself on to a step and rested there. The Doctor joined him.

'We've no way of telling,' he said regretfully. 'I'm afraid I don't know the Selachians' capabilities too well.'

'So how do you know those crates will hold them?' The Doctor's look answered the question for him. He didn't.

Ben dwelt on the problem for a while, but it did him no good. He tried to take his mind off it, but it was difficult. The impending threat dominated his thoughts – and whenever he forcibly diverted their course, he arrived at an image of himself and Terri Willis, settling down to life in the future. If anything, that frightened him more than the imminent attack.

'What are these creatures, anyway? Terri said they were like giant walking sharks.'

'There is a similarity between the two species,' the Doctor agreed, 'but not such a close one as the Selachians would have you think.'

'I don't understand.'

'It's called psychological warfare. They add fins to their armour, paint teeth on their ships, that sort of thing. Even their name was chosen to enhance the image. They studied other worlds and decided to emulate the most commonly feared marine creatures among humans. It's what they want more than

166

anything: to frighten people.'

'They're off to a good start,' Ben muttered.

'They have an unhappy history, you see. The Selachians evolved on an ocean world, and are one of the few aquatic races to have developed beyond a Level Two technology.'

'Smart then, are they?'

'They'd have to be. Think about it, Ben. They're water-breathers: to them, even emerging into the air would have been as great a challenge as space travel was to your people. And yet, they have advanced a further step to become one of the major spacefaring races of the galaxy. It's an incredible achievement – but it took them a long time. Too long, as far as they're concerned. For centuries, they suffered at the hands of air-breathing mammals from elsewhere in their system. Culling them became an international sport on some planets.'

'So now they're taking it out on everyone else?'

'Essentially, yes. Over generations, they developed exoskeletal battle armour. Some of them underwent the most horrendous surgical procedures to fit into their mobile weapons of war. Then, in the midst of one year's major culling festival, they emerged from the depths to exact their revenge.'

Ben shivered at the thought. 'I don't know whether to feel sympathetic or not.'

'Save your sympathy for us,' said the Doctor. 'The Selachians' world was cordoned off for a time and people began to forget them. But they never forgot. Without warning, they launched a fleet of ships at their immediate neighbours. The ensuing wars were long and bloody.'

'And the Selachians won, I take it?'

The Doctor nodded. 'And the bloodshed didn't stop there. They've become fanatical, Ben. They fancy themselves a civilised people, but the terrors and resentment of the past have made them paranoid and ruthless. It's a dangerous combination. Their overwhelming concern is to ensure that they will never be abused or helpless again. In that cause, they're determined to make themselves the most powerful and feared race in the cosmos. They still think themselves disadvantaged against air-breathers and they're desperate to acquire technology to equalise the balance. Many people have been killed by them, many worlds ransacked for what they can contribute.'

'If they aren't really sharks,' said Ben, 'what are they?'

The Doctor thought for a moment before answering. 'If they're related to an Earth creature at all, I'd say it was the dolphin.'

'The dolphin?' He suppressed an urge to laugh. 'Doesn't sound too bad to me.'

'Just don't mention it to their faces.'

'Why not?'

'Because they'll rip off your head and swallow it!'

'Ah.'

In the ensuing silence, Ben's thoughts drifted back to all the terrible stories he had heard about sharks. They had been his single biggest worry when, as a fifteen-year-old boy, he had first run away to sea. He remembered cowering under tarpaulin, the smell of tar, old rope and sawdust in his nostrils, feeling queasy as the cargo hold rocked and creaked about him. He had dozed for minutes at a time, his dreams filled with the fear of discovery if he was lucky; with the more illogical but greater fear, if not, of plunging into the icy sea, surrounded by bloodthirsty predators, thrashing about to escape but unable to move, and running out of breath and time. The reality of naval life had long since dispelled such images. In all the intervening years, Ben had rarely seen a live shark close up, and had certainly not been endangered by one. Until now – when, ironically far away from the sea, their threat loomed larger and nearer than even a teenage runaway could have dreamed.

A sudden, shocking rending of metal came from beyond the fortified door. The terrible sound seemed to last for ever and grated on Ben's fraught nerves. But, finally, there was silence again. 'They're on their way,' he said quietly.

'I think they've arrived.' The Doctor was straining to listen, although Ben could hear nothing. 'You'd better go back to the TARDIS. I'll wait here.'

'Hold on!'

'No time to argue, Ben. Make sure the evacuation's going smoothly, hurry people along. I'll keep watch. The Selachians are trapped on this level, but it won't last. When it looks as if they're going to break out, I'll follow you. Now go!'

Polly watched nervously as Hayes stared out of a corridor window. 'The warcraft's moving in,' she reported. 'The Selachians must have gained access to the station. They're allowing it to dock.'

'We've got to get out of here!'

'Not without the disks.'

Frustrated, Polly turned to Dorothy, who still lay slumped against the wall. 'Why don't you just help us? We're all in trouble now. We live or die together!'

She had evidently been thinking about it. 'All right,'

she said, nodding sulkily. 'I'll tell you where my disk is.'

'Progress at last,' said Hayes. She strode over to Dorothy and took her arm, hauling her to her feet. 'But you'll do better than tell me. You'll show me. Which floor is it on?'

'A7 – one of the unused residential levels.'

Hayes rolled her eyes. 'Six floors up, with the lifts down. It would be! Come on, we'd best hurry.' She took off at a sprint, almost physically dragging the slower Dorothy behind her. Polly fell into step alongside them. 'We're parting company at the stairs,' Hayes told her. 'There's no need for us both to risk our lives. You can go back to the dining room and get ready to leave.'

'No way!' she said, before she had time to realise how attractive a proposition it was. Still, she couldn't agree. Hayes wanted her out of the way; once she had the disk, Polly doubted she would see her again. 'I'm coming with you,' she said firmly.

Hayes shrugged. 'Your funeral.'

They barrelled through the stair doors and Polly strained over the railing to see what was happening on the level below. The angle was all wrong and a pile of boxes blocked her view. She crossed her fingers for Ben's safety and followed Hayes and Dorothy upstairs. It was only just occurring to her that they had put the approaching Selachians between themselves and the TARDIS.

Ben hared around a bend in the staircase and collided with Henry Mace, who was running just as frantically in the opposite direction. He grabbed the rail to steady himself, just in time, but Mace tumbled backward with a shriek. He bounced off several steps and came to rest in a sobbing pile. Ben felt guilty about the accident, although they had both been equally culpable. He started forward, but his advance alarmed Mace enough to make him forget his pain and to leap to his feet in terror. 'It's you, it's you! I knew all along. You're the murderer and you're coming to kill me. Stay back!'

'Hey come on mate,' Ben coaxed, spreading his arms wide to show he posed no threat. 'It was an accident.'

'You killed someone in cold blood and you say it was an accident!' Mace shrilled, aghast.

'No, don't be stupid.'

'Don't call me -'

'I've no time for this,' Ben shouted. 'We've got to – hey!' His explanation of the proposed evacuation was cut short as Mace took fright and darted off. Ben cursed under his breath and clattered down the stairs after him. They passed the entrance to Deck B1 and the safety of the TARDIS beyond, and continued downward. Surprisingly, Mace stayed ahead: his fear lent him unusual speed and the day's exertions were beginning to tell on Ben.

He followed Mace on to Deck B4 and stopped at the first junction he came to. He had lost sight of his quarry. As he was debating his next course of action with himself, Thomas popped into view beside him. 'Begging your pardon, sir, but Ms Willis has requested that a message be sent to all personnel on board the station.'

'I know,' said Ben dismissively, 'we're to get back to the dining room straightaway, right?'

'Indeed.'

'Hold on a minute, Tom.' The hologram waited with an expression of polite expectation as Ben pondered on his options. He hadn't liked Mace from the moment he had first seen him, and to go after him now would mean risking his own life thanklessly. He might not be able to help, anyway: the immature thespian had shown no signs of being reasonable thus far. He was more likely to flee again than to hear what Ben had to say – or he may attack his would-be rescuer. All logic told Ben to forget him and to save his own skin. But you didn't just abandon a shipmate, not even an obnoxious one. He couldn't leave Mace to the Selachians' mercy, not after all the Doctor had told him.

With a show of reluctance, he turned back to Thomas and asked, 'Which way did Henry Mace go?'

'To your left, sir,' said the hologram.

The Doctor steeled himself as footsteps approached the door from the far side. It opened, just fractionally, but found itself impeded. If he listened hard enough, he could hear the husky breathing of three or more Selachians immediately behind it. They didn't exchange words. He waited and hardly dared breathe himself.

He heard nothing more for a while and he drew closer to the barricade, his ears alert for further clues. He wondered what the creatures were up to. He hadn't expected them to be so easily dissuaded. Perhaps, he considered, they were still searching for the path of least resistance; perhaps they weren't yet aware that the elevators were not functioning. It was a nice theory, but it didn't ease his worries. The silence unnerved him and he wanted desperately to know what was going on beyond his sight.

A second later, he got his wish. The door exploded outward with incredible force, crushing and scattering the crates behind it. The Doctor was taken unawares by the ferocity of the blast. A gust of stale air flung him away and he was buffeted by flying planks and dust. He came close to being tipped over the stair-rail, but he grabbed it in time and altered his course, although he wrenched his arm so that his right shoulder felt dislocated. He hit the wall with considerable force and knelt, doubled over, spluttering and gasping. As he struggled to bring his respiration back under control, he squinted upward and saw a giant figure looming through a grey cloud. 'Oh no,' he moaned. 'Oh good gracious, oh dear. Oh, crumbs…'

The Selachians had arrived.

CHAPTER 10

PRISONERS

The dust was settling, to reveal a scene of devastation.
The Doctor wiped away tears with his jacket sleeve. He
could see more clearly now, but he almost wished he
couldn't. The leading Selachian pushed its way through
the mangled remains of his barrier and halted before
him. It was as short as the Doctor himself, but far
broader. Its eyes could not be seen – the result,
presumably, of an invisible one-way viewscreen – but a
red replacement was stencilled on to each side of its
bullet-shaped head. Beneath this, an equally fake down-
turned mouth was crammed with sharp white teeth.
But for its colouring, and its stumpy arms and legs, the
Doctor could have been staring at the underside of a
common Terran shark. Tubular guns ran along each of
its forearms and a large, sharp fin grew from its back.

It regarded the Doctor dispassionately – or, at least, its
all-concealing armour prevented an expression from
filtering through. Conversely, he could see his own fear
distorted and reflected in its polished golden surfaces.
Many more of its kin poured out of the door from the
docking level and split wordlessly into two streams.
Half climbed the stairs while the others descended,
pushing past their comrade without sparing its prone
prisoner a glance. Their bulk forced them to proceed in
single file. As they walked, the sound of sloshing liquid
came faintly to the Doctor's ears. Their suits would, of
course, have to double as life-support apparatus outside
of an aquatic environment. The fins, he imagined, would

also have more than just a psychological function: they probably housed equipment for breaking down air molecules and thus reoxygenating the limited amount of water available to them.

His captor raised its arm deliberately. It curled its stubby fingers into a fist, but the main threat didn't come from there. The Doctor was left staring down the circular barrel of its arm-mounted weapon. He threw up his hands in a gesture of surrender, which he hoped it would recognise and accept. It kept the gun trained on his head for long, agonising seconds. Then it spoke.

'You are a prisoner of the Selachian Empire. Stand.' The Doctor nodded his understanding dumbly and did as he was ordered. It was a difficult manoeuvre, as he kept his hands raised throughout.

The Selachian's voice had a tinny, indistinct quality and it echoed slightly. It was speaking through water, of course, but the Doctor's guess was that a throat microphone picked up its sub-vocalisations and transmitted them to a concealed loudspeaker. 'Our schematics of this station show a sizeable meeting area on the third from lowest level,' it said. It was talking about the Interplanetary Bar on Deck B8, he realised. He nodded again: a mute confirmation. 'That is where we will gather the human plankton. You will take me there.'

Dorothy Adler was rummaging behind a dressing table in a bedroom on Deck A7. Hayes watched her from the doorway, while Polly waited in the corridor. She was too nervous to be still and she hopped impatiently from foot to foot. 'How much longer is this going to take?' she asked, when she could bear it no longer.

'I've nearly got it,' returned Dorothy, indignantly. She

put all her weight into pulling the heavy piece of furniture an extra inch away from the wall, then she got down on her knees and strained once again to force her flabby arm into the widened gap. 'The idea wasn't to make it easy to find, you know.'

'If I even begin to suspect you're stalling,' growled Hayes, 'I'll slit you open and feed your intestines to your shark partners!'

'What a colourful way you have with the English language, dear,' said Dorothy sourly. 'Perhaps, when this is over, we could form our own writing partnership. I rather enjoyed my dry run.'

Hayes scowled and crossed the room in a few quick strides. She towered over Dorothy and was surely about to issue more threats. Then the older woman smiled and produced a square of plastic, about two inches wide and long, still trailing white tape from where it had been attached to the back of the dresser. This, thought Polly, had to be one of the two disks that had caused all their problems. It certainly seemed to be what Hayes wanted. With neither a further word nor a change of her grim expression, she snatched the object smartly away and deposited it in the inside pocket of her pinstriped jacket. She pivoted on her heel and marched back out of the room.

'Don't I get a "thank you"?' called Dorothy, to her back.

'Ms Wright and I are taking this disk and getting away from the station before the Selachians kill us both. I honestly don't care whether you accompany us or not. Just make up your mind fast!' Hayes turned to Polly. 'Come on, we've wasted too much time already.'

Hayes set a brisk pace back to the stairs, and Polly gratefully kept up with her. No more than a few seconds elapsed before Dorothy thundered down the corridor after them, at a much greater speed than Polly would have thought her capable of. 'You will keep me safe, won't you?' she pleaded. 'I've kept my side of the bargain.'

Hayes didn't answer, but Polly felt only sympathy for the wretched woman despite her misdeeds. 'Of course we will,' she said, smiling reassuringly.

'Speak for yourself,' Hayes muttered. 'If the Selachians are on board, because of the time she's cost us, I'll make sure I'm not the first course on their menu!'

Ben was exhausted. He had been searching for the past fifteen minutes, running in circles and becoming increasingly desperate as Henry Mace remained obstinately hidden and time passed at an alarming rate. He ached to know what was happening upstairs in his absence, but he also felt a nagging worry that the answer might be too dreadful for him to contemplate. He stopped and studied a wall map, hoping for a lifeline of some description to present itself – and his fears were suddenly realised.

The sound of a metallic tread was Ben's first indication that he was no longer alone. He backed away instinctively as he turned, and was horrified by the sight of an armoured, humanoid shark approaching fast. 'You will surrender yourself to the Selachian Empire,' it hissed. But Ben's first impulse was to run, and he went with it. His decision, he thought later, might have been different had he known the thing was armed. Its in-built weaponry had not been immediately evident – and the panic engendered by its design had been an illogical one, throwing up images of being ripped to pieces by its teeth rather than brought down by its technological superiority. He learnt better as a hot, sizzling, yellow blast struck the ground between his feet and propelled him into the air in an almost comical leap. A second later, he was around a corner, shielded from harm, and he saw no reason to resist his strong urge to keep on going.

He turned two more corners at random before he allowed himself to slow down and think again. If he kept on hurtling around the deck like this, he was sure to run straight into the monster again – or into one of its fellows. He needed a plan. He asked himself what the Doctor would do and concluded that he would whip up some super-weapon to use against his enemies, using whatever materials were handy.

'OK, Ben Jackson,' he muttered to himself to keep his spirits up, 'you might not be a scientific whiz, but you can knock something together to give you a fighting chance.' All he needed, he thought, was a distraction: something to slow down the Selachians enough for him to get past them and to the TARDIS, three floors above.

He began to try doors, but found the first three locked. The fourth opened on to a cupboard, but it was disappointingly bare. Then a broad grin stretched across Ben's face as he saw what he was looking for in the corridor itself. He snatched the small red fire extinguisher from its wall mountings and gave it a cursory inspection. It was surprisingly light, and simple enough to use: he had already worked out the basics in a second, when he had brought Henry Mace's improvised weapon under control. The thought reminded him of his uncompleted mission to find Mace. For all he knew, though, he might be a prisoner of the Selachians already. Ben's priority now was to rendezvous with the Doctor. They could work out the rest later.

He found another map and picked out a route to the stairs. He held the nozzle of the extinguisher like a gun as he walked, and wondered if he looked as ridiculous as Mace had done. At least, in his hands, the device had more practical value. The Selachians had to have eyeholes in that armour of theirs, he reasoned. Let's see how effective they are when they can't see.

He was soon to get his answer. The sound of heavy footsteps reached him from around the next corner, and he knew one or more of the monsters was approaching. He cast about desperately for somewhere to hide, to avoid the confrontation or at least to give himself the advantage of surprise. There was nowhere.

So Ben summoned up all his courage, leapt into the connecting corridor, aimed the extinguisher, and blindly fired.

Polly flung a hand to her mouth to stifle a scream. Her little group had rounded a corner and come up short at the sight of the armoured form of what could only be a Selachian. Its back was to them, and for a second Polly thought they might be able to quietly retrace their steps and avoid its attention. Such hopes were thwarted as Dorothy Adler pushed her way between her two captors and ran to the creature, yelling for help. Polly's instinct was to flee, but she had barely gone a dozen steps when she realised she was alone. She turned back, but Hayes was no longer in sight. The suicidal fool had gone after Dorothy!

Polly froze, her mind reluctant to abandon Hayes but her nerves unwilling to follow her desperate course. The decision, thankfully, did not need to be made. Her colleague hurtled back into view, barely avoiding a beam of yellow fire which crackled through the air behind her and blew a chunk of plaster out of the wall. 'Run!' she screamed, as if Polly needed the encouragement.

The next few minutes were a blur of corridor walls and, in the small part of her mind that could still think clearly, Polly bemoaned the increasing familiarity of such a scenario. She had faith in the Doctor and Ben, she really did – but if the former persisted in landing them in such danger, how long could it be before her luck ran out and even he was unable to save her?

She had no idea where they were going, but she trusted to Hayes's detailed knowledge of the Galaxian's layout to keep them on whatever course she had chosen. She concentrated on keeping up, despite the shrieking muscles in her legs and the attempts of her heart to smash its way through her ribcage. They saw no further sign of Selachians, but there was no doubt in Polly's mind that they were being pursued all the same.

After what seemed like an eternity, Hayes shouldered open a door and Polly stumbled gratefully into the room beyond. They spent a few minutes just recovering their senses and panting from their exertions. Polly sank to the floor and put her head between her knees.

When she looked up again, she saw that they were in a small cubicle, not much larger than a telephone box. In fact, it was a fitting comparison. Hayes was already sitting on a long wooden bench and punching a series of numbers into what appeared to be a larger version of the communications console in Polly's room. 'What are you doing?' she asked.

'Sending out an all-frequencies distress signal,' said

Hayes. 'With luck, it'll be picked up by the Terran Security Forces.'

'What can they do?'

'I don't know. Issue threats, maybe. Scare the Selachians off. Something, I hope – we need all the help we can get.'

Polly wasn't about to argue with that, although she doubted Hayes's motives. What if she was calling in more agents from her own mysterious organisation? What if her primary aim was still to get both disks for herself? It was something to worry about later, she decided. They were on the same side for now, united by an immediate threat.

Hayes held down a switch and spoke tersely into a metallic grille. She briefly outlined the situation, gave the hotel's coordinates and requested urgent assistance from anyone in the vicinity. Then she operated a few more controls and explained: 'I've placed the message on to a loop. It'll keep on broadcasting until somebody stops it.'

'What now?'

'We get out of here fast.'

Hayes headed for the door, but Polly stopped her. 'What if we run into those things again? Why can't we hide here for a while?'

'Because I'll feel safer in a room with more than one exit. More to the point, the Selachians will trace our transmission. It won't be long before they find out precisely where we are.'

'Oh.' Polly stood aside as Hayes pulled open the door and stuck her head out into the corridor. She checked both ways, then hurriedly withdrew. She had turned quite pale.

'Too late,' she said. 'They're here.'

The extinguisher bucked in Ben's hands as its white payload erupted furiously. He struggled to keep it under control and aimed at the Selachian's head. His plan appeared to be working. It stopped, blinded, and attempted to deflect the stream with one hand while wiping foam from its viewscreen with the other. Ben kept up the onslaught and the Selachian changed tactics. It straightened out its short arms and let fire with both barrels. Ben saw what it was doing in time and dodged the twin blasts, more by luck than judgement. He had to go, before it could try again. Stooping low and clutching the extinguisher to his chest, he tried to duck past it while it was still confused. But it was too fast.

It moved to cut off his path – and, before Ben could reverse, its hand was around his left arm and gripping painfully. It tried to catch hold of his right, but he evaded its flailing grasp and brought the extinguisher around in an arc, driving it heavily into its armoured head. The impact sent vibrations up his arm and he dropped the improvised weapon. The extinguisher sported a large dent, but the Selachian's armour remained in pristine condition. Left with no other method of defence, Ben kicked at the creature's shins (hurting no one but himself) and fought in vain to prise open its steely fingers. It was unmoved.

It reached down and took hold of his right leg, above the knee. Ben cried out as it lifted him easily and held him, squirming, above its head. Then it casually flipped him over, took two steps and hurled him. To Ben, a sudden blur of sickly motion ended when his back hit the floor, hard enough to knock the breath from him and to crowd his vision with black spots. He fought to remain conscious and to stem a rising tide of nausea.

He wanted to do something as the Selachian closed in for the kill, but his body felt bruised all over, his chest was tight as if being crushed by a boulder and he had no energy to lift his wooden limbs.

He stared down the barrel of a blaster attachment, numbly, and thought of Polly. Then he heard his captor's voice, dully, as if from the other side of a partition. 'As I said before, you will surrender yourself to the Selachian Empire.' It was not going to kill him.

Relief washed over Ben like the warm sea lapping against a golden beach. He allowed himself to drift into unconsciousness.

'Geoff was so brave,' Daphne twittered breathlessly. 'He broke free of that terrible monster, but it chased him into a common room. It dragged me along with it – it was horrid. Geoff threw a chair at it, but it just bounced off. It was really strong, you know.'

The would-be hero was lying on the floor of the Interplanetary Bar, while the Doctor used his handkerchief to apply water to a purple bruise on his temple. Hornby flinched from his touch. 'Don't worry, the damage is superficial,' the Doctor assured him. 'I'd say you've had a lucky escape.'

Daphne had been on edge since her arrival, unable to stay still. She was recounting her escapade again, this time to the recently arrived Terri. 'I was so scared. I thought it was going to shoot Geoff, but it punched him instead. I thought it had killed him!'

Bryan Melrose sat a short distance from the gathering, freed now from his bonds. He glowered at the foursome and said nothing.

'When I suggested treating this like a game,' the Doctor admonished his patient gently, 'I didn't mean to the extent of endangering your life. The Selachians are a very real threat. You'd be a fool to defy them openly.'

'Good thing they need us alive then,' said Terri. 'The only thing they're interested in is getting those disks before the station burns up. They won't kill us until they find out where they are.'

'And here's the one person who might know,' said the Doctor. Across the room, a familiar ritual was being repeated. Two Selachian guards stepped aside from the doors as another pushed in the latest captive. It was Dorothy Adler, and she was none too pleased.

'We made a deal. Do you hear me? I demand to speak to your superior!'

The Selachian ignored her. It left, and the doors clattered shut behind it. Dorothy made as if to follow, but the guards smoothly retook their positions and barred her way. She let out a heartfelt grunt of exasperation, then turned and strode down the steps to join the others.

'I wouldn't dwell on it if I were you,' the Doctor counselled. 'Mr Melrose suffered a similar disappointment. Selachians don't make good business associates, I'm afraid.'

'They'll have to respect me - I have what they want.'

'Are you sure about that?'

'This is all your fault,' Daphne accused her miserably. 'You're a terrible woman! Oh Doctor, what do you think they'll do to us?'

'I really couldn't say, Daphne.'

'Shouldn't we do something?' Hornby tried to sit up, but winced sharply and let his head roll back on to the floor. His visible weakness detracted from his rallying call. 'There are six of us now, to two guards. Couldn't we overpower them and get to our ships?'

'I want better than three-to-one odds before I try tackling those things,' said Terri, echoing the Doctor's sentiments.

Then another Selachian entered, and this one was carrying the unconscious body of Ben Jackson. The Doctor's hearts leapt in fear and he jumped to his feet and strained to catch any sign of movement from his companion. The monster rolled Ben on to a bench and, to the Doctor's relief, he twitched and muttered something under his breath.

'What have you done to him?' he cried. The Selachian turned away dismissively, only fuelling his mounting sense of outrage. 'You call yourselves civilised?' he bellowed. 'The Cybermen are more civilised than you! At least they're interested in a bit more than just acquiring weapons, waging war and building up the illusion of importance in an otherwise pathetic, insignificant, backwater race!'

'Doctor…' warned Hornby, in a terrified whisper. But it was too late for caution. The Doctor had got the creature's attention. It turned back and regarded him for a long moment, unmoving. He subsided, panting from his emotional outburst and beginning to realise he had pushed things too far.

It seemed like an age before the Selachian spoke. 'Your voiceprint is known to us. You denied our warcraft access to this station. Your execution has already been promised.'

It raised one arm slowly, and the Doctor felt quite sick as its blaster attachment rose to his eye level. He was no match for a Selachian physically. If it wanted to kill him now, there was nothing he could do to stop it. He would die an ignominious death – and who would get Ben and Polly home then?

It held the weapon poised for a while longer. Then it said, 'You will die once your usefulness is over.' As it turned and lumbered away, the palpable tension in the room was released like steam from an open valve. The Doctor sank, drained, into a seat and mopped at his brow with the damp handkerchief.

'Excellent!' said Dorothy, drily. 'An object lesson in how to stand up to the Selachians.'

'Well,' the Doctor conceded shakily, 'I suppose even the wisest man can act like a fool sometimes.'

Polly's stomach tightened and a feeling of dread came over her. 'Did they see you?' she asked Hayes, but she didn't really need an answer. Her colleague's expression told the story well enough.

'Come on,' Hayes urged, 'give me a hand with this.' She had hold of the heavy bench from in front of the communications console, and she was trying to turn it sideways. 'If we can wedge it between door and console, we can delay them for a few seconds.'

'What good's a few seconds?'

'I'm in no hurry to die. What about you?'

Polly wasn't, and the two women quickly manoeuvred the bench into position. None too soon, as it transpired. The door handle turned, but the creatures without couldn't gain access. Not yet.

Hayes produced the master keycard from her pocket and tossed the white plastic square to Polly. 'Take this. There's an access point to the service ducts beneath the console. Open it.'

The prospect of escape lifted Polly's spirits, but only for a moment. Something large and heavy slammed against the door from outside, and it bent in its frame. The bench held, but barely. She was galvanised into action, fumbling with the card and almost losing it as she dropped down beneath the console and searched for a lock. She hadn't seen the invaders yet, but she imagined them bristling with weapons and rippling with incredible muscles. Her throat felt dry as she worked feverishly. Her fingers felt numb and it took her twice as long as it should have done to swipe the card through its slot. With a soft click, a small panel swung open.

'Well go on, get in!' squealed Hayes from the door, where she was adding her own weight to the losing side of the predetermined struggle. It shook with a second blow, and this time it opened a crack as its guardian was knocked halfway across the tiny room and the wooden bench splintered. Polly needed no further urging.

The space beyond the hatch was dark and cold, and she didn't know what she was falling into as she swung her legs over the rim. She couldn't afford to think about it, couldn't let fear delay her. She closed her eyes and pushed herself through. The drop was shorter than she had expected, and she landed with a jarring impact. She twisted around in the confined space and saw that her head was still level with the opening. Hayes was still fighting to keep the Selachians out, although the impromptu wedge was fast turning into matches.

'I'm through, come on!'

'No time. Go without me. They haven't seen you, they might not come looking.'

And with that, the bench gave up the fight, the door was torn from its hinges and Hayes was thrown to the floor. A squat, armoured figure strode into the room. From this position, Polly could see only its lower half; she hoped that, in return, it hadn't seen her yet. She ducked, but couldn't resist raising her head again a second later, to see what was happening. She gasped as she found herself face to face with Hayes, who had moved her body to block the hatch from the Selachian's view. They stared at each other, and a desperate thought occurred to Polly.

'The disk,' she mouthed silently. 'Give me the disk.'

'You are a prisoner of the Selachian Empire,' the newcomer hissed from above.

'Don't shoot,' said Hayes sullenly. 'I give up.' She turned away and clambered slowly to her feet. In the process, she contrived to kick the service hatch shut and to plunge Polly into a stifling darkness.

Ben surfaced from troubling dreams about sharks, to find the Doctor's concerned face hovering above him. His body ached all over, but his first thought was to find out what had happened and what he could do. The Doctor cried out in alarm as Ben determinedly swung his legs off the bench and used a table to prop himself up. 'Don't worry, Doc,' he said through gritted teeth, 'I'm a bit winded, that's all.'

He looked around the assembled group and noticed first of all that Polly wasn't present. Before he could ask after her, however, a sullen Hayes was brought into the room by a Selachian escort. It gave her a hefty push towards the other prisoners, then turned and left, without speaking. Ben regarded the two silent door guards, but reluctantly concluded that it would be suicidal to challenge them.

'Where's Polly?' the Doctor whispered urgently, when Hayes was close enough.

'Safe. The Selachians don't know about her.' She took the Doctor's shoulder and propelled him to one side, conspiratorially. Ben could only just make out what she was saying. 'Have you still got the plasma cartridge from my gun? And the gun you took from Matlock?'

'Ah.' The Doctor knew what she wanted, but he was reluctant to provide it.

'Come on, Doctor,' Terri urged, 'we're on the same side now, aren't we?'

Hornby was seated across the table from Ben, nursing a bruised head. He raised his voice in support. 'If you've got a gun and Ms Hayes knows how to use it, then hand it over and let's get out of here!'

Finding himself in the minority, the Doctor relented with bad grace. 'Oh, very well.' Hayes turned her back to the guards so her body shielded the ensuing transaction. 'But it'll take more than this to blast our way free,' the Doctor warned. 'Keep it hidden until it's absolutely necessary.'

'I do know how to handle a gun,' said Hayes, smiling as she slapped the small power pack into place and the now functional weapon disappeared into her jacket.

The door opened again, this time to admit a trio of Selachians. The foremost of them had a blue band painted across its golden armour, from left shoulder to right hip (if they had such bones, Ben thought; Earth sharks, of course, had cartilage instead). Judging by its demeanour, the markings had to indicate that it was in charge. The entourage halted in unison, with its leader one pace ahead of the others. 'You will stand when an officer enters the room, plankton!' it instructed. Its voice was louder than that of the Selachian Ben had fought – more obviously amplified. Its consonants were indistinct, and the increased reverb only added to the difficulty of deciphering its words.

Only Geoff Hornby and Bryan Melrose were sitting,

and they chose wisely to obey the command. Both stood, though Hornby teetered dizzily and put his hand on a chair back for support. Daphne McAllister whimpered and shrank behind the Doctor. Dorothy Adler folded her arms and stared unflinchingly. She didn't want to show weakness, which Ben knew was a mistake. He certainly had no intention of angering their captors again unless he had no other choice.

'We are here to collect two disks,' the officer hissed. 'You will tell us where they are or be eliminated.'

It was met by a stony silence. Everyone looked from one person to another, as if wondering who would place themselves in the firing line by speaking first. The exception was Dorothy, who continued to glare. 'Don't you think we should be discussing credit transfers before I hand over the merchandise?' she said pointedly.

'Earlier agreements made with human scum have no relevance. The new deal is this: we take the weapon or you die.'

'But we don't know where the disks are,' said the Doctor mildly, 'so you see we couldn't hand them over if we wanted to.'

'We will see if you are so obstinate once the first execution has been carried out.' The Selachian raised one of its blasters and allowed its arm to sway back and forth, taunting its impotent targets. A cold flush broke across Ben's face.

'There's no need for this,' the Doctor insisted, but the Selachian ignored him.

'I wonder,' it hissed, 'who should have the honour of dying first.' It allowed its aim to linger on each of them in turn. On Dorothy: 'The piece of plankton who still thinks itself our equal?' On the Doctor: 'The fool whose

191

death has already been promised?' On Daphne, who went rigid with fear as a small tear trickled down her cheek. On Melrose: 'The agent whose incompetence has forced us into this action?' On Hornby, then Ben: 'The two who would match their physical strength against ours?' On Terri, and finally Hayes. 'You are all equally deserving of oblivion!'

It snapped its arm around and fired, with startling speed. Daphne screamed and the Doctor wailed in helpless dismay as a jet of lethal yellow fire struck its chosen target square in the chest.

When the dust had settled, the Selachian's first victim was dead, but its gun was still levelled at the survivors. 'You have ten seconds to reveal the location of the disks,' it said, 'or more will perish.'

CHAPTER 11

NO MERCY

Dust tickled Polly's nostrils and she fought against the urge to sneeze. She had been cold at first, but now the dark service duct felt unbearably warm and close. It seemed like hours since she had been shut in here, but the hushed, flat tone of the Selachian voice that had told Alison Hayes not to resist arrest was a fresh and unsettling memory. She hardly dared move or even breathe. Phantom itches broke out on her face and legs, but remained unattended to. Polly strained her ears for any sign of the monsters returning, but there was none.

The situation felt unreal. Nothing like this was supposed to happen to an aspiring debutante from the fashionable London set. Once upon a time, the biggest worry in Polly Wright's life had been the creeping awareness of her exploitation by the modelling industry; her biggest regret at moving on from there had been the monotonous routine of a secretarial job with Professor Brett. Now she had excitement aplenty, but her worries had multiplied a thousandfold too. At the age of twenty-four, she was constantly scared for her life and for the health of her friends, and that couldn't be right. She had to pinch herself sometimes to be sure she was awake, not simply dreaming on her parents' sofa while an action movie or Professor X flickered across their monochrome TV screen.

Polly was living in a fantasy, but a happy ending wasn't guaranteed. In fiction, she might have crawled through the service ducts, spied on the Selachians, learnt their plans and staged a last-minute rescue of her travelling companions. In reality, the prospect seemed an unpleasant and unrealistic one. She was more likely to find herself stuck in the narrow shafts or running out of oxygen or trapped behind locked access panels on other decks. She would certainly feel safer in the corridors, where detection was more likely but at least she could run. And the best she could hope for was to find the Doctor and let him sort things out for her. She had faith in him to keep her alive, given a chance.

Nothing had stirred now for some time. Still, as she tentatively eased open the hatch back to the communications room, she couldn't help but imagine that she would find herself staring at armoured feet. She held her breath, and released it slowly and gratefully as the room proved to be empty. Stale air was replaced by fresh, and its cold touch pricked at the droplets of sweat on her brow. She hoisted herself out of the hole with trembling arms and lay on the floor, emotionally drained, listening for sounds of motion from without but unable to hear a thing over her own heartbeat. When she finally plucked up the nerve to stand and to peer around the edge of the door, she found the corridor deserted. Hayes had been right: the Selachians were not aware of her presence. They had presumably searched the hotel and rounded up its occupants, but had missed her hiding place. She was safe for now. Or so her head was telling her, though its voice was a small one compared with the electric tension in her nervous system.

Even if the Selachians didn't find her on a second sweep of this floor, Polly couldn't help her friends without first heading into the creatures' midst. It took all the courage she had to overrule unwilling leg muscles and to walk towards the stairs.

Daphne screamed again and subsided into hysterical, racking sobs. The Doctor felt only numb. He had failed in his duty to save another human life. Bryan Melrose was dead, his corpse horrifically disfigured by the searing action of the Selachian's gun. He remembered what he had discussed with Ben: how the monsters were keen to maintain their image. They didn't just kill their victims: they killed them horribly. Melrose had toppled into a circle of deep-blue light, which washed over pale skin and dark blood and made his fate seem surreal and somehow distant. It was as if the instant of vengeance was captured for all time as a warning to others.

'You didn't have to murder him!' he spat, shaking with contained anger.

'We do not tolerate failure. Nor shall we allow air-breathers to withhold information from us. You have four seconds left.'

'And then what? You'll kill someone else? And then someone else? We won't be of any use to you when we're all dead.'

'He's right,' said Dorothy, stepping forward boldly. The Doctor hadn't expected this, but he subsided and watched her through narrowed eyes. 'But then, most of these people can't help you anyway. I brought the disks here to trade. Upon presentation of the agreed payment, I will hand them over. No one else has to be involved.' The Doctor could see her tactics and he didn't approve. She was letting the trio of Selachians know that she alone had the information they wanted; she was the only one they couldn't afford to dispose of.

'Our position has been made clear. You will surrender the disks or your colleagues will die.'

'And I have been equally clear. Do your worst.'

'No!' the Doctor cried, pushing her aside. The Selachian leader snapped up one of its weapons and he found himself staring fixatedly down its barrel, instead of confronting his enemy face to face. He threw up his arms and bumbled through his speech with less confidence than he had intended to show. 'This woman is no friend of ours. She'll happily see us all die. You will do no good by killing us, it won't make her talk.'

'Can't you threaten to torture her?' The timidly made suggestion came from Hornby, who looked as if he regretted it as he drew attention from all quarters. The Selachian leader had to physically turn to see him, and the Doctor made a note of its restricted field of vision for possible future use. Hornby continued hurriedly, committed now. 'I mean, I wouldn't condone it or anything but, like the Doctor said, it's no use shooting us. Mrs Adler knows where the disks are and as far as I'm concerned she should hand them over and save our lives. You wouldn't have to actually hurt her, just tell her you'll, er, bite off her arms.' He tailed off nervously. 'Or something.'

The leader swung around to face Dorothy again. 'An excellent suggestion,' it said coldly. It lifted one arm and drove it forward, gesturing to its subordinates to advance. 'Mutilate her!'

Dorothy fell back before the oncoming creatures. She seemed to have lost the power of speech and just kept mouthing, 'No. No.' Her legs went next and she sank to her knees, tears welling in terror-filled eyes. The Selachians continued their advance unperturbed.

'This is inhuman!' the Doctor yelled.

'You believe we should aspire to the weaknesses of your race?'

The Doctor watched in horror as the Selachians halted on either side of Dorothy and took hold of an arm each. Then, to his relief, their leader signalled them to stop and addressed the trembling captive. 'You will tell us where the disks are, or we will break you. There will be no more warnings.'

Dorothy tried to say something, but tears were running freely down her cheeks and she choked on the words. 'I think you should tell them,' the Doctor urged. 'They'll find them one way or another. It's not worth being hurt or killed for. Remember, where there's life…'

Dorothy nodded meekly and, on her second attempt, managed to force out an answer. 'She has one of them.' She nodded towards Hayes, and the Selachians immediately let her arms go. Her body collapsed and she sobbed into the carpet. Alison Hayes became the centre of attention. She stood her ground, but her fear was not quite hidden behind her stoic expression.

'Is this true?'

'It is,' she replied evenly. 'I have one disk in my pocket.'

'And you kept it to yourself as these things threatened us?' exploded Terri. 'Well thanks a lot, madam. I'll do the same for you one day!'

'You do realise what the Selachians can do with a weapon like this, don't you? I was acting to safeguard millions of lives, not just our few!' Hayes was right too, the Doctor thought. Logic said they should sacrifice themselves to prevent the disks from falling into Selachian hands. Emotion begged him to let the monsters have what they wanted, and this was a more attractive argument. He preferred to go with the third alternative: hope. They were beaten for now – but, so long as they lived, they could reverse their setback somehow.

'But now,' said the leader, 'we will have your disk. If you do not give it freely, it will be taken from your smouldering corpse.'

Hayes acceded a little too readily – and, as she reached slowly into her jacket, the Doctor realised what she was about to do. He met her gaze and shook his head almost imperceptibly, his eyes urging her to abandon her futile plan. She turned away and he looked to Ben helplessly. It was clear that he had seen and interpreted the signals between them and his body was tensed, awaiting action.

Hayes produced the stubby white gun and, in one fluid movement, brought it to bear and fired. In the same instant, the Doctor yelled, 'Down, everybody!' He appended a cry of 'Ben, no!' as he saw what his companion was about to do.

The next few seconds were a blur of motion. A thin white jet of concentrated plasma struck the Selachian leader's chest and scythed across it, cutting a neat line into its golden armour. Its entourage brought up their guns and the guards left their posts and thundered across the room. Hayes ducked for cover behind the bar. Daphne screamed and froze, and was dragged bodily beneath a table by Terri. Dorothy cowered on the floor, exposed, and buried her head in her arms. Ben brought a chair down on a Selachian's back, but with no effect. The leader fared less well: water gushed from its armour and it thrashed about in desperation. One of the guards lifted it and bore it speedily away. Hornby turned one way and then another, paralysed by indecision. He picked up a chair but, seeing the results of Ben's attack, did nothing with it. The Doctor cannoned into Ben, knocking him out of the way of a retaliatory blast, which hit a table and blew away two legs. Hayes surfaced and fired again, but missed. The Doctor took Ben's arm and pulled him towards the unguarded doors. Two Selachians split up to approach Hayes from both sides. Hornby found himself in the path of one, panicked, and smashed his chair over its head. It carried on relentlessly and, with nowhere to run, he flung himself at it and fought uselessly. Ben saw his plight, broke away from the Doctor and leapt on to the Selachian's back. The Doctor was torn between aiding his pointless effort and making good his escape. If he could only reach the TARDIS, he might concoct something with which to end this. He cast around and saw a Selachian bearing down on Hayes. It moved with lightning speed and gripped her wrist even as she fired again. The blast seared its shoulder, but didn't breach its protective shell. Ben and Hornby, meanwhile, were carried like dead weights. There was a crackle and an ozone smell and they cried in pain as electricity coursed through the Selachian's armour, snapping their bodies rigid and flinging them clear. Daphne screamed again as Hayes was thrown to the floor, behind the bar and out of the Doctor's view. He was glad of that small mercy, at least. Her attacker aimed its guns downward and fired both barrels at close quarters. The Doctor rediscovered his legs too late and found his route to the exit blocked. And then it was all over.

Hayes's executioner stooped out of sight and straightened, a moment later, to display two items. One was Hayes's gun, which it crushed in a mighty fist. The other was a blue computer disk, and it brandished this triumphantly. All three of the remaining Selachians then moved into positions around their scattered, defeated foes. 'You will rise,' one ordered, and nobody was in the mood to resist. Daphne and Terri emerged from beneath their shelter; Terri helped the stunned Ben to his feet, while the Doctor did the same for Hornby. Dorothy stood, sulkily, after a sharp prod from a Selachian toe. One of the creatures seemed to have inherited the role of leader, as it did all the talking now. 'We have one disk, although two of your pathetic kind died to keep it from us. We will have the other. You can avoid further bloodshed by revealing its location.'

Nobody spoke, and the Selachians closed in deliberately so that their six prisoners were forced into a tight group, back to back. The Doctor found himself next to Dorothy. 'I really think you should tell them,' he said nervously.

'I don't know where it is.'

'Oh no, you must do!' wailed Daphne.

But Dorothy looked and sounded too scared to be lying. 'I don't. Neville and I hid one disk each. I don't know where he put his, but he was taking it back there when Hayes killed him. I searched his body and it wasn't there. Either he hid it before he died -'

'Or somebody else took it later,' the Doctor concluded for her. His mind was ticking over as he tried to fit this new information into his partially assembled mental jigsaw. In particular, he wanted to know why Neville Adler had apparently retrieved his disk and then decided to return it to its place of safety. But, intriguing though the puzzle was to him, he had more immediate concerns.

'All this is irrelevant,' the Selachian snapped. 'We will return to our original arrangement. One of you has the knowledge we require, so you will perish one by one until you reveal it.'

'What is wrong with you?' the Doctor erupted angrily. 'Can't you see that we genuinely don't know where the disk is?'

'Then you will die. You have already earned worse for your assault upon our commander.' The acting leader walked slowly around the group, its line of fire sweeping across each of them in turn. They shrank into an ever-decreasing circle, until their backs were pressed against each other's. The Doctor craned his neck left then right to keep their tormentor in view. Daphne whimpered as it passed her.

Part way into its second circuit, the Selachian halted. It announced simply, 'You will be next!' and the Doctor felt a sense of helpless dread as, with a cruel and unnecessary fastidiousness, it sighted down its blaster at the head of its appointed victim.

It had chosen Ben.

The long walk downstairs had been a tense and frightening journey for Polly. She had expected to encounter Selachians at every turn and the twisted railing, gaping doorway and tattered remnants of a barricade outside the docking level had filled her with trepidation. It seemed a war had been fought there, and she wondered if there had been casualties. The emptiness of the dining room on B1 added to her misery and she knew before she unlocked and entered the TARDIS that there would be no one inside. The evacuation had been aborted and, alone in the softly vibrating console room, Polly feared she might be the only person left alive on the station. She didn't want to leave the safe isolation of the ship, but she had no choice.

Back out in the dining room, she called up Thomas and wondered why she hadn't thought to do so before. She kept a watchful eye on both doors as she whispered her question: 'Where is everybody?'

'The answer, in all cases, is on Deck B8.' The vampire spoke at his normal volume, to Polly's horror. She calmed down as she processed his reply: they were seven floors away from anyone who might hear. 'All but three are situated in the Interplanetary Bar. Lord Henry Mace and two of our Selachian visitors are immediately without.'

'How many Selachians are in the bar?'

'Three, madam.'

'Is everyone OK?'

'I can no longer detect heat traces from Alison Hayes or Bryan Melrose,' Thomas reported. Which, Polly supposed, was a polite way of announcing their deaths. The report saddened her, but she was relieved too. She had imagined worse. At least the Doctor and Ben were alive.

But, if they were trapped in the bar with three Selachians present and two more watching the entrance, what could she do to help them?

Ben stared at his own impending death, helplessly. His muscles throbbed and his skin still burnt from his electric shock, but he straightened his back and shoulders and glared defiantly at his executioner. He was determined to hold on to his dignity until the end. He would not see his ship again now, although somewhere in the back of his mind he had always known that would be the case. He had known it would come to this.

But the killing blast was never let loose. His reprieve

came in the form of an unexpected arrival. It was another Selachian, and it had an announcement to make. 'We have the second disk.' The gun was lowered and Ben felt his legs beginning to shake. His immediate reaction was not so much of relief, but rather of disbelief. His luck, it seemed, had held out again.

The Selachians moved as one towards the doors and Ben noted, not for the first time, how their moves were coordinated without the apparent need for words. Were they telepathic, he wondered – or perhaps just well drilled and practised in situations of this kind? Their leader halted on the threshold and turned to face its six prisoners. 'You will be pleased to hear,' it said with a sneer in its voice, 'that our commander has reached the aquatic environment of our warcraft and has been restored to full health.' Telepathy, Ben decided. Or a radio system in their helmets.

'I'm pleased for you,' said the Doctor drily.

'Air-breathers are weak! Even with your best weapons, you are no match for us. However, you attempted to cause us harm and an example must be made. You will die.'

'But you've got what you wanted,' Hornby blurted out, aghast. 'Why can't you leave us alone? We aren't the ones who attacked your commander – and anyway, you started it!'

'Don't waste your breath,' said the Doctor mildly. 'They were planning to kill us anyway. They had their agent mine the hotel, remember? They don't want to leave behind anyone who might be able to reproduce the weapon, concoct a defence against it, or even testify to their having it. As I told Dorothy, you can always trust a Selachian to renege on its promises.'

'We have made but one promise to you, plankton, and

we intend to keep it. This station is in a decaying orbit. Our computer projections indicate that it will be destroyed in approximately forty-six of your minutes. We will leave you to your fate. Your ships have been jettisoned from the docking bays, so there can be no escape. In the meantime, your temporary survival will give us an opportunity to conduct a most interesting experiment.'

The Selachian made to leave but, as an afterthought, it turned back and added, 'And, if you harbour hopes of being rescued by your colleagues, you may disregard them. We are aware that two more of your loathsome kind are on board and we will not leave until they have been exterminated.'

They were talking about Polly. 'No, you can't!' cried Ben.

The Doctor was fairly hopping in alarm. 'Why don't you just leave them to die with the rest of us? We can… we can say our final goodbyes.'

'Your own deaths will be a swift and painless expediency. Your friends' deaths, beforehand, will be your true punishment.' So saying, the Selachian departed.

Its pronouncement left an aching void in Ben's stomach. 'Doctor, what are we going to do?'

'What difference does it make?' grumbled Dorothy. 'We're all dead anyway. It's just that someone else gets to go first.'

The Doctor was pacing anxiously. 'No, we're not beaten yet. The Selachians don't know about the TARDIS. As soon as they've gone, we can go straight to it and leave.'

'But they're going to kill Polly!' urged Ben.

'I know. And I've got to do something, even if there's

no hope.' The Doctor turned and dashed towards the doors. And into them. 'Oh no,' he lamented. He pushed and pulled to no avail and, as he spun to face the others again, his eyes were wide with dismay. 'We're locked in!'

Polly heard movement on the stairs below and she ducked quietly on to the nearest deck, B7. She stood with her back pressed against the wall, trying not to breathe and praying that the approaching Selachians wouldn't visit this floor. They didn't.

As their footsteps passed, she could hear Henry Mace chattering nervously. 'You will let me go once I've done this for you, won't you? I didn't have anything to do with bringing the disks here or hiding them, I promise. I don't even know what's on them. I heard they were important and I found one on Neville – ah, I just found one. I thought I'd better take it for safekeeping. And I thought you were the best, erm, people to give it to.'

'You will be rewarded,' a Selachian voice promised him. Polly felt a hot flush of anger. Mace had taken the disk before she and Hayes had got to it and the coward had surrendered it to preserve his own life.

When she was sure the group had passed, she returned to the staircase and cautiously descended. She stopped in her tracks, though, as she came in sight of the door to B8 – and the Interplanetary Bar – even as another Selachian stomped through it from beyond. Her only advantage was that it didn't appear to have seen her. It was examining its own lower arm and, a second later, she saw why. A seamless panel popped open to reveal a tangle of... wires? The more she looked, the more she thought they were alive; they had the repellent appearance of spindly, elongated maggots.

A soft bleeping sound emerged from the machinery/creatures and Polly withdrew from sight. She padded back upstairs, as swiftly and softly as she could manage, and retook her hiding place on the next level up. Interminable seconds passed before the regular bleeps came back into her hearing. They grew louder as the Selachian drew closer, until she felt it must be directly behind the door. Then, perplexingly, they grew louder still and faster – and Polly realised that their volume and tempo had increased with proximity.

The logical conclusion was a few seconds in coming so that, even as she became aware of her peril, the Selachian was bursting through the door to confront her. Its tracking device now emitted a continuous, high-pitched shriek. It brought up its other arm to point its gun at her, and she knew there was no hope of escape.

Polly screamed.

The Doctor was on his knees in front of the doors, using an eyeglass to peer through the narrow crack between them. His examination proceeded at an achingly slow rate and Ben's impatience mounted. Polly was in danger out there and, until the Doctor could free them, he could do nothing.

Terri moved to his side and sympathetically brushed her hand against his. He shrugged her away, then belatedly realised how rude he had been and offered her an apologetic look. Terri seemed to understand, although she couldn't have appreciated this blatant display of how much another woman meant to him. 'Why don't you call up Thomas?' she suggested. 'He could at least tell us where Polly is and whether the Selachians have found her.'

'Oh, good idea!' enthused Hornby, and Ben agreed. He darted across to one of the information points at the bar and punched the button that summoned the holographic vampire. He appeared instantly, but the news he imparted was not to Ben's liking.

'Doctor,' he cried, fighting down an almost overwhelming sense of dread, 'they've got her. She's alive but she's with one of those creatures on the next floor up. You've got to hurry!'

The Doctor leapt to his feet and, for one joyous second, Ben thought he had succeeded. But his face was a mask of hopeless misery. 'They've attached a locking device to the other side. I can't open it from here.'

'You've got to!'

The Doctor bounded down the steps and towards the bar. He produced a screwdriver from his pocket and prised open an information terminal. Thomas coughed politely. 'Erm, may I remind you, sir, that you are damaging -'

'No, you may not. With the circuits in here, I might be able to cobble together a sonic device to trip the lock remotely.'

Ben was dismayed. 'How long will that take?'

'Too long, I'm afraid. Thomas, where is Polly now?'

'She is on the stairs with a Selachian escort, proceeding upwards between Decks B5 and B4.'

The Doctor breathed a sigh of relief. 'They've taken her prisoner.'

'But they might do anything to her,' Ben protested.

'They haven't done anything yet - which indicates that they need her. She's safe for the time being. Thomas, I want you to keep tracking her and tell me if the situation changes.'

'Acknowledged, sir.'

The Doctor pulled a handful of circuit boards from the terminal's innards and began to poke at them as he continued to talk. 'In the meantime, we have our own problems to worry about. The Selachians mentioned "an experiment". I imagine they intend to test out their new weapon.'

'On us?' guessed Hornby.

'Oh no,' moaned Daphne.

'But they've only just got the blueprints,' Terri pointed out. 'How could they assemble a prototype so quickly?'

'Well, that rather depends on what the weapon is.' The Doctor turned to face them and Ben saw a familiar knowing glint in his eye. 'Do you want to tell them, Dorothy, or should I?'

'Excuse me, sir,' interrupted Thomas, 'but Ms Wright has just arrived on Deck B1.'

When the Selachian had first instructed Polly to accompany it, she had felt only relief that her life had been spared. Now, however, the emotion was wearing off and, as she was marched by the medical centre, she began to worry about what her captor did have in mind. It directed her into a small office, and she suppressed the urge to scream as she found three of its brethren already present within the claustrophobic room. She was more surprised, however, to see Henry Mace seated at a wooden desk between them, typing awkwardly at a grey plastic computer keyboard. He looked up and saw her, but didn't acknowledge her arrival. He returned to his work, but his fevered brow and jerky movements suggested that he was doing so under duress.

One of the Selachians bore a wide blue diagonal

stripe across its golden armour. It appeared to be the leader, as it turned to Polly's escort now and demanded, 'Why have you brought her here? She was to be slain.'

'I believed she may prove useful. Her face and form are within the parameters we identified as being... pleasing to human animals. She could replace Melrose as our liaison operative.'

Blue Stripe stepped forward and cupped Polly's chin in one huge hand. She flinched from its touch, but forced herself to stare back at it. 'Your choice is a good one,' it approved. 'She has spirit, as well as human beauty. But she will learn to serve as did her predecessors. She will fear the alternative.' Polly wanted to pour scorn upon its notions, but she was too scared to speak. It was probably a good thing, she reflected: she had to prolong her life as long as possible until the Doctor could find a way to rescue her.

The Selachian leader addressed her directly for the first time. 'You have arrived at an opportune moment, plankton. You may witness a demonstration of our might.'

'What are you going to do?' she asked, her voice sounding faint.

'We are about to test our new weapon on one of your colleagues.'

'But you can't have built it so soon!'

The Selachian actually laughed: a horrible, staccato, guttural sound. 'Stupid human!' it berated her. 'The disks don't contain the weapons' blueprints: they contain the weapon itself!'

'I don't understand.'

'You will. Your friend here will activate the weapon, under our instructions. In return for his servitude, we have allowed him to choose his own victim from those remaining on the station.'

'You've what?' Polly was appalled. She felt as if a small animal was clawing at her stomach from the inside. 'You don't have to do this,' she entreated Mace.

'I think you'll find I do, my dear. Somebody is going to die, and I have rather a vested interest in ensuring that it is not me.'

Angered by his seeming indifference, she told him, 'If you hadn't handed over the disk -'

'The same logic applies, I think. I'm sorry, dear. I genuinely didn't intend for things to come to this pass.'

His eyes met Polly's, and she was alarmed to see the unexpected depths of fear and agony locked into them. She saw his predicament from within, then: Mace was being forced to commit murder, to decide who should live and who should die. She actually felt sympathy for him, but her thoughts were nonetheless dominated by the fact that Ben and the Doctor were among his candidates for destruction. Her voice failed and she could only croak one single word, to release the question which burnt painfully in her breast.

'Who?' she begged him.

CHAPTER 12

THE ASSASSINATION PROGRAM

The Doctor was perched on a stool beside the bar, hands working at tangled wires in his lap, though he rarely glanced down at them. He was managing to put together his electronic lockpick while simultaneously holding court. Ben found himself in an attentive, semicircular group alongside Daphne, Terri, and Hornby. Even Thomas maintained an expression of polite interest. But Dorothy sat some distance away, her arms folded sulkily.

'There were one or two details I couldn't quite get to add up,' the Doctor explained. 'Things to do with the Adlers, mostly. We know why they came here and we also know they had the best motive for murdering Ted Matlock. But they had a perfect alibi for the time of his death.'

'I was in their room with them,' Ben reminded the others.

'A few minutes ago, Dorothy said something to shed a little light on the problem. We had assumed that Neville had died while looking to retrieve his disk from its hiding place. In fact, he was taking it back there. But why – unless he had been using it?'

'For what?' asked Terri.

'Ah, there we come across another discrepancy. The Adlers, we're told, were engaged in weapons research – and yet their field of expertise appeared to be computer programming. Dorothy saved the whole station from a terminal in her room when Melrose's bomb threatened to bring it down. She and her so-called husband could easily have killed Matlock from just such a distance.'

'You mean they programmed the computer to commit murder?' Ben was revolted, astonished, and even a little embarrassed by the revelation. He remembered sitting in the Adlers' room, sipping tea while Dorothy tapped away at her keyboard as calm as anything. No wonder she had insisted on inviting him in: like a fool, he had been testifying to her innocence ever since, acting as her unwitting dupe and throwing the others off her scent.

'Precisely, Ben. Ms Hayes was never told the nature of the Adlers' weapon, and she made the perfectly logical assumption that the two disks contained its blueprints. I believe they actually hold the weapon itself: a program which can turn a computer system against a chosen victim. Mr Matlock was electrocuted inside an elevator, with nobody nearby, because the Galaxian's systems themselves diverted power through the doors or the control buttons.'

There was a stunned silence, which was broken by Dorothy Adler's deliberately slow handclap as she stood and crossed the room to join them. 'Well done! It took you long enough, but you've arrived at the truth at last.'

Ben was chilled by her blatant unrepentance, but at the same time he was almost relieved. Dorothy had shown herself to be an unpleasant, ruthless woman; to find out she was the killer after all allowed him to feel more comfortable with the former suspects he had begun to think of as friends. Or more.

'Of course,' she continued, 'under better circumstances, with more time to plan, the crime would have been untraceable. We could have loaded our program into any computer, anywhere on Earth or its outposts, and it would have found its way here.'

'It locates its victims too?' The Doctor was altogether too appreciative for Ben's liking.

Dorothy, however, seemed flattered by his interest, and she was certainly enjoying the opportunity to brag. 'Almost every computer system is connected these days, Doctor. If it isn't on a network, it will no doubt have a back door somewhere, or its owners will visit websites and collect messages from across the world. Our program can find its way around all those access points. It leaps from system to system at a phenomenal speed, collecting information until it is sure of its victim's location. Then it will strike, with whatever means are available. There is no escape.'

'You'd have to abandon civilisation altogether,' the Doctor breathed, struck by the magnitude of her achievement.

'Even then, it could narrow down your position and send a drone to do the job. It might take some time, but I can promise you: once your details are entered into the assassination program, you're dead.'

'It's a clever piece of work,' the Doctor complimented her. 'A very clever piece of work indeed.' Then his demeanour changed in an instant as he spat, 'And an unconscionable abomination!'

'It's a work of genius, Doctor! My colleague and I have earned a place in history. We have perfected the ultimate murder weapon.'

'Well I hope you're proud of yourself.'

'I am,' said Dorothy smugly. 'Very proud.'

* * *

'Who are you going to... to...' Polly couldn't say the word.

Nor could Mace seem to answer. He cast his eyes downward, even as the Selachian leader interceded. 'Be silent,' it commanded, 'and resume your task. I am anxious to see how our acquisition functions.'

'Why can't you do it yourself?' Polly challenged, the hopeless situation forcing a mutinous spirit to rise within her.

'The assassination program will be adapted to run on our superior computers. For now, the air-breather's spindly fingers are best suited to this primitive human system.'

'I've installed the program,' Mace reported, his voice quivering slightly.

'Then activate it.'

He nodded obediently and input a series of commands. His clumsy two-fingered typing was unbearably slow, and Polly was uncomfortably aware of the Selachians' laboured breathing as she watched and waited.

'I... I have to define a target now.'

'Then do so.'

Mace tried not to react, but he was a little too straight-faced and tight-jawed to appear wholly unaffected by the callous instruction. A pulse rippled the skin of his flabby neck. 'Do so,' the leader repeated, with more force this time.

He swallowed, and stalled: 'It's asking for all kinds of details. Name, height, weight, distinguishing features...' Polly looked at the screen but could only see a string of indecipherable characters. It was some futuristic computer code, she decided. How long would the Selachians employ her – and keep her alive – if she couldn't interpret something so apparently basic for this era?

'It needs only enough details to differentiate its victim from other plankton,' the leader said impatiently. 'Choose your subject and give it what information you have.'

Mace's fingers hovered over the keyboard and he seemed to be willing himself to obey. But, again, he wavered. 'I only met these people today. I don't even know the real names of some of them.'

'You know the current location of all. Along with an assumed name, that should be adequate. Complete your task without further delay, or you will perish and the other human will take over.'

Polly shivered at the thought and wondered what she would do in such a position. She couldn't condemn a living, breathing human being to death; she just couldn't. She remembered how, even as a schoolgirl, she had felt a warm glow of pride when her country all but abolished the death penalty. The Doctor had reinforced her belief that all life was sacrosanct. She would rather die, she concluded, than take a life herself. In Mace's case, however, the threat had overridden what few principles he might have had.

She wanted desperately to know what he was telling the computer to do. To her, though, it seemed he was pressing random keys, inputting gibberish. When he had finished, he sat back with sweat glistening on his forehead. He at least had the decency to look ashamed. 'I've done it,' he said unhappily. 'I gave you the disk and now I've done your dirty work for you too. Will you let me go now?'

'You are untrustworthy human scum,' growled the Selachian leader. 'What made you believe you were worthy of existence?'

It raised its gun, and Mace had less than a second to

draw breath for a scream of terror before it shot him at point blank range through the head.

For an instant, it was dark in the Interplanetary Bar.

Of them all, only the Doctor and Dorothy fully realised what the brief power failure presaged. The latter froze in wary anticipation, while the former leapt up frenziedly and brushed the components of his almost-completed sonic device from his lap. He had hoped for more time than this. As always, the Selachians had been too efficient for his liking. 'Stay close together!' he instructed.

'They've activated the weapon, haven't they?' said Ben.

'I'm afraid so. Thomas?'

'I have no knowledge of anything amiss, sir.'

'No, I didn't think you would have. But for a moment there, your central processing unit was too busy with an enormous influx of data to attend to its other responsibilities.'

'If you say so, sir. And, incidentally, Ms Wright has just been escorted out of the office on Deck B1.'

'Is Mace still with her?' asked Hornby.

'I can no longer detect his heat signature.'

'They've killed him!' cried Ben.

Daphne gasped in sudden realisation. 'The lights flickered just before… before Matlock…'

'Indeed. Now form a circle, everyone. Back to back and link arms. Hurry.'

'But Doctor, they've killed Mace!'

'I know, Ben, and there's nothing we can do.'

'But Polly…'

'Ms Wright is heading once more towards the stairs,' reported Thomas.

'There you are, Ben, she's safe for the moment. Now please do as I ask!'

Ben hesitated, but did as he was bidden, holding out his arms for Daphne and Terri to take. Hornby followed suit, but Dorothy shook her head derisively. 'What do you think you're trying to do?'

'I'm trusting that even you have enough basic compassion to have included a few safeguards,' said the Doctor. 'Or will your program go after its victim regardless of the cost?'

'It will be careful not to harm another human being.'

He was glad to hear it. 'In which case, I suggest you join us. Or has it not occurred to you that you're the Selachians' most likely target?' He extended his arm towards the scientist and, losing her nerve, she scampered over and inserted herself into the chain.

He had lied to her, of course. He had consistently defied the aliens since their arrival, marking himself out as the group's primary agitator. In part, it was simply his nature to stand up to those who would ride roughshod over the rights of others to peaceful existence. He also felt it his responsibility, though, to draw trouble from those less able to cope with it than himself – including his companions. He actually hoped he was the computer's intended victim. If it was anybody else, he wasn't sure he could save them.

So far, at least, they were all alive – and he had bought himself time. Dorothy clung to his right arm, Hornby to his left, and the uncomfortable circle swayed as any one of its constituents shifted his or her balance.

'Ms Wright is now on the docking level,' said Thomas presently.

With the silence thus broken, Ben spoke up too, interrupting the Doctor's cogitation. 'What's all this in aid of anyway?'

'Safety in numbers, Ben. The hotel's computer is now primed to kill one of us, but there's no way of knowing who. So long as we remain in contact like this, it will find its job difficult. It can't use gas, it can't even cut off life support. According to Dorothy, it won't do anything to endanger the rest of us.'

'And you trust her?' protested Terri.

'She is staking her life on it.'

'Oh, this is horrible,' whimpered Daphne. 'What are we going to do?'

'Stay calm,' said the Doctor firmly. 'So long as we remain in a cluster and don't touch anything, we're reasonably safe.'

'But we can't stay here for ever,' said Hornby. 'How are we going to get out before the station crashes?'

'Or before those creatures hurt Polly?' Ben added.

The Doctor was glad that no one could see his expression of uncertainty and disappointment as he confessed, 'I had rather hoped not to be asked those questions yet.'

'I'm sure,' said Terri drily, 'but if we don't hear the answers within the next thirty minutes, we never will.'

Polly crossed the docking level, still sobbing quietly and surrounded by the four Selachians so that she had no choice but to match their pace or be crushed by them. Their leader's casual slaughter of Mace had caused her to be physically sick, but she had received no sympathy. One Selachian had punched a button on the computer and the Adlers' two disks had popped out into its grasp; the group had then made haste towards the floor above and Polly had been forced to accompany them. Her throat was still burning, she had had to wipe her mouth on her arm and her stomach threatened to repeat its eruption whenever she thought about Mace's corpse and the bubbling red pool where its head should have been. Her revulsion was equalled by the increasing certainty that such a fate awaited her too.

The realisation that she was leaving the hotel did nothing to assuage such fears. Her captors took her through two ragged holes where once airlock doors had been, along a cylindrical metal tube of about ten yards in length, and through two more, similar doors which hung ajar. And then they were on the Selachian warcraft.

For a moment, she was dazzled by its unexpected elegance. They had emerged into an enormous hallway and Polly's shoes clacked against a polished grey marble floor. The high roof was supported by fluted columns with inset golden strips. The walls were interspersed with beautiful watercolour pictures in tastefully gilded frames. The centrepiece was a huge swimming pool in which clear water sparkled and rippled to an artificial breeze. Either the Selachians had very human tastes or this area had been deliberately designed to appeal to air-breathing visitors. The latter option made more sense. The aliens greeted their would-be business partners with courtesy and signs of opulence, before betraying them.

Many white doors led off the hall, and one Selachian – the one that had captured her, she thought, although there was no way of knowing – guided her across to one of these and through. She glanced over her shoulder to see the rest of the group, its leader included, sliding into the pool. Then her view was obscured as her escort shut the door and announced, 'These will be your quarters.'

Polly looked around the room and tried to hide an expression of distaste. It was smaller than her bedroom in the TARDIS, but the presence of a bed, table, sink and desk – this last complete with a computer terminal – suggested that she was expected to live, work, eat, and sleep here. The surfaces had not been dusted for some time and there was an unpleasant damp, musty odour. A man's suit lay crumpled on the floor and a dirty cup stood next to a crusted coffee stain on the worktop. She didn't fancy clearing out the effects of the late Bryan Melrose. She would have protested about the conditions but for her belief that the Doctor would take her away from this soon.

Until he did, she had to keep on the Selachians' good side. 'What will my duties be?' she asked, as if she intended to perform them.

'To do as you are told.'

'Oh.'

'In many cases, you will be responsible for our first contact with prospective partners. You will open negotiations and sometimes meet clients to execute transactions.'

'And to execute the clients,' Polly muttered. The comment came out louder and sounded more sarcastic than she had intended. For a moment, she feared it might bring reprisals.

'I will return in four hours,' the Selachian said. 'By then, you will have familiarised yourself with our data storage system.'

'Fine,' said Polly, trying to sound as dutiful and efficient as she could to compensate for her slip-up. She could see no sign of a filing cabinet, though. 'Where is it then?'

She realised her mistake instantly. The Selachian said

nothing and she couldn't see through its helmet, but she felt its suspicion glaring through the metal. Her eyes strayed to the grey plastic box on the table and she concealed her fear. 'The computer, I mean. Oh, there it is. Right under my nose, silly me.'

'You are familiar with secretarial work?'

'Oh absolutely,' she insisted. 'I was Professor Brett's personal assistant in London. He was one of our cleverest computer scientists, you know. He used to say he didn't know how he'd got by before I came along.' All of which was true; she had only omitted the fact that the reference was almost two centuries out of date.

'I will return in two hours,' the Selachian decided. It departed then and Polly was disappointed – but not too surprised – to hear the sound of the door being locked behind it. Alone now, she allowed herself to show all the signs of terror that she had been holding back. She sank on to the bed – the mattress was threadbare and she could feel its springs – and shook uncontrollably.

A minute later, she realised the floor was shaking too, vibrating to the rhythm of distant engines. She could hear a throbbing hum. The ship was taking off, and Polly shivered at the thought of being separated from her crewmates and from the TARDIS by an interstellar distance. For the first time, she thought about what her life would be like if the Doctor and Ben couldn't rescue her.

She felt helpless and very alone.

Ben shook his left foot, trying to rid it of the sensation of pins and needles. His action unbalanced Daphne and the circle swayed and shifted again. He was becoming impatient and he itched to do something productive.

The deadline for the hotel's destruction was looming. More importantly, every second they delayed sentenced Polly to another second in the Selachians' company. Thomas had reported that she was boarding the creatures' warcraft, before he had been stricken by a sudden fault and had blipped out of existence.

'The computer must have requisitioned his power supply,' the Doctor said gloomily, 'no doubt for some death trap or other.'

'Look Doctor,' said Ben, 'what are the chances of turning your sonic gizmo there into a remote controller?'

'Not hopeful, I'm afraid. Not without more equipment.'

'And if he goes feeling inside any machines, he might get his hands fried off,' said Terri unhelpfully.

'So what are we going to do?'

'I've come to the conclusion,' said the Doctor, slowly and with reluctance, 'that the sonic device is our only hope after all. I'll simply have to complete it to my original specifications.'

'So one of us will have to go to the door to use it?' said Hornby.

'Oh, that's a good one,' snorted Dorothy. 'We all sidle over there together, do we? And what if the computer electrifies the lock?'

'It can't,' said the Doctor, 'not if we remain linked. It can't kill one without killing all.' But he didn't sound sure.

'Then it puts enough heat through the coils in the door frame for whoever's touching it to stick,' said Dorothy, seeming to relish the gruesome image. 'Or it blows up the locking device in his face.'

'You've made your point. Whoever picks the lock will

be exposing themselves to danger, I admit.'

Despite the warning, Ben was cheered by the prospect of taking practical action. 'Right. Only one of us is at risk, yeah? Well I'll take a one-in-six chance. If you can get that thing finished and show me how to use it, I'll get us out of here.' He tried to break free of the group but, while Daphne let him go, Terri held on stubbornly.

'Are you mad?' she remonstrated, pulling him back into line.

'She's right, Ben,' said the Doctor. 'The Selachians were ready to kill you, remember?'

Ben pouted. 'You're going to try yourself, aren't you?'

The Doctor phrased his reply carefully. 'Under normal circumstances, yes, I would rather place myself in jeopardy than anyone else. But then I have become rather a focal point for our friends' anger.'

Dorothy laughed. 'Listen to our courageous leader. He wants some idiot to put their life on the line, but it's not going to be him.'

'He's right,' countered Hornby. 'If the Selachians chose anyone to die, it would have been the Doctor. Or you.'

'So it makes sense for me to do it,' said Ben firmly. He pulled away again and, this time, he managed to throw off Terri's restraining hold. Daphne looked momentarily lost and afraid, then she clutched at the lifeline of her old schoolfriend's free arm and the circle was closed, with Ben on the outside.

He hesitated then, not sure what to do. He felt cold, and not only because his shoulders missed the heat of warm bodies pressed against them. It had been easy to sound brave when he hadn't really thought through the consequences – when he was just reacting as always to an opportunity to prove himself useful in an environment in which he was otherwise lost. Now, having isolated himself from the safety of the group, he had to deal with the real possibility that he had condemned himself to a death which he probably wouldn't see coming.

'No!' the Doctor shouted. He pushed and pulled and almost toppled the whole circle as he forced it around until he was facing Ben. 'You're almost as likely a target as I am. What if the Selachians want to punish both of us by murdering you and making me watch?'

'What if, what if?' scoffed Dorothy. 'Are you going to keep us here all day playing guessing games, or will you let him try it? Look on the bright side: if the computer incinerates him, the rest of us know we're safe.'

The Doctor ignored her. 'Taking unnecessary risks isn't brave, Ben. In fact, it's a very stupid thing to do.'

Ben was stung by his forceful words, although the concern from which they were born was very visible in the Doctor's face and manner. 'Someone's got to do it,' he muttered. He turned his head away sullenly, but found himself facing a life-sized effigy of a green, humanoid, tortoise-like creature. Its eyes too seemed to accuse him.

'And I won't let you volunteer. I won't... I won't complete the device for you.'

Ben sighed and made a show of acceding. In truth, he was glad by now of the excuse to go back on his ill-advised plan. Before he rejoined the others, though, he stooped to pick up the abandoned, half-completed device. He was frozen by the Doctor's strangulated cry.

'It's still connected to the main power supply,' he said, indicating a stretch of multicoloured wires back to the gutted terminal. 'Touch that, and you'll give the computer the best shot it could hope for.'

He backed off, eyeing the tangle of components as if it could bite him. The Doctor disengaged himself from Hornby and proffered his hand. 'Hold on to me. It can't send a current into you then.' Ben obeyed, and reached for the device again. Despite his lifeline, he flinched from touching it at first. Then he lifted it gingerly by one corner and almost flung it back to the Doctor who, in turn, clasped it with both hands and gave it a vicious yank so that the wires came free at the other end.

Ben rejoined the circle between the Doctor and Hornby and watched as his companion performed an engineering miracle with no tools but two hands and a screwdriver. At one point, he popped the handle of the latter into his mouth and craned his neck to prod at a tiny circuit board nestled in one palm. Ben couldn't imagine how he could work accurately under such conditions. His arms twisted and squirmed so that it was difficult to keep hold of him, and Ben's ribs regularly became the unwitting targets of his flailing elbow. Dorothy suffered similarly, but she was quicker to complain.

At last, the Doctor tossed away a handful of wires and brandished the remainder, now twisted into an insane conglomeration. It looked, thought Ben, as if he had cooked up a plate of spaghetti using wires instead of pasta and had pulled out a handful at random. But he had faith in the Doctor's abilities: it would work.

'It's ready,' he announced. 'Or as ready as it will be. It has a limited, self-contained power source, but it will burn itself out after a few seconds. We'll only get one chance.'

'Which leaves the question of who'll use it,' Ben reminded him.

'Ah, yes.'

'I've been thinking,' said Hornby in a quiet voice, 'and I don't know if I can. I mean, I attacked the Selachians twice. What if they've decided to take revenge and put my name in the computer?'

'Ha! So it begins,' said Dorothy. 'Anyone else got an excuse to give? We might as well just sit down and wait to die. How about you, Daphne dearest? Fancy going to heaven before the rest of us?'

'Oh, I couldn't,' Daphne squeaked. 'I'm sorry, I couldn't. I just know I wouldn't be able to make my legs move. They feel like jelly already. I'm sorry.'

'There's no need to be,' the Doctor assured her. 'It's a great deal to ask.'

'Which only leaves one. What is it to be, Ms Willis? Developed an unexpected paralysis? Looked cross-eyed at any sharks lately?'

'I'll do it,' said Terri, as if to spite her.

Ben's stomach sank, but he told himself not to intervene. Logically, Terri was the best choice. Apart from Daphne, she was the least likely person of them all to have been marked for death. Still, he railed inwardly at the unfairness of a situation that forced her, of all of them, to put her life on the line. He actually caught himself wondering how he could survive without her, but he made himself deny the thought. He couldn't stay here.

'Are you positive about this?' the Doctor asked.

'I know what I'm doing – and somebody has to do it.' Terri left the circle and moved slowly into Ben's field of vision, stopping before the Doctor.

'Then it's appreciated,' he said, handing over the sonic device. Terri wasn't looking at him, though. Her attention was reserved for Ben, and the Doctor watched in polite silence as they stared at each other but couldn't quite bring themselves to speak.

'Well?' said Dorothy finally. 'Are you going to spring the lock or are you just waiting for it to melt in re-entry?'

Tearing her gaze from Ben, Terri turned and began to walk across the room. After four confident steps, she faltered and looked back over her shoulder. Her hard features were softened in a wash of red light, and Ben wondered if he would see them again. He tried to convey sympathy and encouragement in a simple glance. He remembered how he had felt upon leaving the circle himself, and he imagined she was experiencing those same awful sensations. There was a tight knot in his own stomach – but, as she took another tentative step and then another, it began to unravel one strand at a time. At last, she reached the doors without incident. The worst moment of all came then, as she reached out hesitantly and, in a teeth-clenched moment of decision, clamped her hand on to the metal handle. Ben flinched and closed his eyes involuntarily. But she didn't cry out. She didn't fall. She turned instead, and the flicker of her lips betrayed the beginnings of a relieved smile.

'All right Doctor, I'm here. Now how do I work this thing?'

The Doctor had begun to allow himself hope. On his directions, Terri had held the sonic device against the doors and oscillated it through a range of frequencies. She dropped it as it heated up and eventually destroyed itself; however, it had endured long enough to do its work. They all heard the clunk of the Selachians' locking mechanism disengaging, and an even more satisfying thump as it hit the floor outside. The Doctor congratulated himself and resolved to begin work on a permanent version of the device when he got back to the TARDIS. It would circumvent so many complications.

'Don't touch the door frame,' he warned everybody as they threaded their way out of the bar in a chain. 'Now, watch out for anything that might be used as a weapon – ventilation grilles, electrical appliances, anything – and give them a wide berth. Keep hold of each other, stay as close as you can and walk slowly.'

'Not too slowly. We've got about fifteen minutes left.'

'I'm well aware of that, Mr Hornby, and it should prove ample. We'll take an elevator to Deck B1. Terri, you aren't in danger from the computer so I want you to operate the controls.'

'OK.' Terri moved ahead and pressed the call button.

At which point, Daphne screamed.

The group broke apart instantly. The Doctor felt Ben's hand leaving his and he cried out in panic. 'Stay together!' But his lone voice went unheeded. Daphne and Dorothy had both leapt for cover, while Terri and – more unwisely – Ben were scrambling to place themselves in front of the others.

Thomas had materialised in the doorway of the Interplanetary Bar. But he looked different. He looked dangerous. His insubstantial form was fizzing with energy and discharges like miniature lightning bolts leapt from him to die in the air around him. His expression was twisted into a dark grimace of loathing, and the Doctor's fear was almost eclipsed by his astonishment that the Adlers' program was powerful enough to enable the computer to do this.

There was no time to do anything but take shelter, as electrical fire crackled in Thomas's eyes. But, a split second later, the Doctor experienced the hearts-stopping realisation that he wasn't its intended target after all. He could only yell out his anguish as twin bolts of high-voltage death were let loose from the holographic vampire's eyes – and struck Ben Jackson full in the chest.

CHAPTER 13

TARGET

Ben fell to his knees and was surprised not to find himself dead. The bolt had earthed itself straight through him and he was tingling all over. He also felt giddy, and he closed his eyes and rocked to dispel the sensation. Instead, he burst into paroxysms of laughter. In the back of his mind, he expected Thomas to follow his failed attack with a killing blow but, to his distant horror, he was unable to react to the sobering thought. Daphne's screams, the Doctor's plaintive wails and Dorothy's laughter merged in his ears and shrieked through his head like persistent sirens.

He felt himself being hauled to his feet and, focusing through orange blotches at a slow-motion scene, he saw that Terri was lifting his crumpled body. His muscles refused to work and he lolled in her arms like a rag doll. Dimly, he remembered her taking his hand as Thomas fired. It had been too late to prevent the blast from being unleashed, but the computer had at least toned down the voltage in deference to its effects upon the woman. She had saved Ben's life – and she was in the process of so doing again.

'Get behind me!' she yelled, flinging him aside as the hologram advanced. For a second, he thought she had thrown him straight at it; then he registered the implausible sight of his own dishevelled form stumbling towards him. He was jolted back to reality by the twin catalysts of a panic-driven adrenaline rush and an unexpected collision with the mirror on the back wall of an elevator. Alert again, but using the wall for support, he twisted around to see what was happening and what he could do. The answer to the latter was nothing. He was trapped in the tiny cubicle, with nowhere to run, and his would-be guardian was backing nervously towards him as Thomas bore down on her. Terri cursed as the vampire leapt forward and sailed through her as if she wasn't there. He and Ben were alone in the lift now, and Thomas's eyes glowed as he prepared to fire again. Ben took a tip from his attacker's book and propelled himself in the only direction possible. The hologram dissipated as he passed through it, found Terri's hand and drew her into a tight embrace. He wanted to cling to her for ever, and he was only vaguely aware of the rattling of the doors as they cut the pair off from the rest of the group, including the visibly alarmed Doctor.

Terri saw what was happening and she twisted in Ben's arms to reach the button for Deck B1. She pressed it, but the movement unbalanced them both and they fell, rolling over on the floor until Terri ended up on top and Ben lay on his back beneath her and laughed again. 'S-sorry,' he stammered between hard-won breaths, 'I'm a bit shaky. Electric shock.'

'You're telling me. I caught the tail end of it too, remember?'

'Yeah. Thanks for that.'

Then a puzzled look crossed Terri's face. 'We're going down!'

'I beg your pardon?'

'The lift. I pressed B1, but it's taking us down.'

They scrambled to their feet, their exhaustion forgotten. Terri punched the button for their preferred destination several times, but it was already lit and there was no sign of their direction being reversed. 'Well, the sneaky pile of junk!'

'The computer must have worked out where the TARDIS is,' Ben realised as they came to rest on B9, 'and it's keeping us clear.'

'Until it can get another shot at you.'

'What if it won't open the doors?'

'It has to.' Terri raised her voice, as if hoping the computer would hear and respond. 'If it locks us in here, we'll both die. It'll have violated its prime directive or whatever it wants to call it.'

'Do you think it cares?' Ben muttered.

'Anyway, it has more chance of separating us – and killing you – if it lets us out.'

'Thanks for the cheering thought.'

The doors slid open, and they started and leapt back into each other's arms as they were greeted by Thomas. He stood, firmly blocking their exit, unmoving and unblinking. A halo of energy coruscated about him. 'On second thoughts,' said Terri, 'I could get used to living in this lift – for all of the next fifteen minutes.'

At which point, they were thrown to the floor again.

The lift doors had clapped shut in front of the Doctor with the finality of a guillotine blade, sealing the fate of his young charge. He stared at his own distorted reflection, and its distraught expression, in the dull silver surface. Hornby placed his arm around the weeping Daphne and Dorothy watched with a smirk.

'I must say, I've exceeded my own expectations. Quite a resourceful program, isn't it?'

The Doctor glared at her. His mind was racing, already accommodating the new situation and working out a fresh strategy. Terri was with Ben, which was something. She was level-headed and capable: she had saved his life, when the Doctor himself had not been close enough to do a thing. He had to credit them both with enough sense to stick together and to head for the TARDIS. There was no reason why he couldn't lend a helping hand, though.

'I want the three of you to go to the dining room,' he ordered, 'and wait for me outside my, ah, blue box.' Daphne's mouth dropped open, but he forestalled her objection. 'It's perfectly safe. The Selachians have left and the computer isn't bothered about any of us. But I think you should take the stairs just in case. And hurry: our main concern now is to get off the station before it's destroyed.'

'And what about you?' asked Hornby.

'I'll be along in two minutes – there's something I have to do first. Now shoo, go on!' Having sent them on their way, he rushed back into the Interplanetary Bar and over to where he had left the innards of a terminal displayed. He reached into his pocket for the screwdriver, but thought better of it. There was no need for finesse this time. He plunged his hands into the circuitry and set about doing all the damage he could. Which, as it turned out, wasn't much.

The Doctor was hurled away spluttering as something exploded in the heart of the console. For a moment, he thought his own sabotage had been responsible, but then the gyroscopic systems failed again and he was thrown head over heels back into the seat of a miniature, open-sided space shuttle. Its engine wheezed into action and the ride began to jerk up and down. Too close, a blue lamp was shaken free from its fixing and fragmented upon impact with the bar top. Only now did the Doctor realise how warm it had suddenly become. They had hit the planetary atmosphere and the heat would soon surpass design tolerance levels. Even now, components were malfunctioning and the already overburdened operating system was beginning to lose control.

The hotel settled back into an upright position, but it maintained an ominous vibration. As the Doctor pulled himself out of the shuttle model, he saw that the station had twisted round to give him an unsettling view of the approaching Earth. It was close enough to fill the observation window and he quailed at this reminder of his proximity to an unpleasant death. He returned to the terminal and lifted out a handful of circuit boards, snapping them free from their moorings. If he had guessed right, his act of mayhem would have hopelessly corrupted Thomas's generation routines. If the computer wanted Ben, it would have to find another way to get him.

He could do no more. He had lingered here too long already, and other people's lives depended upon his returning to the TARDIS in time to evacuate. He crossed his fingers and offered a silent prayer to the gods of his own people. Then he headed for the door, but was caught off guard by a second violent tremor. He lost his footing and flapped his arms uselessly to keep his balance. His head glanced off the corner of a table and his last thought was of the necessity to stay conscious, for everyone's sake.

The Doctor blacked out.

Ben blinked and then Thomas was gone. His first, paranoiac thought was to check over his shoulder in case the hologram had reinitialised itself behind him. But all he saw was his own reflection, and Terri's, in the mirror – and the doors, sliding swiftly together. Terri rushed to place herself between them; their tiny motors whined as her body blocked their movement. Then the station shook for the second time, as if the computer was deliberately trying to throw her clear of the elevator, to separate her from its intended victim.

It didn't work. Terri braced herself in the aperture, with shoulders and foot, and maintained her position. Ben, on the other hand, was flung to the ground. As he levered himself up, he found himself staring through the slats of an ankle-level heating grille. One of the Doctor's earlier warnings came back to him just in time. A hot cloud was blasted out into his face and he closed his eyes and held his breath but still ended up with a throat and chest full of choking, stinging poison. He coughed up bile and his eyes streamed. He stumbled blindly into the lobby, pushing Terri ahead and feeling the doors' feeble efforts to close on him as he passed through.

Terri stayed close, standing guard, as he bent double and breathed deeply until the wheezing in his chest subsided. Eventually, she took his shoulder urgently. 'We have to go. We're eight floors away from this TARDIS of yours and there isn't much time. The systems are beginning to break down – and can you feel it getting hotter?'

Ben could, although it hadn't occurred to him before. He was sweating all over. 'What's happening?'

'Our orbit's holding, but we must be skirting the atmosphere's edge. The station can't cope for long. The gyroscope must be under a great strain as it is. It'll be wrecked for good soon, and then we'll all be in for a long drop.'

'Wait a minute, what's happened to Dracula?'

'Who cares? Come on, Ben!'

They headed for the stairs. A drinks machine gurgled at them as they passed its alcove and Ben shied from it, fearing a jet of scalding liquid. Eight flights seemed a long way to travel, if every innocuous appliance was to pose a threat. A further worry had occurred to him too. 'The computer knows where we're going, and it's made sure there's only one route to take. It's got plenty of time to set a trap.'

'But, like you said, we've got no choice.' Terri led the way upward and Ben stayed as close to her as possible. As they passed B5, a light fitting exploded and showered him with hot glass. It gave him a fright, but was otherwise ineffective. So long as he was accompanied, it was as much as the computer could try. It seemed to Ben like an act of frustration: an all-too-human reaction to his obstruction of its goals. Or perhaps it was a genuine fault – another symptom of the hotel's impending demise.

Ben left the stairwell at Deck B4, almost dragging the surprised Terri along behind him. 'What do you think you're doing?' she cried.

'I don't fancy walking into whatever that thing's preparing for me upstairs. I've thought of another way up.'

'It had better be quick. There's less than ten minutes left.'

Ben knew it. He was dreadfully hot now; his wet hand threatened to slide out of Terri's grasp, and he was sure his face must look like a shining beacon. He had not been on this level before and he hoped its layout was the same as that of B1. If it wasn't, he had doomed them both.

Then, suddenly, Terri shrieked and Ben's jaw gaped

open at the scarcely credible sight before them. It was a fireball, huge enough to fill the corridor, shedding yellow shards of flame as it rolled around the next corner and towards them, skipping and bouncing off walls as if made of stone. It bore down on them at an incredible speed and Ben wondered if he had walked straight into the computer's trap after all. He let go of Terri's hand and turned to run. Instead, he found himself being shoulder-charged into the wall. She held him there, his nose pressed against the plaster, as the fireball rattled towards and through them, then vanished. 'You risked a lot on a lucky guess, didn't you?' he panted, when she had released him.

'It's a case of knowing where to look.' Terri nodded upward. 'One of Thomas's projectors is up there; it was following the fireball's progress. It wasn't hard to deduce that it was a low-level hologram. Anyway, how many times do you have to be told the computer won't harm me? I doubt I'd have escaped with a bit of smoke damage if that thing had been real. It was just trying to split us up again.'

'You think this is the first computer that's tried to kill me?' said Ben glumly. 'I'm just wondering how long it'll wait before it decides to do us both in and hang the consequences.'

Terri laughed. 'I was forgetting what year you come from. Computers don't work like that, Ben: they obey their programming. And if you've recovered now, we'd better get on. Where are we going anyway?'

'There's a zero-gravity chamber around this next corner,' Ben said, as he allowed himself to be led away. 'It spans a few levels. We should just be able to float up to B1.'

'I like it.'

'And in my experience,' he added as they broke into a jog, 'most computers do as they flippin' well please.'

Polly could almost have cried, she was so exasperated. She had seen enough movies in which the hero escaped from a locked room with a simple piece of plastic: it had looked easy. But, after ten minutes of sliding and wiggling her makeshift lockpick every which way in the obstinately narrow gap between door and frame, she had run out of patience. Admittedly, she had no credit card and was forced to work with a tea-sodden cardboard coaster left behind by Melrose. One day, she thought, she would have to ask the Doctor to teach her a few of his own escapology tricks. For now, she was trapped.

She was determined not to remain idle, though, and she seated herself at the computer. She was smart enough, she prided herself, and quick on the uptake. And, as she had told her captor, she had worked as a secretary. Surely the idea of technology was to make such work easier, not more difficult. An hour and a half was plenty of time to pick up the basics, and then she would be able to delay the end of her usefulness for a while. Or perhaps even, she thought hopefully, turn the Selachians' own technology against them – send out a signal to the Doctor or something.

Her first disappointment, however, came as she inspected the keyboard. Its letters were arranged alphabetically; more logical than the usual method (the old-fashioned one, she supposed), but it would slow her down incredibly. She hunched over it and got to work, tentatively trying each key and button in turn. Ten long minutes passed in a crawl before her experiments yielded fruit.

'At last!' she cried, almost leaping out of her seat in excitement. She had found the on switch. It was on the back.

The Doctor clambered to his feet. He didn't know how long he had been out, but the stifling heat suggested that he was almost out of time. His head was aching and his every nerve was shrieking at him to lie down again until the pain of living had passed. But he wasn't just responsible for his own life: he was the only person in the hotel with a TARDIS key. Daphne, Hornby and Dorothy – and, with any luck, Ben and Terri too – would be waiting for him to save them and he couldn't let them down. It was his job; his vocation, no less.

His legs balked at the short flight of steps up to the doors. He held on to the railing and blinked furiously to drive the muzziness from his mind. The rational part of him tried to re-establish control. It was aided as he glanced over his shoulder and the sight of the fast-approaching Earth gave him a new strength fuelled by terror. Its land masses were clearly visible now and he suffered another disappointment as he saw that the station's course had changed. They were heading for a crash landing in Western Europe.

Even as he stumbled out of the Interplanetary Bar, the Doctor found himself thinking of others. He prayed that the station might burn up completely in the atmosphere: the devastation, if any substantial part of it was to hit a populated area, could be tremendous. He considered the problem, running over what he knew of its design and construction, to keep his mind occupied as his legs propelled him upstairs. It was, he concluded, a thankfully minor possibility. There was nothing he could do about it anyway. The Hotel

Galaxian was going to crash. The only difference he could make was to ensure its occupants' survival and continued health. He vowed to do so, however tight the deadline. Nobody would end up as cinders floating around in Spain if he could help it.

Terri went first into the chamber, and kept a firm grip on the rungs in the wall. They couldn't afford to go drifting off – not with less than five minutes to complete their journey. Ben followed awkwardly, straining his muscles in unnatural ways as he tried to get on to the ladder without letting go of his human shield. As he surrendered the comfort of the parapet, he realised that the absence of gravity rendered the task easier than he had made it. He let Terri do the climbing, propelling herself upward easily and with little effort, as he clutched at her hand and floated after her.

As she reached the topmost door, Ben transferred his grip to her shapely ankle and kept a steadying hand on one of the rungs, so as not to unbalance her as she clambered out on to Deck B1. He remembered pursuing Melrose through this room, in an even more urgent situation. It seemed a long time ago.

He was beginning to feel more comfortable. The computer hadn't pulled any more tricks, and it hadn't been able to make a serious attempt on his life since its initial attack outside the bar. They were almost home. Terri was out in the corridor now, lying flat on her stomach so she could reach down and keep hold of him, his ever-present lifeline. He kicked down against a rung and floated up to join her.

And, suddenly, the computer switched off its antigravity field.

Had Ben or Terri received any warning whatsoever, it wouldn't have been a problem. As it was, they couldn't react to Ben's regained weight in time. He fell like a block of cement, and almost dragged Terri after him before their hands parted. He plunged towards the floor, some five stories below, and reached out desperately for one of the rungs as it shot by. He cried out as he wrenched his shoulder painfully, swung around and hit the wall. The breath was knocked out of him and he lost his grip, but he had slowed his rate of descent so that his next attempt was successful. His head spun as he flattened himself against the too-flimsy rungs and held on for his life. They weren't designed to bear weight. Only belatedly did he wonder if the computer was capable of routing power into them. But if it was, he realised, he would have been dead now.

He looked up to see Terri climbing back on to the ladder and finding it difficult. From this vantage point, he could see how her plastic foothold bent alarmingly beneath the sole of her boot. He felt he should shout something heroic about leaving him and saving herself, but the words were knocked out of him as the support beneath his own feet snapped. He kicked and scrambled and hoisted himself up, to the protestations of his arm muscles. He found purchase again and tried to spread the load by distributing his limbs across four rungs. It left him in an uncomfortable, vulnerable position.

'Go back,' he urged Terri, the stress of the moment afflicting his jaw and making him shout through clenched teeth. 'I'll make my own way up.'

'But if I'm not there, you're a target!'

'I don't think it can do anything,' he insisted, although

he wasn't confident. 'There are no ventilation grilles here, nothing electrical. It can't get to me. It's just hoping I'll fall to my death.' And it might get its wish too, he thought, as the plastic loop beneath his left foot began to give way and he shifted weight on to his right.

By now Terri was spread-eagled hazardously with feet on two of the uppermost rungs and her left hand clinging to the parapet while she strained towards Ben with the right. 'Try and reach me,' she called, tantalisingly close but too far away. He climbed gingerly; each support in turn protested at being made to shoulder more than its fair share of the burden, but they held. Ben readopted his posture of relative safety, a little further up now, and gazed up at Terri again. He would have to repeat the manoeuvre three times to reach her. He became uncomfortably aware of the heat and wondered how much time was left. The worry galvanised him into a second effort. But, this time, as soon as his left foot was adrift, his left handhold broke. He scrambled to reverse the setback, but was unbalanced down one side and fell. He hit every rung on the way down, and by the time he was able to get a proper hold again, he was nearer to Deck B2 than to B1.

'I'm not going to make it,' he called to Terri. 'I'll have to get off down here.'

'I'll come down and fetch you,' she promised.

'You don't have time!'

'You can't get upstairs on your own. You'll be a sitting duck!'

'I'll be all right,' Ben lied. 'I know what to watch for.'

'No!' If Terri's defiant cry took him by surprise, her suicidal leap into the room almost stopped his heart.

She plummeted towards him, and he fleetingly entertained the notion of catching her as she passed, even though it would doubtless have ripped him free of his supports and killed them both.

And then, suddenly, she was bobbing alongside him with a broad grin on her face.

'You took a chance, didn't you?' he said, when he had recovered enough to speak. He untwined himself gratefully and they held hands again. 'The computer might have let that one go as your own fault.'

'Yes, well, it was a calculated risk. Shall we go?'

'I think we'd better,' said Ben, pushing down on a rung to send them both upward. 'Only this time, maybe I should get out first.'

The window in the dining room faced the same way as the one in the Interplanetary Bar. The first thing the Doctor noticed as he skidded through the door and to an undignified, haphazard halt was that he could see Earth's mountain ranges. The heat was intense now. He could probably measure the time remaining to him in seconds.

Daphne had worked herself into a state of near hysteria, and she sobbed with relief at the sight of him; Hornby clasped her to his side supportively. Even Dorothy seemed grateful for his timely arrival. But, to the Doctor's immense dismay, Ben and Terri were not present. He looked into Daphne's ashen, hopeful face, but he had no words of comfort for her. She broke into a fresh wave of tears.

The Doctor produced his key and ushered the trio into the TARDIS. He followed, but bumped straight into them. He had neglected to warn them about his ship's interior dimensions and they had all halted just beyond the doorway, at first expecting to be able to go no further but then simply staring in astonishment at the huge white console room. He was used to such a reaction, but there was no time for his practised explanations now. He hurried to the instruments and set coordinates almost at random, for a position in space beyond the danger zone. He also disengaged the temporal circuits: he couldn't afford to leave this time, not with Polly still stranded.

'Where do you think you're going?' Dorothy stopped him as he headed back towards the door.

'I won't leave anyone behind if I can help it,' he said darkly.

'You're insane! Do you think you can find them now?'

He didn't. He had even managed to destroy the computer program that could have directed him to them. 'They could be on their way,' he insisted. 'I must give them as much time as possible.'

'You're putting us all at risk!' she cried.

He fixed her with his most hateful glare. 'I don't think I can take all the responsibility for that, Mrs Adler!'

Polly had made two heartening discoveries. One was the existence of pull-down menus; the other was a mobile grey box with which she could access them, by moving an arrow about the screen. This wasn't so difficult after all, she decided as she quickly got the hang of a spreadsheet program. The Selachian wouldn't return for over an hour yet, and already she thought she had learnt enough to be able to bluff it. Time for a little more work on the escape plan.

She glanced down the main menu for useful entries. 'Locks' and 'Doors' didn't appear, to her chagrin, but she was pretty sure she'd been imprisoned by a manual system anyway, and the Selachians weren't stupid enough to have left an electronic 'key'. No, she had to rely on Plan B. She grinned as she found an entry for 'Communications', brought her handy arrow to bear and pressed one of the buttons on the grey box. She recoiled from the screen in terror as a frame opened and a helmeted Selachian face appeared inside it.

'Your request is denied,' it hissed, its voice coming from a tiny speaker in the computer itself. 'We have committed no crime and see no reason why you should be allowed to board.'

The picture shrank, as another frame sprang into existence beside it. In this one was a head-and-shoulders shot of a thick-set man with piercing green eyes and a black moustache. He was wearing a black uniform – similar to the one in which Melrose had been clothed for the murder game – and a sturdy, reflective helmet on which the letters 'TSF' were stencilled in blue. 'We are answering a distress call and investigating the destruction of one of our space stations,' he said. 'You are obliged to grant us entry under the terms of the First Galactic Treaty.'

Polly experienced a mass of conflicting emotions. She was relieved to see that the Selachian wasn't addressing her, and she could feel her quickened heartbeat resuming its normal pace. A further source of hope was the realisation that the message she and Hayes had sent had finally been answered: the police – or the Terran Security Forces, Hayes had called them – were here. But the revelation of the Galaxian's destruction was like a shard of ice penetrating her stomach, even though she had known it was inevitable. It seemed to have happened so quickly.

Could her friends have possibly escaped?

'We observed the demise of your construct, but we were not responsible,' said the Selachian. 'Nor do we have any information relevant to your inquiry. In the interests of continued peace between our governments, you will not obstruct our lawful business further.'

The uniformed man disappeared, and Polly held her breath as she awaited his answer. When his image returned, it was wearing a resigned expression. 'Your concern is noted,' he said quietly, 'and we will not detain you. Good day.'

'No!' she yelled at the screen. Then it occurred to her that she would be better off saying it to the policeman directly. A message beneath the two pictures read J – JOIN CONFERENCE and, almost without thinking, Polly stabbed at the key and shouted, 'Don't believe them. They destroyed the Galaxian and they've kidnapped me. Help, please!'

This time, there was no doubting that both parties were aware of her. The officer, somewhat taken aback, said, 'Hold tight, ma'am. We're on our way.'

'Treacherous plankton,' the Selachian growled, 'you have earned a painful death!' Polly sobbed with fear and lashed out at the off switch, just to remove its fearsome visage from her sight. She was left in silence, dread prickling at her nerves as she realised what she had done. She was trapped in this room: could her saviours arrive before the Selachians did? She doubted it.

She had one hope left. She turned on the computer again and feverishly negotiated her way back into its communications mode. Contact with the other ship must have been severed, as she was now presented

247

with a simple menu. She opted to send out an all-frequencies call and spoke urgently into the speaker grille.

'Doctor, it's Polly. I'm on the Selachian ship and I'm in trouble. If you can hear me, please come quick. Please, Doctor, I think they're about to kill me. I need you now!'

CHAPTER 14

WATERLOGGED

Polly's message echoed around the console room, driving Ben into an impotent frenzy. It sounded as if she was calling from the next room, and it was hard to accept she was separated from him by an uncrossable void. He didn't want this to be the last time he heard her voice.

The Doctor was worried too, and he worked frantically at the controls. Time had slowed to a crawl and, despite his haste, he seemed to take for ever. Ben's patience finally wore thin. 'Didn't you hear her?' he cried, raising his fists but thinking better of driving them into the console. 'She's in trouble, you've got to hurry!'

'I'm going as fast as I can, Ben. You know how temperamental the TARDIS can be. If I rush this, we could end up on the wrong side of the galaxy.'

'But she's in trouble,' he reiterated helplessly.

'And she's done the right thing by sending a signal,' said the Doctor gently. 'Remember how we landed at the Galaxian? I can follow her transmission back to its source and, erm, almost ensure we materialise in the right place.' A note of barely concealed panic entered his voice and he added, 'Now, please, let me get on with it.'

Ben saw the logic in his request – and an opportunity to do something. He took his position by the console. 'You'll need my help again then. The numbers on this display, right?'

'Ah, no.' The Doctor bustled past and physically lifted Ben out of his way. 'I'm sorry, Ben, there's no time.' He sidled into a corner, feeling miserable and useless. Terri joined him, snaking an arm through his, and he forced a smile for her sake.

The Doctor was a blur of motion. Hornby, Daphne, and Dorothy watched in silence; Dorothy had expressed her disapproval at being taken to the warcraft, but the Doctor had assured her she would be in no danger if she remained in the TARDIS. 'I will certainly do so,' she had said archly, 'and I won't be foolish enough to expect your return.'

Ben felt dizzy and tired, and strangely hollow. He was being kept upright by adrenaline, he realised. The Doctor's reference to their last perilous journey reminded him that he hadn't rested properly since he was shaken out of bed by the unexpected collision. Hard to believe it had been less than twenty-four hours ago: in the intervening time, he had been attacked, threatened, rendered unconscious and almost electrocuted – twice. Most recently, he and Terri had been forced to race hand in hand across the hotel dining room, struggling to keep their footing as the station entered its final approach and was buffeted by atmospheric turbulence. They had run a gauntlet of shifting floors and tumbling furniture, and the expression of horrified anticipation on the Doctor's face as he waited by the TARDIS with arm outstretched was etched on Ben's mind for ever. It had seemed only seconds after they had attained the safety of the ship that they had watched the Galaxian's demise on its scanner, hovering a safe distance away. The spinning construct had glowed white-hot, then crumpled. It was a less spectacular sight than Ben had expected, but it left him with a sickly feeling.

There had been a general outpouring of relief then. Daphne and Terri had hugged each other tightly and both had cried. But the Doctor had remained apart from the celebrations. 'We still have a job to do,' he had said. 'We must retrieve the weapon before the Selachians use it again. And, just as importantly, I must rescue my companion.'

The central column ceased its undulations and the familiar sound of materialisation reverberated in Ben's eardrums. The TARDIS juddered to a halt and his gaze met the Doctor's, neither daring to voice his concerns. The Doctor's hand wavered over the scanner control for a second, but he pressed it down firmly and all eyes travelled to the screen, high up on the back wall, where an image was being formed. It was indistinct, and Ben couldn't make out what he was seeing. It was green and mottled and it seemed to pulsate. It looked like a giant living wall, but closer inspection was thwarted by the picture's murky quality. Something grey drifted across it and he realised, with a pang of dismay that hit like a hammer blow to the chest, what was wrong.

'We're underwater!' he cried.

'Oh dear,' said the Doctor, entwining his fingers fretfully, 'I believe you're right.'

Polly had tried to move the bed across the room, but its cast-iron frame made it too heavy for her. In any case, she had seen the remnants of the last barricade with which the Selachians had been confronted. Nor was there anywhere to hide. In desperation, she flattened herself against the door, although she would never be able to keep it closed against a determined onslaught.

To her surprise, though, there was no sound of

movement from outside. A minute passed, and she wondered how it could take so long for the creatures to get here: they were only a hundred yards or so distant in their pool, weren't they? For an instant, she allowed herself foolish hope. Perhaps they weren't coming after all. Perhaps, for some unguessable reason, they had decided to spare her life.

But then she heard the approach of metallic footsteps. She closed her eyes and took a deep breath, controlling a powerful urge to scream. The Selachians drew nearer, with their promise of swift execution. And then she heard a small explosion, followed by more footsteps and a scuffling which confused her totally, and then the most welcome sound she could have heard, short of the Doctor's voice. A shout: 'Terran Security Forces. Stay where you are!'

'I'm in here,' she yelled, pounding on the door with her fists. 'They've locked me in here. Help!' Whether it was a wise idea or not, she wasn't sure, but she couldn't stop herself.

'You have no rights on this vessel,' a Selachian hissed, uncomfortably nearby.

'We do, if you're holding an Earth citizen hostage,' said somebody else. His voice grew louder as he spoke and Polly almost cheered as she heard the sound of the lock being disengaged. She stepped back as the door was opened, to reveal the officer with whom she had spoken earlier. But her grateful expression froze on her face as she saw a Selachian behind him, raising its gun. She didn't even have time to shout a warning. She screamed as her rescuer's smouldering corpse toppled into her arms, and chaos broke loose.

Polly stood in the doorway, staring, for far longer than she should have dared. In those terrible, elongated seconds of paralysis, she bore reluctant witness to a massacre. Four officers had boarded the Selachian vessel. The airlock door through which she had been marched hung open, its lock eviscerated, and a docking tube extended to a similar portal beyond. One by one, four officers were cut down. Each hideous death seemed to occur in slow motion, each mutilated body taking an eternity to hit the floor. Polly prayed for each fatality to be the last; that the tide of battle would turn. Only two Selachians were present, one the blue-striped leader, but their weapons cut through padded uniforms and boiled away tissue with horrific ease. In contrast, the standard-issue rifles of the Terran Security Forces made not a dent in the aliens' casings. The outcome of the conflict was never in doubt, but the speed with which it was resolved left Polly breathless and numb with disappointment.

And then they came for her.

She whimpered and tried to conceal herself behind the door as the victorious creatures strode across the battlefield, stepping casually over the simmering remains of their prey. But it was a futile gesture. Whatever they wished to do to her, she was powerless to prevent it. She still had faith in the Doctor: he would be here for her soon. But this time, for the first and last time, he would be too late.

The TARDIS was on the warcraft, of course. Ben kicked himself for not realising that an aquatic race would fill their ship with water. But the Doctor solved the problem of how they would function in such conditions by disappearing into the bowels of his own ship and returning with two lightweight harnesses. Ben looped the belt of one about his waist and kicked off his shoes. Terri helped him to fasten other straps around his shoulders and to adjust their buckles until the main component of the rig, a white metal cylinder, rested comfortably against his back.

'It's not as heavy as I expected,' he said.

'It doesn't store air like the tanks you're familiar with,' the Doctor explained. 'It houses equipment to extract oxygen from the water.' Ben was about to comment on the likely size of such machinery, but then this miracle was hardly different from the many others he had seen. Incredible miniaturisation seemed to be a constant feature of post-1966 technology.

Terri unthreaded and straightened Ben's airline, and handed him his oxygen valve and transparent goggles. Then she clapped her hands together and said, 'Right. Where's my tank?'

The Doctor looked up from the console in surprise. 'I had intended for Ben and I to go out alone.'

'You've got more equipment?'

'Yes, but –'

'Then I'm coming.'

Dorothy laughed. 'You're like lemmings, all of you, following your leader out to certain death. You had no chance against the Selachians on dry land; what do you think you can do to them in their natural environment? They'll rip you apart!'

'She's got a point,' said Ben. 'You'd only be risking your own life by coming with us.'

'So you're thinking of staying indoors too, are you?'

'They've got Polly,' said Ben stubbornly. 'I have to go.'

'So I'm coming with you. Or have you forgotten how many times I've had to save your life already today?' She didn't say it unkindly, but Ben could feel himself turning bright red all the same at this unwanted

254

reminder of his uselessness.

The Doctor broke the ensuing silence. 'There's no time to argue. Ben, show Terri to the right-hand storeroom, you'll find more scuba gear there. And hurry – I'm reconfiguring the TARDIS's force field to let us out without letting water in. It'll take a few minutes, but then we really must go.'

Ben turned to Terri again, but despite this and Daphne's similarly beseeching look, she was adamant. He hated the idea of placing her, as well as Polly, in jeopardy – but he had seen enough of the future to know that his chivalrous attitude was considered old-fashioned now, so he bit his tongue and said no more.

By the time they returned to the console room, only five minutes later, the Doctor was wearing his own harness, the face mask resting on top of his head, and he was hopping from foot to foot impatiently. 'Come on,' he urged, ushering them towards the doors, 'we haven't time to lose. Now, I'll deal with the weapon. I want you two to find Polly and bring her back here. Ben, you'll have to share your oxygen with her on the way back. You do know how to do that don't you? Good. Once you're in the water, I suggest you head upward where possible. The Selachians must have a dry room, probably a deck, for receiving visitors – and logically it will be at the top of their ship.' He paused on the threshold and turned to address his other three guests. 'If we're not back in an hour...' Then he tailed off, as if realising how hopeless a situation that would leave them in. 'We'll be back in an hour,' he announced instead. 'Mr Hornby, Daphne, I want you to keep an eye on our friend here. Don't let her touch anything. Now, are you two ready? Splendid. Let's go.'

And with that, he cuffed his mask down into place

and leapt through the doors. Ben and Terri followed him, caught up in his breathless urgency. Ben flopped down on to his stomach and found himself being caught and carried on a warm tide. He clamped his teeth firmly onto the oxygen valve and began to suck dry air from the tank. By the time he got his bearings, the Doctor was already out of sight and they seemed to have drifted a long way from the TARDIS.

The Doctor reached out and ran his hand, almost reverently, over the coarse green surface. It was warm to his touch and it shifted slightly, not with the throbbing of machinery but with the gentle rhythm of respiration. His hypothesis was confirmed. Despite the hazardous situation, he felt a tingle of joy at the discovery of a new life form. The warcraft, beneath its impenetrable shell, seemed to be one enormous creature – or perhaps an amalgam of several. Of course, an aquatic environment had forced Selachian science to take an unusual path. Their technology was not created but grown – genetic engineering on an almost unprecedented scale. He felt sad, though, that such a race would never appreciate the beauty of what they had accomplished. To them, these poor mindless beings were simply an exploitable commodity. They were blind.

He shook himself and suppressed his natural admiration. He had a job to do. He pushed himself softly away from the green wall and squinted to see through the clouded water. He could make out the shadowy hulks of many more organic consoles, protruding – no, growing – from the walls, but he could not guess their individual purposes. He kicked his feet to send himself towards one. He would find his way around these systems only by closer inspection of each component in turn. It would delay him, true – but then the discovery that Selachian science was so incompatible with human technology was a lucky one. It would be some time before the assassination program could be adapted for the monsters' use. By then, the Doctor hoped to have introduced a virus into their computers – one that would corrupt the data on the disks as soon as they were used.

It was an easier and safer alternative to a full-frontal attack, which would almost certainly have failed. The Selachians wouldn't expect him to be capable of launching a covert operation from inside their own ship, so surprise was on his side.

He only needed to avoid detection until his task was complete.

Ben and Terri's progress was slow. Despite Ben's powerful need to find Polly, and his fear that it may be too late already, he was only too aware of the consequences of discovery. Assorted misshapes reared up constantly out of the gloom and the pair made an unspoken agreement to keep close to the slimy, revolting lumps of the ship's instrument banks, to use them as cover lest one of the shapes turn out to be an enemy scout.

Their caution proved well advised. Ben stared at an approaching mass for several seconds before he was sure that it was, in fact, moving towards them. It seemed both too small and too slow to be a Selachian, but he wasn't about to take chances. He tapped Terri's shoulder and pointed, and they took refuge behind a green outcrop. Ben knew the dangers of holding his breath with an oxygen tank on, but he tried to make his respiration slow and shallow, minimising the risk of telltale bubbles. For a few seconds, anyway. Then he forgot all about such things and just watched in fascination, as a creature more weird than he could have imagined swam by.

His first impression was of a bizarre cross between a man and a salmon. Its skin was pink and smooth, its mouth a thin straight line, its eyes narrow and unblinking beneath a wavy, undulating crest. It had no nose (of course), but a series of gills flapped open down its sides. It was a spindly thing, and Ben couldn't help but think that he could have snapped it with his bare hands. He revised his opinion as it drew level and he saw how its flexible body twisted lithely to propel itself onward. For an aquatic creature, though, it didn't seem too accomplished a swimmer. Its movements were awkward, almost lopsided. Its long, thin arms appeared to do most of the work, three tapered fingers (tentacles?) at the end of each hand cleaving water with sure strokes.

And then Ben saw what its problem was. Its symmetrical, graceful form came to a sudden stop, just below what he automatically thought of (incorrectly, he was sure) as its hips. The cutoff was too harsh, too straight, to be natural – and he knew with certainty that legs or a tail had been amputated. The movement of the stump seemed to confirm this: it thrashed as if trying, through force of habit, to work an appendage that was no longer there. Ben felt a sick, miserable rage at this casual mutilation of such an inoffensive creature. And then he caught a glimpse of gold and, as it passed his hiding place, he saw an array of gleaming metallic nodules down its back.

He felt even more sick then, as something the Doctor

had said flooded back into his mind: something about the persecuted denizens of an ocean world undergoing terrible operations to fit into defensive battle armour. He was looking at a Selachian, in its natural form – and he was seeing what it had been forced to do to itself in the name of protection from its air-breathing tormentors.

For a long, unsettling moment, he was almost sure that he was on the wrong side in this battle. But then he remembered Polly.

Polly let out a breath, closed her eyes and swallowed hard as the two Selachians pushed past her and into her quarters. She considered running, but where could she run to? Instead, she watched as the leader took a pen in its giant digits and used it to stab out a sequence of keystrokes on the computer. 'It is as our systems reported,' it said, as a stream of information flashed across the screen. 'The program has failed to terminate its victim. He left the human station by means unknown and his location cannot be ascertained.'

Despite her own peril, Polly felt a smile tugging at her mouth. Whoever Mace had targeted had evaded death, and his departure by 'means unknown' could only point to the Doctor's TARDIS.

The second Selachian stepped forward and held out a small, green, waterproof casket. 'Shall we proceed with the replacement test as discussed?' The leader gave a sharp nod, and its subordinate opened the container and shook its contents out on to the desk. Polly drew a sharp intake of breath at the sight of the Adlers' two disks.

The leader turned to her. 'This time,' it hissed, 'we will be able to observe the efficacy of the weapon first-hand.' And Polly realised then that she had not escaped death at their hands after all. They had merely chosen a slower means of execution.

'Run,' the leader challenged. 'Try to outdistance our weapon, for what good it will do you.' And she did – but first, in a desperate, split-second decision, she reached out and snatched the disks even as an armoured hand made to close around them.

Polly fled, earning valuable seconds as her bold action surprised her captors. She threw the door shut behind her, but a sizzling blast sliced through it. She squealed and tried to gain some distance, leaping over the half-melted corpses of her would-be rescuers. But, halfway across the marble-tiled hallway, an old problem came back to haunt her. Where could she run to?

She started in one direction, but uncertainty halted her and she stumbled a few paces in another. She stopped again, almost sobbing at the hopelessness of it all, and found herself by the poolside. Or rather, she realised now, it was an access hatch to the lower decks. Of course, it made sense that the greater portion of the ship would be waterlogged. She wondered how many more Selachians were down there. Dozens, probably; maybe hundreds.

And then she saw the outlines of two dark figures swimming up towards her and, glancing back, she saw that the first two Selachians were approaching from behind. She was surrounded.

The Doctor hadn't even begun his work when he became aware of a disturbance in the water behind him. He flipped himself forward and rolled over, coming up behind a gangling, pink-skinned creature as it launched itself into the space he had just deserted.

He was barely surprised by this revelation of the Selachians' unarmoured appearance, and he knew better than to underestimate the abilities of his attacker. He was in its environment, after all, as Dorothy had said. Had it been prepared for trouble, and wearing its battlesuit, he would have been dead already; as it was, he still faced that unpleasant prospect. It reorientated itself with unfortunate speed and came at him, snarling to reveal a neat row of tiny but deadly sharp teeth. The Doctor kicked himself backward, but the Selachian was upon him in an instant and he fought to keep it away, his hands around its throat even as it sought to fasten its own long fingers about his. Its strength was plainly greater, so he dropped his hold and dived beneath it, hoping to take it unawares with the manoeuvre. It came after him, and he twisted and turned at random to keep its flailing hands at bay. So long as it was denied leverage, he might have a chance.

His pursuer made a series of high-pitched, squeaking sounds which the Doctor took to be a curse or threat in its own language. It drew almost level with him from above, and reached out to throttle him again. And he remembered what Jacques Cousteau had once told him about dealing with sharks. He pitched downward and kicked up with both feet, catching the Selachian a glancing blow across the snout. It flinched away and he made for the cover of the nearest console. But even as he swam, he tasted water and he spat the oxygen valve out, realising that his air hose had been cut in the struggle. The severed end was too far away to reach his mouth.

He weaved his way through a maze of organic instrument banks, his tank leaving a trail of bubbles in his wake. He thought he had given his pursuer the slip, but it couldn't be long before it reported back to its colleagues and a search party was organised. Worse still, he had been unable to draw a good breath before losing his air. His lungs already ached with the effort of holding in a pitifully small supply.

If he didn't surface soon, he wouldn't need any Selachians to finish him off.

Ben felt a surge of hope as the emerald sky lifted, giving him a longed-for opportunity to swim upward. Terri had seen it too and they struck out together, Ben's spirits rising ever more as a white rectangle of light was defined through the murky water. It seemed to slip farther away as he approached it and he could hear a shrill, distant siren. Then, after an eternity, he emerged into a colonnaded hallway and was greeted by the terrifying sight of four corpses, a screaming Polly and two advancing, armoured Selachians.

Ben tried to shout out, but lost his valve and took a mouthful of water. Time slipped through his fingers more quickly than it had a right to and the monsters closed in. He hauled himself on to dry land and swayed under the sudden weight of his tank. Almost without thinking, he ripped off his face mask and slapped the quick release mechanism on his belt so that the cylinder fell with a clang. He was only dimly aware of Terri doing the same beside him, so concerned was he with leaping to Polly's rescue. He never stopped to consider the futility of taking on the Selachians again.

Ben shoulder-charged the nearest creature, but failed to move it. Instead, he bruised himself, bounced off its golden casing and nearly fell over. But, as it turned its attention to him, Terri swooped in, grabbed Polly's hand and pulled her away. He could hear Terri crying out,

'The disks, give me the disks!' but his eyes were focused on the Selachian with the blue stripe as it brought both weapons to bear. Ben kept moving, and howled as twin blasts ripped into the floor beneath him and churned its marble covering.

'Get the tanks, Duchess!' he yelled, though his voice sounded muzzy in his own ringing ears and he wasn't sure his message would get through. 'Dive into -' Then his throat gave in to the dust of the Selachians' blasts and the water he had taken, and a hacking coughing fit interrupted his words.

A hand closed around his forearm and he was dragged to Terri's side. They backed away together from the two Selachians, and he realised that Terri was holding the disks in front of them like an inadequate shield. The monsters had fixated upon them. They didn't fire – too wary, as Terri had no doubt hoped, of melting the prize with their indiscriminate discharges – but they kept on coming relentlessly, and the pair were being backed into a corner. At least they had forgotten Polly: Ben could see her, behind the Selachians, holding one of the discarded oxygen tanks and hesitating by the water's edge.

And then a commanding voice bellowed 'No!' and Ben's heart soared to see the slight but reassuring figure of the Doctor, dragging himself up on to the marble tiles. Immediately, as was his wont, he became the centre of attention – and as the Selachians half turned to inspect the new arrival, Terri took her chance.

At first, Ben didn't know what she was doing. Even as she gave him a hefty push and he reeled towards and into the Selachian leader, he didn't want to believe what his senses were telling him.

One golden arm swept him casually aside and he hit the floor with a bone-jarring impact. The Doctor had lost the moment, and his commanding presence: he was racing into the affray like a demented goblin. Terri was heading for a circular doorway, and Ben saw a rigid tube extending from the airlock beyond it and realised that another ship was docked on to this one. The leader brought up its weapon and aimed for her back, but the Doctor reached around its bulk and jerked its arm up so it shot its subordinate instead. The stricken Selachian took two paces back and an unearthly squeal crackled through its suit's speakers. Its armour was blackened and smoking, but it remained standing, brought its guns to bear, and fired.

Ben yelled out Terri's name as she was winged by a well-placed (or lucky?) shot and spun to the floor, her mouth open but her cry of agony trapped in her throat. Polly screamed Ben's name in turn, as another blast was launched in his direction. He tore his eyes from Terri – he had to be concerned with himself now – but the image of her, an arm outstretched towards the door, her fingertips an inch from escape, was burnt into his retinas. In the confusion, the Doctor somehow got past the Selachians and scooped up the disks from where they had fallen. But the monsters closed in on him inexorably, even though one was still unsteady on its feet. Ben howled in anguish as his friend disappeared behind them – but then the top of the Doctor's head bobbed momentarily into view and, a second later, the disks flew over the Selachian leader's shoulder and described a perfect arc into Ben's hands. He hesitated for a moment, but as all eyes turned to him, he panicked, turned and pitched the Adlers' precious weapon into the ruinous (he hoped) water.

Immediately, the leader thundered by and dived after them. Polly leapt out of his path and to Ben's side. The remaining, injured, monster was still for a moment, and the Doctor yelled at his companions to follow him.

The trio came together at the airlock, and the Doctor and Polly raced through without pause. Ben held back, agonising over Terri. Was she still breathing or was it just a cruel trick of his imagination? 'Come on Ben,' the Doctor urged, 'leave her. She's dead!' He grabbed his shoulders and pushed him into the tube, even as the Selachian recovered its wits and fired again. The outer door took the brunt of it, as the Doctor slammed it firmly shut. Thankfully, it was made of strong material. It buckled but did not break.

Polly was already at the far end of the short, white, ridged corridor, and the Doctor hared after her. Ben lingered, staring at the barrier beyond which Terri lay, his mind a conflicting mess of emotions and desperate reasoning, all fighting with a screaming imperative to ensure his own survival. It had happened so quickly. How could she be dead? What had she been trying to do? Had she betrayed him, or had it been some desperate plan?

He tried not to think about it, and ran. First Polly and then the Doctor leapt through the circular opening into the other ship, whatever it was. He made to follow – and, with unexpected speed, the portal irised shut and Ben was cut off from the others. And trapped in the docking tube.

At first, he thought there had been some mistake. He hammered against the unyielding expanse of grey metal, but to no avail. Then a terrible realisation dawned on him and he knew what was happening. The awful hiss of clamps disengaging proved it. Already, air was beginning to flow past him and towards the narrow, but widening, fissure between the tube and the ship's hull.

Dorothy had explained how her assassination program would track its victim from system to system. It had caught up with him, even here.

And it was about to finish its job.

CHAPTER 15

NO ONE CAN HEAR YOU SCREAM

For a second, Polly had actually thought it was over. She had attained the relative safety of the Terran Security Forces vessel, and the Doctor had followed her into the shabby, dark interior of the ship. They still had to regain the TARDIS and – if the water hadn't damaged them – the disks. But they were out of immediate danger and, with the Doctor and Ben beside her again, Polly couldn't believe any hurdle was insurmountable.

And then it all went wrong.

She flung herself against the closed airlock door and tried to slip her fingernails into the grooves in its surface, to prise it apart again. She was unsuccessful. The Doctor was equally frantic: he was tapping away furiously at a control pad on the wall. Polly could hear Ben banging against the resolute barricade from the far side, and it brought frustrated tears to her eyes.

'I can't do anything!' the Doctor exclaimed, with a helplessness that Polly found all the more dreadful for its rarity. 'The computer has locked me out. I'd have to dismantle the whole thing to get around it.' He turned from side to side, flustered and indecisive, and apparently saw nothing to help them.

'Do something,' Polly sobbed. 'You've got to do something, Doctor!'

Ben stopped knocking.

Ben had no choice. Only certain death lay before him, so he had to go back towards almost certain death on the warcraft. But the decision was made too late. He was fighting against air pressure with each painful, slow-motion step, and as the tube retracted from the side of the mysterious ship that had once offered so much hope, he lost his footing altogether. He fought for breath as he was dragged, feet first, towards a circle of blackness. The terrible wind coaxed tears from him and forced his eyelids to close. And he hit something, and thought in his blindness that he had been expelled into space and had glanced off the side of the docked vessel.

He felt ridged metal against his cheek and his besieged stomach told him gravity had reasserted itself. It also expressed its disapproval of this sudden change in circumstances. He lay, gasping for breath, and listened as footsteps approached. He didn't have the strength to look up and see whose they were. He soon found out.

A steely hand took his collar and hoisted him up, leaving a ragged tear in his shirt. The free end of the tube, he saw, had been sealed by an airtight shutter. Selachian reinforcements had arrived and had opened the airlock at their end, ironically saving his life as the program's directive not to harm others had kicked in.

'Bring him,' ordered the leader, framed by the circular doorway. Ben's escort thrust him roughly down the white pathway and back on to the warcraft. It pushed him again as he crossed the threshold, and he stumbled and fell by Terri Willis's side. Looking up through misty eyes, he made out the forms of at least five Selachians. The leader loomed over him, brandishing both disks, and a droplet of water fell from one and struck his nose. 'If the information on these is corrupted,' it threatened, 'you will have earned a slow and agonising death.' It stalked away then, and Ben was given a brief respite in which to recover his senses.

'As opposed,' someone croaked, 'to a quick and agonising death if not.'

'Terri!'

'Hello, Ben.'

'I thought you were... I...' Ben tailed off and choked back a sob as his initial euphoria was quelled by a re-examination of her body. Her right side was a mangled mess, her skin was a deathly white and blood trickled from her mouth. She didn't have long. 'Stay still,' he said hopelessly, 'I'll get help.'

She almost laughed. 'A nice thought... bit late, though. Don't worry, Ben, it only hurts when I... breathe. Shouldn't... last too long then.'

'Terri,' he whispered. He cursed himself for being tongue-tied, for not being able to say anything when he was facing his last chance to say the right thing. He wanted to curl up into a ball and cry.

'You should worry, anyway... tried to... kill you.'

Her eyes were closed now and her words were fading in and out of hearing. 'No,' he protested weakly.

'Don't take it personally... just the job... what I had to do. I... actually liked you in the end there, Ben.'

And then the light fled from her body, and he wept over her – for seconds? minutes? it seemed like hours – until the Selachian leader returned and he struggled into a sitting position and glared up at the monster with increased venom and a determination not to give in.

'You have been lucky,' it announced. 'The weapon is intact.'

'A funny definition of luck,' Ben spat.

The leader gave a silent signal, and two Selachians moved to each side of him, took an arm each and hauled him upright. He stared into the leader's faceplate and tried to imagine the pink, spindly creature within. It didn't help. 'You must, however, be punished for your acts of sabotage against the Selachian Empire.' It left a suitably dramatic pause and then gave the instruction: 'Rend him!'

The creatures pulled in opposing directions and Ben gritted his teeth and pulled back, determined not to cry out, to expose his weakness. He felt sweat pouring down his forehead and he knew he was losing the uneven struggle. His arms threatened to pop out of their sockets and the muscles in his back and shoulders felt on the verge of tearing.

And suddenly, unexpectedly, he was freed, and the momentum of his own efforts carried him forward and almost pitched him to the floor. He realised, belatedly, that the warcraft was shaking. The Selachians had been taken by surprise, and he used their confusion to his advantage. He pressed his leg muscles into service, converting his fall into a headlong dash for the water and the decks below. But, even as he dived, the leader recovered its wits and jumped with him, clinging to his back and driving him down so as to force a painful landing which almost knocked the breath out of him.

They sank like stones, a metal-sheathed arm around his neck. His lungs began to burn and his vision was clouding. The life was being choked from his body.

Polly stared out of the forward portal at a side-on view of the great black Selachian vessel. It was turning slowly away from them, and she had the awful feeling that it was about to engage a warp drive or a hyperspace engine or something and shoot out of sight, taking Ben beyond rescuing. She resisted the temptation to interrupt the Doctor with her fears; instead she crossed her fingers and silently willed him to work faster.

They were in the cramped cabin of the Terran Security Forces ship, which the Doctor had been dismayed to find unoccupied. Muttering something about control codes, he had discarded his wringing-wet frock coat and useless tank, rolled up his shirtsleeves and dived beneath an old, rusted instrument bank so only his legs protruded. For several minutes, all Polly heard from him was the occasional grunt of, alternately, frustration or satisfaction.

At last she could contain herself no longer. 'What are you trying to do, Doctor?' She winced in sympathy at the sound of his head hitting the underside of the console. Then he slid back into the open and looked up at her ruefully.

'I've succeeded in gaining control of the main computer functions,' he explained. He leapt to his feet and began to operate the various, unlabelled levers and switches as if he had been handling them for years. 'Now I can override the airlock door control and persuade the Selachians' systems to re-extend their docking tube.'

'We're going back to their ship? But what can we do there?'

'Improvise, mainly.'

'Doctor, do you think Ben's...' She neither wanted nor needed to complete the question.

'He's a resourceful young man, Polly,' said the Doctor gently. 'With luck, he'll have found his way to safety.' He returned to his work and she vowed not to disturb him again. The resolution lasted less than ten seconds.

'Doctor, look!' she cried. 'What's happening?'

The warcraft had veered suddenly off course, and its left side tilted downward as if a heavy weight had been dropped on it. It appeared to be juddering, and its smooth forward motion had been reduced to fits and starts.

'Oh no,' the Doctor moaned, transfixed by the spectacle. 'Oh my giddy aunt, no!' Then he attacked the console in a cyclone of renewed urgency. Polly kept well clear of him, chewing on her knuckles to keep herself from screaming. She didn't need him to explain that, for whatever reason, the Selachian ship was in its death throes.

And, if it was destroyed, it would take Ben and the TARDIS with it.

The water was churning fiercely and a huge mossy lump of machinery sailed into the Selachian leader and almost dislodged it from Ben's back. With the last vestige of his strength, he wriggled and broke free. His lungs and stomach were on fire and he wasn't sure which way was up any more. He finally surfaced, greeting the cold air with great, racking breaths, light-headedness, considerable relief and the realisation that he had to get off this ship before it blew. He forced his eyes open, almost expecting to see a line of armoured sharks at the waterside, waiting to finish him off. Clearly, though, they had more immediate problems. What he did see was one of the TARDIS's diving harnesses, knocked over the edge by the increasingly frantic shaking of the stricken vessel. He seized upon it like a drowning man finding a piece of driftwood, except that his weight caused it to sink and to drag him down with it.

He thrashed about in momentary panic, fumbled blindly for the valve and bit down, sucking from it hungrily. He desperately needed to rest, to sleep, to breathe long and deeply from real, fresh air. But if he didn't find his way back to the TARDIS soon, he would not breathe anything again.

Ben's sense of direction was usually good, but the turbulence of the water, and the hindrance of silt and lichen thrown up by it, stole the ability from him. He had neglected to find a face mask, and tiny particles stung at his eyes so he could only keep them half open. In the end, he swam almost blindly, convinced he was near the TARDIS but having no idea of which direction it might lie in. To make matters worse, he was suddenly aware of the increasing difficulty of each succeeding breath. His tank was running dry: its oxygen generation system must have taken a knock. Either that or his mounting panic had made him gulp down air at a faster rate than it could cope with.

He took one last, good breath and hit the release mechanism. The white cylinder drifted out of sight and he was left on his own, too far from the surface to find replenishment there. His only hope lay in reaching the TARDIS within the next minute. But he had worked out his location now; at least, he thought so.

He struck out towards where he was sure the Doctor's ship must be, but was stopped short by the sight of three Selachians – armoured ones – cutting across his path with powerful strokes of their arms and artificial legs. He thought they had seen him – but if they had, they did nothing about it. He withdrew, just in case, and lost most of his air in alarm as something green and heavy tumbled towards him from above. He hit the floor and sent up a cloud of sand. The dislodged console landed on his legs, but he managed to pull himself free of it. He covered his eyes and waded through the cloud, knowing he would not reach his destination now.

And then he was able to see again – and, by some miracle, he saw that his series of mishaps had brought him to the TARDIS's very doorstep. The incongruous machine nestled at the mouth of a nearby crevasse, the landscape about it totally changed from when he had last seen it. He didn't dwell on the stroke of luck that had kept him from making a big mistake: he simply swam, for all he was worth, towards the welcoming blue box and hoped that somebody was watching for him on the scanner screen and waiting by the door controls. As it turned out, somebody was.

He staggered into the harsh white embrace of the console room and hit the switch to close the doors behind him, ignoring Daphne and Hornby's questions about the whereabouts of his companions and Dorothy's protestations at the shaking which affected them even here. He just wanted to pass out, but alarm bells rang in his head. The TARDIS's shell was as good as invulnerable but, if the warcraft was about to explode, it would be sent flying. That, he recalled dimly, was how the day had begun – and this time, the Doctor wasn't here to set things right. If only he'd been able to learn how to pilot the ship, to remove it from the danger zone...

Ben could feel himself losing consciousness and, as a last-ditch, desperate measure, he reached for the dematerialisation levers. He didn't know where they would end up, or in what state, if he threw them – but anywhere, anywhen and anyhow was better than this.

And then the tribulations of the day took their toll. His legs buckled and his eyes involuntarily closed. Later, Ben would recall sliding towards the floor – and pulling the levers down with him – but not hitting it.

He tumbled into deep dreams.

The Doctor suffered an unbearable instant of agony as the Selachian warcraft exploded. He closed his eyes and clenched his fists and ignored the bucking of the tiny cabin: though he had moved the police ship swiftly away, it had been caught on the periphery of the blast and its automatic systems were struggling to compensate. He prepared himself for a devastating psychic shock – and, when it didn't come, he was suffused with the warm feeling of hope. He opened his left eye and then his right, and inspected the drifting debris critically. Finally, he took Polly's arm in a fatherly manner. She was rigid with shock, but she had seen the eager look on his face and she knew all wasn't lost yet. She turned to him with wide, appealing eyes, but he didn't know what to say. He needed to comfort her, but he didn't wish to raise false expectations. Instead he kept his gaze riveted on the forward portal, and she followed it there.

The TARDIS wasn't dead. He would have seen some indication of it if it was: more than likely, its police-box form spinning away to its inevitable destruction. But, more conclusively, he would have felt it too. Its death throes would have resounded in his mind, a final plaintive message communicated to a faithful owner by telepathic circuits. It had escaped the explosion – of this he was certain – but if it had drifted into another time, another space, he might never see it again all the same. It would be a lonely life without it, he reflected: a sad, claustrophobic existence.

But in some darkened recess of the Doctor's mind, which he accepted without quite understanding, he could feel his vessel's heartening presence, not too far away. He told himself it might be a trick of his fraught nerves, a phantom echo amplified by desperate hope –

but he couldn't stop a broad smile from stretching across his malleable features, even before his eyes relayed to him the welcome sight of the steadfast blue box, rematerialising in the midst of the wreckage. Polly saw it a moment later, and she cheered and whooped with an elation that proved infectious. It was some seconds before another worry occurred to her, and she was serious again.

'Do you think Ben made it on board, Doctor?'

'Well,' he said, squeezing her hand reassuringly, 'I'd be surprised if anyone else had worked out where the dematerialisation levers are; at least, not without resetting the coordinates in the process.' He crossed his fingers behind his back, where she couldn't see them, and just thanked his stars that he had disabled the notoriously drift-prone temporal circuits before his last short hop.

'Oh, I do hope he's OK,' said Polly, with heartfelt concern.

'We'll soon find out,' the Doctor muttered, and he searched the main instrument panel for any sign of a tractor beam.

Ben dreamed of sharks and spies and mad killers, but in a strangely detached way. They danced across his vision, but seemed blurred as if he was separated from them by a cloudy, impenetrable shield. His mind explained to him how it was merely sorting through the images of the day while he slept, and how they couldn't harm him any more. He was safe, wrapped in a white cotton-wool shell, and they could neither see nor reach him here.

But they had seen Terri, hadn't they? And reached her. And killed her. And Ben was screaming at his loss – inside, where nobody could hear him. But at what loss?

She had not been what he had thought she was. His notions of a life with her had been fantasies, and he would have run from such a situation anyway. It was over now, and he was… home?

Where was he, exactly?

Not wrapped in cotton wool, although he had been right about the colour. His protective cocoon opened up around him and he was mildly surprised to find himself in a white room. He could see every detail, though he still lay with his eyes closed. He recognised the meticulously ordered ranks of glass bottles on the dressing table and the neatly hung clothes in the wardrobe. The distinctive wall pattern of grey circles nagged at him with its familiarity, and yet it still took him a while to realise that he was in his own bedroom in the TARDIS. He wasn't used to seeing it in this context: his dreams had always been of his home and his ship before.

And then it occurred to him that this time was no different. Images of home. His ship. And his initial surprise soon gave way to a warm glow of belonging. He embraced this unique occurrence and reimmersed himself contentedly in welcome sleep, which was dreamless now.

It was some considerable time before he was aware of his surroundings again.

The Doctor closed the scanner on a scene of roiling crimson skies and spitting volcanoes, and turned to Geoff Hornby and Daphne McAllister with a sheepish grin. Daphne looked worried, and he reminded her again that he had fixed the TARDIS so as to prevent it from travelling into the future or past. It was only a matter of time before he got the spatial coordinates right, he promised. And they took off again, much as it irked him to do so. It wouldn't be fair to expect his temporary passengers to wait while he explored, but he hated the thought of leaving behind another enthralling new world with its myriad undiscovered possibilities. Perhaps just one tiny expedition, if they didn't reach Earth on his next attempt?

Hornby and Daphne chatted to each other in the corner, and the Doctor glanced up at them between calculations. Quite when it had occurred, he wasn't sure, but they seemed to have become very close. Of course, it was natural for them to do so after all they had been through together. Just look at Ben and Polly, he thought. They had also been relaxed and refreshed by a good night's sleep and a hot bath, though Daphne was still not entirely happy. It would take time. Hornby had found the most awful shirt in the TARDIS's wardrobes: a clashing patchwork affair, none of the squares on which quite matched his yellow trousers. The Doctor grinned inwardly. He might not have Polly's fashion sense, but at least he would never dress like that.

'There's one thing I don't understand,' said Hornby thoughtfully – as luck would have it, distracting the Doctor at the most inopportune moment possible. He sighed and braced himself for what would doubtless be the first of many explanations. Why were human beings always like this? 'What made the Selachian ship explode?'

'Hmmm.' Actually, he had wondered that himself. 'Well, I am still waiting for a first-hand account from Ben, of course. But my guess is, the Adlers' weapon caught up with him and its safeguards were only meant to apply to humans. I certainly wouldn't put a touch of xenophobia past our Dorothy. Once Ben was alone – or rather, once he had become the only surviving human – on the ship, it didn't feel the need to be careful any more.'

'But what about us? We were on board too.'

'Ah yes, but the Selachians had no surveillance devices below water – they thought themselves unassailable there, you see – so even when the program entered their systems, it had no way of detecting the TARDIS. In fact, my guess is that Ben was down there too, at the end. The computers couldn't pinpoint his location precisely, or get to him, so they blew up the whole ship. An extreme solution, maybe, but expedient – and perfectly within the program's parameters.'

'Is it all over, then?' asked Daphne timidly. 'Or might it follow Ben here too?'

The Doctor shook his head. 'The TARDIS's systems don't have the sort of gateways needed by the program to spread. Anyway, the Selachian computers won't have detected Ben's escape. They'll believe him dead, and they'll relay their triumph to every other infected system. It might take a few days, or even weeks, but the assassination program will eventually delete itself. So long as Ben doesn't return to 2136, he'll be in no danger. Don't you agree, Mrs Adler?'

He had seen Dorothy lurking in the doorway and she entered now, responding to his question with an indifferent shrug. Daphne eyed her with distrust and drew closer to Hornby for protection. 'No nearer to getting us home, then?' Dorothy taunted.

'Don't see why you're in such a hurry,' said Hornby resentfully. 'We're handing you straight over to the authorities.'

She retorted with a short, confident snort of a laugh. 'And how long do you think they'll keep me? My organisation knows exactly which strings to pull. I'll never even come to trial.'

'Like they'd help you, after you betrayed them.'

'You're forgetting, Mr Hornby, I'm their only hope of getting the weapon after all.'

The Doctor was alarmed. 'You can't duplicate the program on your own?' He subjected her to a probing stare, and she returned it levelly but betrayed the slightest hint of doubt in her eyes. He smiled. 'No, I don't believe you can.'

'What you believe is immaterial. You're talking about morality and practicalities, Doctor – both, I'm sad to say, outmoded concepts. I can't overstate what an organisation like mine would do for even the chance of owning a weapon like the assassination program. They'll forgive anything.'

'Doctor?' Daphne looked to him for a shred of hope, but he could provide none. Perhaps Dorothy Adler's mysterious employers wouldn't be so gullible as to believe she could still help them, or that she wouldn't betray them again if she could. Better still, perhaps they'd see the futility of spending so much, of taking such risks, for what was no more than a devious, impersonal killing machine. But he doubted it. His centuries of experience with human nature suggested that she was right. She could probably walk away from this with hardly a regret, but for the riches lost to her. And, in her wake, she would leave the incinerated remains of Ted Matlock, Neville Adler, Alison Hayes, Bryan Melrose, Henry Mace and Terri Willis, with not even a tear to shed for her former partner in crime.

There was silence in the console room as the Doctor set the final coordinates and the TARDIS embarked upon its next voyage.

Some time later, Polly stood in the corridor outside Ben's room, longing to knock but finding it difficult. What could she say to him? Of course, people had died during their misadventures before, but somehow it had never seemed close enough to touch them. An unwanted part of her opined that it was only the same for her this time. She had wanted Ben and Terri to be separated, hadn't she? She had wanted him to return to the TARDIS with her and the Doctor and nobody else, to resume their journeying as if nothing had happened. But she couldn't be so callous. She cared for Ben, and she felt for him – and, as much as she had resented his closeness to Terri, she couldn't deny it. She could only imagine what he was going through now, and it seemed selfish to be considering her own feelings. As if she even knew what they were.

So she hesitated. And she waited. And she paced.

And she started guiltily as the door was flung open and he appeared on the threshold. Ben seemed tired, and he had clearly just woken. He hadn't attended to his hair: usually neat and straight, it now grew tangled and wild. His white shirt – the one he had been wearing when Polly and Daphne had carried him from the console room and put him gently to bed – was askew and badly creased. He was surprised to see her there. He looked at her through reddened eyes and blinked, bemused. And something undeniable drew them together.

They embraced tightly, and didn't let go for a long time. Polly felt tears dribbling down her cheeks and they put her confusion into perspective. Ben was a friend. A special friend, her best friend. Whether that was just because he was the only one who could identify with her mad experiences of the past months, or because of something more, it didn't matter. Not now. He needed her, and she was here for him. The rest would be clear in time.

'I should have cottoned on sooner,' said Ben, speaking in a careful, thoughtful monotone as he perched on his bed and sipped gratefully from a mug of hot, sweet tea that Polly had prepared for him. He had a cold, numb sphere in his chest where his feelings about Terri's fate ought to have been. But by talking about it, he hoped to set things straight in his mind and, perhaps, to prick at its surface, to see what might lie beneath. Polly, bless her, was listening attentively.

'Terri wanted the disks for herself – she made that pretty clear at the end. I don't know why. She was probably working for another of those top-secret government-type organisations – a rival firm to Ms Hayes's or something.' The theory brought back a memory: he was with Terri on the docking level, taking a break from preparations for the forthcoming attack. She had said something about having a job to do, and he had wondered at her meaning. And then there were the gaps in her computerised records. And one more thing: 'It was her that knocked me out, it must have been. You know, outside the Adlers' room at just about the time old Matlock was getting done in. Of course... Hayes thought we were Selachian agents, come to get the disks off Neville and Dorothy. If Terri thought so too, and she saw me leaving their room, she probably thought I had the things on me. It's all making sense!' He grinned at his triumph of deduction, but let the smile fade as a depressing thought occurred to him. 'So she just used me. When she found out I didn't have the disks, she decided to stick with me until one of us picked them up. And, by the time she found out we weren't working for the sharks at all, she'd probably realised that the Doctor was likely to get hold of them anyway. She didn't care about me. She only cared about getting what she wanted.'

Polly took his hand and said firmly, 'You're almost right, Ben. That's the type of person she was, and you just happened to be in her way. But I saw the pair of you together – and I know she saved your life, how many times? She didn't have to. I think you made her like you a lot more than she could afford to. But she wasn't good enough for you, Ben. You deserve better.'

He was struck by the tenderness in her voice, and her caress as she reached forward and stroked his bedraggled hair back into some semblance of order. 'Pol,' he said awkwardly, 'what do you think about the future? I mean, what do you see there, for yourself?'

'I don't know, Ben. I honestly don't.'

And he looked into her eyes and she into his, and he was positive then that the same thought was uppermost in both their minds. They were from such different walks of life: could they grow old together, have children together, make each other happy? Then a sudden rush of fear and self-doubt caused him to wrench his gaze away and to bury it in his cup. And the moment passed. Polly stood and said with (forced?) cheer, 'I expect we'll just follow the Doctor, wherever he takes us. Straight into more trouble, I shouldn't wonder.'

Ben dared to push the point. 'And if we end up back in London?'

'Then it's back to real life, I suppose – although I don't know how. But it has to happen eventually, doesn't it?'

'Eventually.'

They exchanged smiles and Polly left. Ben lay back on his bed with a heavy sigh, head resting on cradled hands, and he felt his sadness lifting a little. He wondered where the TARDIS would take them next – and for the first time, he hoped it would not be to his home and to the difficult decisions that had to be made there.

Not just yet, anyway.